Shifting Sands at the Beach House

Diamond Beach Book 2

MAGGIE MILLER

D1738337

All she wanted was one last summer at the beach house...

Claire Thompson's trip to the family beach house has gotten far more complicated than she'd ever expected. Grieving her late husband's sudden death, Claire and her daughter, along with Claire's sister and mom, are struggling to make sense of the mess he's left them with.

How on earth did he have another family she never knew about? How did he keep that secret for so many years? Claire fights with her feelings as she tries to find a way forward. All she really knows is that her husband wasn't the man she thought he was.

All she can hope for is that he'll do the right thing in his will and leave Claire enough to live on. She already knows she's going to have to sell the beach house. Will she have to sell her home, too? She hopes not.

But every day it feels like the sand is shifting beneath her feet and Claire is doing everything she can to stay upright. Will it be enough?

Chapter One

Roxie stared at her mom, trying to wrap her head around what Willie had just told her. "Your late ex-husband left you seven and a half million dollars. You're sure?"

"No, of course not," Willie answered. "That's why I told the attorney I'll believe it when I see it in my account. But what if it *is* true? Why would his lawyer lie to me?"

Roxie thought about her mom's fourth husband, who'd also been her last. Zippy had been a working magician with his own stage show and seemed to be in good shape financially, from what she could tell during the brief visit she'd made to Las Vegas to meet him. But she wouldn't have pegged him as having that kind of dough laying around. "Was Zippy really worth that much? I knew he was well off, but..."

"You saw his house in Vegas. You stayed there. It was pretty big and very fancy. That whole pool setup wasn't cheap."

"Sure, but a big house with its own lazy river on a nice property doesn't mean there's money in the bank. Sometimes people live above their means. Especially showbiz people."

"That's true, but the lawyer told me Zippy owned the rights to a bunch of magic tricks, tricks he invented. Once he found out he had cancer, he put them up for auction to the highest bidder."

"Magic tricks raise that kind of money?" Roxie shot her mom a skeptical look.

Willie nodded. "Apparently, they do. At least the ones as good as what Zippy came up with. And he's been creating tricks and selling them to other magicians for years. But in his last days, he finally let go of the ones he'd kept for himself. The big ones. And they were worth the most."

"Well, good for him." Roxie couldn't imagine her mother was really going to come into that kind of money. "Good for you, too, if it actually happens."

Willie gazed off into the distance. "I can't believe he left all of that to me."

"Didn't he have kids?"

Willie nodded. "He had a son from his first marriage. He must be forty or fifty by now. Decent guy. I think he was a general contractor in Reno. Anyway, the lawyer told me that he'd been taken care of, too. And Zippy left money to the International Brotherhood of Magicians to help take care of those who needed it."

"What a nice guy."

"He really was." Willie put her hand to her mouth for a moment, just sitting there, staring off into space. For a second, Roxie wondered if Willie was going to start crying. Then she looked at Roxie. "If this is real, if the money actually does show up, I know exactly what I'm going to do with it." Her brows rose and she nodded. "I'm setting Trina up in her own shop."

"Oh, Ma." Roxie inhaled. "That would be..." She almost couldn't speak because of the surge of emotion rushing through her. "It would be everything. That would change her life."

Willie touched her newly dyed lavender hair. "She just has to promise to keep doing my hair."

Roxie laughed. "I don't think you have to worry about that."

Willie smiled. "You could be her receptionist.

You're great with people and she'll need the help. Someone she can trust. Or you could at least help her out in some way."

"I would, absolutely. Whatever she needed me to do." A thousand happy images filled Roxie's head. But they were getting ahead of themselves. "Listen, we shouldn't say anything to anyone about the money or the salon. Especially not Trina. What if it doesn't happen? She'll be crushed."

Willie stopped smiling. "You're right. This has to stay our secret."

Roxie grabbed her mom's hand and gave it a little squeeze. "If this is real, and I pray to God it is, that means it won't matter what happens with this house and Bryan's will and his insurance. Trina will be just fine."

"We'll all be just fine, honey." Willie squeezed her daughter's hand back. "We'll get us a nicer place and pay for it in full."

"You know," Roxie lowered her voice. "Claire plans to sell this place. If it ends up belonging to her."

"Does she?" Willie glanced toward the table, where dinner was in full swing. "That gives me all kinds of ideas." She glanced at her daughter. "Would you want this place? I know all the memories can't be good."

"I love this place. Bryan might have betrayed me, but we had good times here." Roxie looked around. "Are you saying you'd want to move here?"

"I'm saying..." Willie trailed off.

Roxie followed her line of sight.

Trina waved at them. "Hey, what's going on over there? You two coming back to finish your meals or what?"

Roxie nodded. "On our way." She tipped her head toward the table while looking at her mom. "We'll talk more later. Remember, not a word."

"My lips are sealed," Willie answered.

They rejoined the others at the big dining table and got back to eating.

"Everything all right, Mimi?" Trina asked.

Willie nodded. "Yes, just some news about Zippy. I'll tell you later, sweetheart."

"Okay." Trina smiled and went back to her food.

Roxie hoped all her mother meant was that she would explain to Trina about Zippy's passing. Not that he'd *maybe* left her a windfall. Roxie did not want Trina to get her hopes up, only to have them dashed.

The child had had enough disappointments in life.

The windfall was something to think about, though. That was more money than Roxie could imagine. Of course, it was her mother's money, but Willie had never been shy about helping out when she could. Roxie had never expected it of her and wouldn't now. Seeing Trina's dreams come true would be enough. But Roxie knew her mother. When she had money in her pocket, she liked to spoil them.

The meal wound down as people finished the last few bites on their plates.

Claire got up. "I'm just going to run upstairs and grab the desserts. Key lime pie and lemon squares."

"Sounds great," Danny said.

Margo, Claire's mother, frowned. "You're serving both? After all the work you went to making those lemon squares?"

Claire's smile seemed strained. "Yes, because not everyone likes lemon, Mom."

Kat, her daughter, pushed her chair back and got to her feet. "I'll help you. You can't bring all that down *and* the whipped cream and plates with only two hands."

As the two women left, Miguel, Danny's dad,

smiled at Willie. He'd been paying a lot of attention to her all evening. It was clear he found her fascinating. And who could blame him? "There is a play at the seniors center later this week. *Arsenic and Old Lace*. I was thinking about going. Would you care to join me? Might be more fun with company."

Willie grinned. "My daughter and I were already going to go. And Margo, too. Why don't you come with us?"

He looked pleased. "I'd like that very much."

"Hey," Danny said. "That's great. Maybe you ladies can keep him out of trouble."

Roxie laughed. "Does that happen a lot?" Danny was a handsome man, but she wasn't interested. Not when it was plain Claire had her eyes on him.

Roxie needed Claire happy, and if Danny could help in that department, Roxie was all for it. Besides, the woman already had enough reasons not to like her.

"Not too much," Danny answered. "But I can't go with him, so having some friends around would be great."

Roxie nodded. She understood and smiled to show him that. Willie could be a bit of a loose cannon at times, too. "Don't worry, we'll all look after each other." She cut her eyes at Miguel. "You think you can handle being the only man with three women?"

Miguel giggled and rubbed his hands together. "Sounds like an evening in heaven."

Roxie snorted. Willie might have met her match.

Chapter Two

Claire pressed the elevator button to take them to the second floor. The doors closed.

"Mom," Kat said. "Danny is a handsome guy."

"I suppose he is." He was. Very handsome. But Claire just nodded solemnly, as though she were merely making a scientific observation.

"So you don't think he is?"

Claire didn't really want to talk about Danny and his good looks. She changed the subject as the elevator stopped at the second floor. "You've been acting a little weird lately, especially toward your aunt. What's up?"

Kat got off and went straight for the refrigerator. "Nothing's up."

Her answer was so quick and short that Claire knew there was definitely something going on.

"Obviously, there is, or you wouldn't be using that tone."

Kat opened the fridge and took out the key lime pie and the whipped cream. "I don't know what you're talking about."

Claire leaned against the island and rolled her eyes. "I'm the last person you should lie to. I know you far too well."

Kat put the pie and whipped cream on the counter as she heaved out a sigh. "It's just..." She shook her head. "I read some stuff in one of Aunt Jules's notebooks that just sort of weirded me out. Like she might need therapy."

Claire doubted her younger sister needed anything of the sort. She was the sanest one of them all. Claire crossed her arms. "First of all, why were you reading Jules's notebook? Seems to me that wasn't something you should have been doing in the first place."

"I know, I realize that. But I can't unread it, can I?"

"No, but you can do other things. Like ignore it and start acting like a normal person again. Or tell Aunt Jules what you did, apologize, and let her explain herself. Because right now, you're treating her like she's done something wrong without giving her the chance to tell her side of the story."

"I can't tell her what I did." Kat grimaced. "It was a violation of her privacy."

Claire bent her head, looking at her daughter through her lashes. "Yes, it was."

Kat looked away. "Just let it be, Mom."

"Sure. So long as you straighten up."

"Shouldn't you be getting the lemon squares or something?"

"I'm serious. Aunt Jules has noticed your attitude toward her as well, so if you think you're hiding it from her, you aren't. You keep it up and she'll ask you about it next."

Kat frowned. "I *can't* tell her what I did."

"Then you need to forget it. Whatever you read *wasn't* your business."

"I know. I really do. And I'm trying. But seriously, the lemon squares."

Claire smiled. The lemon squares were on a plate on the breakfast bar. She'd taken them out of the fridge right before dinner, because she thought they tasted better when they weren't quite so cold. She went over and picked up the plate. "Got them. We need small plates, forks, a knife to cut the pie, a pie server, and a little spatula to serve the lemon squares."

"Then I'm going to need the tray, but it's still downstairs."

"There's another one in the laundry room," Claire said.

"I'll get it."

Toby came out of the bedroom, where he must have been sleeping, and whined softly.

Claire spoke to him. "You want to go downstairs and see everybody?" She scratched his head. "That was quite a nap you had. You slept right through the barbequed chicken."

His ears perked up at the word "chicken," making Claire laugh. "I'll get your leash."

She found it on the dresser in the room her mother and Jules were sharing. She attached it to Toby's collar, then picked up the plate of lemon squares. While she'd been doing that, Kat had assembled everything else on the tray and was ready to go back down, too.

Claire called the elevator and they got on. Toby danced back and forth on his little feet, visibly happy to be included in whatever they were doing.

Kat snickered at his antics. "Tobes, you're a goofball, you know that?"

He let out a little woof as if to say he did know, which only made them both laugh.

The elevator doors opened, and they got out. Toby tried to run but the leash only allowed him so much room.

"Hold on now," Claire said, keeping a careful grip on the leash and the plate of lemon squares.

Jules got up when she saw him. "I guess someone woke up, huh?"

Claire nodded. "He was fussing, so I thought I'd bring him."

Jules took the leash from her. "Thanks. He won't get to be down here too long. I need to get ready and get over to the Dolphin Club."

"I can take care of him," Kat said. She gave her aunt a quick smile, maybe in an effort to show everything was all right between them.

"Okay, thanks," Jules said.

It wasn't like Kat to snoop, Claire thought, but none of them were exactly their usual selves since Bryan's death and then finding out he had another family. That was the kind of thing that turned your world upside down and made you question everything.

She was amazed they were doing as well as they were. The fact that Jules was about to do an impromptu gig to help out a new friend was stunning to Claire. Of course, Jules was on the periphery of what had happened and not directly affected, like Claire and Kat were. Good for her, though, for getting out there.

Jules walked with Claire back to the table. She put the plate of lemon squares in the center and pulled off the cling wrap she'd covered them with.

Danny smiled. "Those look great. Mmm—I can smell the lemon already. And you made these?"

"I did," Claire responded.

Margo, her mom, chimed in. "They're the best lemon squares you'll ever have. Award-winning."

"Really?" Danny's brows lifted. "That's impressive."

Claire shook her head. "Just the church baking contest."

"Which had, like, a gazillion entries." Kat put the tray on the table before taking the pie off. She stacked the small plates next to it. "Who wants pie?"

Miguel nodded. "I want a little slice, but I'm having a lemon square, too."

Danny laughed. "No surprise there."

Willie nudged Miguel. "Bit of a sweet tooth, huh?"

He shrugged, his smile guilty. "How do you think

I got into the caramel popcorn business in the first place?"

Claire plated a lemon square for Danny and handed it to him. "Do you have a sweet tooth, too?"

He let out a reluctant sigh as he picked up the lemon square. "I do. I fight it, but I generally lose. I try to avoid a lot of carbs, especially sugar, but for this, I'm making an exception."

He took a bite of the square. He started smiling after just a few chews. "This is amazing. It's so tart. But just sweet enough to balance that out. It's like eating the best glass of lemonade you've ever had. I love it."

"Thank you." She plated up a few more lemon squares and passed them down. "You know, I could probably figure out how to make a low-carb version of these."

"That would be amazing." He took another bite. "I've been trying to come up with a new flavor of popcorn and this might be it." He looked at his dad. "What do you think? Is lemonade popcorn worth a shot?"

Miguel nodded. He'd already had a bite of the lemon square in front of him. "I say give it a try. If you can make it taste like this, you'll have a winner."

Danny grinned at Claire. "Thanks for the inspiration. Maybe you'd be willing to help me taste test what I come up with? Just to be sure I'm on the right track."

"Really?" Claire nodded. It was nice to feel wanted and useful. It gave her a warmth inside she hadn't felt in a while. "I'd love to."

Chapter Three

*A*fter dinner was finished and they'd all taken time to appreciate the sunset, Trina was helping to clean up when Aunt Jules approached her. "Hi."

"Hi. Do you think you could show me some of your accessories that you'd be willing to let me borrow? I really need to get ready and get to the club."

"Sure, come on." Trina had offered earlier. "Happy to. Stairs okay?"

"Absolutely."

They went up to the first floor together. The door was open, so Trina went in, leading the way to her bedroom. "Do you know what you're going to wear?"

Jules sighed. "That's the thing. I don't have a lot to choose from, since I didn't bring any of my usual stage outfits. I have a nice pair of dark jeans that I'll probably wear, along with my brown ankle boots. Not entirely sure about the rest yet. I do have a black cowboy-style shirt. But it needs something more. A little bling."

"Well..." Trina opened her closet doors. "Feel free to have a look. You can borrow anything you want."

While Aunt Jules rummaged around, Trina opened up her Caboodle of jewelry and hair accessories. Her belts and scarves were looped over a hanger in the closet.

"Hmm." Jules had one of Trina's belts in her hand. "This might work if I had one more piece to go with it."

Trina looked at the belt. It was leopard print with a sparkly buckle. "Oh, I can hook you up with all the pieces you need to go with that. Leopard is sort of my signature. What were you thinking? Earrings, maybe?"

Jules tried the belt around her waist, testing the fit. "I think earrings would be good if they have the right look. I'm not usually an animal print girl."

Trina laughed. "I know. No one on your side is into animal prints, are they. I guess I got all of that."

"You have great style," Jules said.

Trina glanced at her. Jules had been slightly hesitant on the word "great."

"But you think it's a little much, don't you?"

Jules shook her head. "It's not for me to say."

Trina set out a few pairs of her leopard-print earrings. "No, it's okay. I'd like to know what you think." Kat had already told Trina her overabundance of look was probably what was keeping her from having a serious relationship. That it was too much for most guys. And Trina couldn't help but wonder if Kat was right.

After all, Trina had never been in a long-term, serious relationship, and that was *all* Kat had been in.

Jules offered her a little smile. "Does what you wear make you happy?"

"Yes."

"Then nothing else matters."

"But do you think it could be turning guys off?"

Jules's smile dimmed a bit, then it quickly brightened back up. "Maybe. Anything's possible. Guys can be weird, you know? I wouldn't worry about it too much."

"Thanks, but I can't stop thinking about it since

Kat said it. I've never really had a serious relationship and now I wonder if that's why."

"Trina, you're a bright spark in a world that can be pretty dim sometimes. The right guy for you is out there. Have faith."

Trina nodded, her spirits lifted by Jules's kind words. "Thank you." She gestured at the earrings she'd put on the bed. "Any of these work for you?"

"Maybe..."

While Jules looked them over, Trina impulsively added a beaded leopard cuff bracelet with beaded fringe that hung down from the ends. "This is kind of blingy."

"Yes, it is," Jules said. She tried the cuff on. "That would be a nice accent on my fretting hand." She moved her hands like she would if she had a guitar in front of her. "The lights would definitely pick it up."

Trina smiled. "For sure."

Jules held up a pair of long, beaded earrings designed with a leopard print. "These must go with it."

"They do," Trina assured her.

"Then I'm all set. These and the belt and I'm in good shape. Thank you so much."

"You're welcome. I hope you have a great show."

Jules laughed. "Me, too!"

Trina walked out with Jules to the stairs, but they parted at the landing, with Jules headed up and Trina headed back down.

She wanted to see what cleanup was left to do and if help was needed. Didn't look like much when she got to the ground floor. Her Mimi and Miguel were still at the table talking. Her mom was wiping the table down. Claire and Danny were sitting over on the big sectional couch that made up the conversation area. Margo was walking Toby on the edge of the property that was illuminated by the landscape lighting.

Kat was stacking plates on a tray, getting ready to take them upstairs.

Trina went over to her. "What else needs doing?"

Kat gestured with her elbow toward the bowl of potato salad. "There's still food to be brought upstairs and put away."

"Sure, I can help with that." Trina grabbed the potato salad and a basket that had been filled with odds and ends such as extra napkins and the salt and pepper shakers. She followed Kat into the elevator.

Arms tense as she held the tray of dirty dishes,

Kat glanced over. "Did you get Aunt Jules some sparkly accessories?"

Trina nodded. "I did. Leopard belt with a bracelet and earrings to match."

The doors came open onto the second floor just as Kat's mouth came open, too. "Leopard?" She snorted. "I hope I get to see her before she leaves."

"Me, too," Kat said.

Trina put the potato salad down along with the basket of things. "Where's the cling wrap? I'll cover this and put it in the fridge."

Kat set the dirty dishes by the sink. "First tall cabinet door. You'll see it."

Trina got the wrap out, covered the big bowl, and stuck it in the fridge. Then she went to help Kat load dishes into the dishwasher.

"You don't have to help with this."

Trina shrugged. "I don't mind. Makes the work go by faster."

"There's more stuff to bring up, I think. Not much. But some."

"I'll run back down then."

When she returned with what was left of the key lime pie and the whipped cream, Kat was hand-washing the tray she'd brought the dishes up on.

Trina covered the pie, then put it and canister of whipped cream into the fridge.

Hard not to see everything in there was from Publix. Or an actual brand name. Trina and her mom almost always shopped at Winn-Dixie because it was cheaper. Although Publix did have some good sales. Especially their buy one-get one free deals. Nothing Trina's mom loved more than a good BOGO.

Trina closed the fridge and turned to see Jules come out of the bedroom. Trina took in her whole outfit and her makeup, then smiled. "Wow. You look great."

Kat twisted to see her. "Yeah, you do."

Jules held her arms out and did a little spin, her guitar strapped across her back. "Thanks." She pointed at Trina. "Extra thanks to you."

Kat snorted. "I can't believe you're wearing leopard. I like it."

Trina almost fell over. "You do?"

"Sure," Kat said. "It's very stage-worthy."

Trina had to agree. The dark jeans with the brown boots and black cowboy shirt really came together with the leopard-print accessories. Jules had done a gorgeous smokey eye, her makeup heavier than Trina had seen her wear so far, and her hair had been curled in big, loose, beachy waves. Trina approved wholeheartedly. "You look like a star."

Jules held onto her guitar strap as she gave a little bow. She went over to the elevator and pressed the button. "Now I just have to live up to that. See you girls later. Have a good night. Kat, you'll make sure Toby goes out before you go to bed?"

"I will," Kat said.

Jules gave them a wave and stepped into the elevator car. "Thanks."

Kat got out some cleaning spray and a dish cloth and started wiping the counters down.

Trina lingered. "I could take Toby out, too, if you wanted me to. I don't mind."

"You can come with me, if you want."

Trina almost held her breath. She tried not to overreact but that seemed very much like Kat warming up to her. "That would be great."

Kat pursed her lips and nodded, pausing her cleaning for a second. "By the way, Alex found you a date. For tomorrow night."

Unable to stop herself this time, Trina sucked in a breath. "He did?"

Kat nodded, looking sort of smug and amused at the same time. "Some guy named Miles."

"Is he a fireman, too?" Not that it mattered to Trina. She'd go out with just about anyone at least once.

"No, but he's a paramedic."

Trina exhaled. "That's a good job. I like anything that helps people."

And just like that, she had a date.

Chapter Four

Margo stared down at the stubborn little wiener dog at her feet. "Please poop already, will you?"

Toby continued to sniff the random clump of grass near the property line between the Double Diamond beach house and the neighbor's house. Not the Rojas' place. The one on the other side. She wasn't sure who owned it.

She studied it as she waited for Toby to finish his inspection. It was a nice house. White stucco with a blue metal roof and a bright blue door. There were a few lights on and the car in the drive had an Alabama plate. Renters, no doubt. Probably just here for the week.

Toby finally moved on to the next clump of grass, still sniffing like it was his moral imperative.

She looked at the Rojas' house. It was a buttery

yellow with white trim and an aqua door. A very happy-looking place, which fit the people who lived there. Danny and his dad were lovely people. It was obvious to her that Claire liked Danny. And Danny very clearly returned Claire's interest.

At least it seemed he did. His request that Claire help him taste test his new flavor of popcorn could have just been him being nice, but why make such an offer if he didn't really want to spend time with her? He could certainly develop a flavor without Claire's help. Just because he'd been inspired by her lemon squares didn't mean he owed her anything. Lemon wasn't exactly a novel flavor.

Danny seemed to be a smart man. Why would he want to spend time with Claire when she was only here for a brief time? He had to know she'd soon be going back to her life in Landry.

Toby suddenly lunged forward, just a few steps, but enough to strain the leash.

Margo saw the culprit. A small green lizard. She rolled her eyes. Lizards in Florida were as common as birds. "Toby, you've seen more lizards in your life than anything else. How are they still exciting?"

He let out a little woof. The lizard darted away. Toby went back to his patch of grass and seemed to be seriously contemplating a good spot to do his business. At last.

Margo sent up a tiny prayer that Jules's performance tonight would be perfect, and that Jules would be inspired by it. Margo knew her daughter was going through a rough patch creatively. She'd even picked up a few books at the library for her daughter about breaking through creative blocks. She'd left them on Jules's bed. Whether Jules had looked at them, she had no idea.

Toby squatted. She pulled out one of the little plastic bags that were in the cylindrical container that dangled from the leash handle. When he was done, she cleaned up after him, tied up the bag, then carried it to the curb, where the trash can was already out.

Ray must have put it out before he'd left yesterday. That was thoughtful. And very much him. She wondered what would become of Ray if Kat really and truly ended it.

Then again, was Kat capable of doing that? Margo wasn't sure. Her granddaughter had been with Ray for years. Breaking off a relationship like that wasn't easy. She'd be surprised if Kat actually went through with it. She might not be completely happy with Ray, but he was a known quantity. Kat wasn't much on change. Although she had let Trina do her hair—with resounding success.

That was quite a step forward. Where it would lead, Margo had no idea.

"Ready to go in, Toby?" She was. All she wanted to do was put herself in front of the television and turn on one of her crime shows. Dinner had been nice, but she was still in a sour mood from the mistake she'd made this afternoon. The whole idea of getting involved in a book club here in Diamond Beach had been ridiculous.

She didn't live here. She wasn't *going* to live here. The whole effort had been a waste of time. All it had done was make her feel sorry for herself and the life she'd been given. As much as she'd wanted to change and learn to be happy again, it now just seemed like too much work. She'd go to the play with Willie and Roxie, since she'd already committed, but after that she was done trying to put herself on a new path.

She was too old for such nonsense. She was better off sticking to her routine. So what if there was no joy in her life? Maybe that was just as it was supposed to be. She was a widow, twice over.

Claire was in the same situation, though. Why pursue things with Danny when it was just a dead end? Margo narrowed her eyes. Had Claire mentioned her desire to sell the beach house to him? Maybe he was befriending her in the hopes of getting a good deal on the place. Anything was possible, Margo supposed.

She started for the house. Her pants pocket vibrated. She stopped and took out her phone. Toby was happy enough to stop and sniff whatever was in front of him.

She looked at the screen. Conrad was calling her. The handsome former Marine who wrote two columns for the *Gulf Gazette*. The man who ran the bestsellers book club. The man she'd had lunch with. The man she'd allowed herself to think of as a friend after they'd shared a brief afternoon.

She swallowed and made herself answer. Better to tell him she wasn't going to be able to continue attending the book club meetings than to simply disappear. Such a pity. He was one of the first intellectually stimulating men she'd met in a long time. "Hello?"

"Hello, Margo. It's Conrad."

Just the way he said her name, the way he purred it out in that gravelly voice of his, sent shivers over her skin. "Good evening, Conrad."

"Good evening. And as it is evening, I apologize

for calling at this late hour, but..." He sighed and it held an unexpected note of amusement. "Well, the truth is, I can't stop thinking about you."

Her mouth came open to form a response, but she found herself speechless. He'd been thinking about her. Just like she'd been thinking about him. She wasn't about to admit that, however.

"Again," he said. "I apologize, but I wanted—no, I *needed*—to find out if you'd join me for lunch again tomorrow. Maybe we could take a stroll through town. Nothing high-pressure, I assure you. But I very much enjoyed our time together yesterday and I would like to see you again."

Without thinking, she answered. "It was a lovely day."

"Then you'll meet me?"

This was a terrible idea that would go nowhere. Because it couldn't. In fact, it was a complete waste of time. She nodded. "I'd love to."

"Outstanding. Tomorrow, then, twelve o'clock at Brighton's Café?"

"Sounds wonderful." Sounded ridiculous. *She* was ridiculous. But Brighton's Café was a chic little spot in the Hamilton Arms, an upscale hotel that had been around since Diamond Beach was founded. If he was trying to impress her, he'd succeeded.

But then, he'd already impressed her.

"Excellent," he said. "I'll see you. Have a good night."

"You, too." She hung up. She was smiling. Why on Earth hadn't she told him the truth? Clearly, she'd lost her mind.

She took Toby to the elevator. Danny and his father were still chatting with Claire and Willie, although they looked like they were saying their goodbyes.

Danny waved at her. "Have a good night."

Margo nodded. "You, too."

The elevator doors opened. She got herself and Toby on and turned around just in time to see Danny kiss Claire on the cheek.

Margo pursed her lips as the elevator doors closed. Looked like she wasn't the only one losing her mind.

Chapter Five

As Willie got on the elevator, she realized her cheeks ached from smiling all night. She patted her cheeks and laughed softly. When was the last time that had happened? Probably not since she'd spent time with Zippy, may he rest in peace. Miguel was so much fun. Charming and a little devilish, with a wicked sense of humor Willie hadn't been expecting.

That sexy accent didn't hurt, either.

He'd promised to take her out for a dish called *mofongo*, which did *not* sound like something to eat in her books, but he assured her it was a traditional dish in his homeland of Puerto Rico. He said he knew a place in town that made a decent version and he'd been looking for an excuse to go. She'd agreed, game to try anything once.

Miguel was also a great distraction from the

news she'd gotten earlier. Hard not to think about the possibility of actually getting seven and a half million dollars, but she really didn't want to dwell on it too much, in case it didn't happen.

But if it did?

It would be life-changing. For all three of them. Because Willie wasn't about to get that kind of dough and not take care of her daughter and grand-daughter. She'd been about to spend her nest egg on them to make things easier.

That paltry sum of twelve thousand dollars seemed rather insignificant now. She got off the elevator and went toward her room, but the flick-ering lights of the television in the living room at the end of the reading nook caught her eye.

She could see Roxie lounging on the couch, Trina next to her. Willie went in to join them, not nearly ready for bed. "There my girls are. Wasn't that a fun night? Those men are something else, aren't they?"

Roxie sat up a little, but Trina spoke first. "Is that why you're smiling like that, Mimi? Because of Miguel?"

Roxie nodded. "The two of you were getting on like a house on fire."

"We were," Willie said as she settled into her

chair. "And, yes, Miguel is the reason I'm smiling. He's the bee's knees, as we used to say. Haven't met a man that fun in quite a while." She leaned toward her granddaughter. "He's going to take me out to dinner for something called *mofongo*."

Trina tilted her head. "What's that?"

"I have no idea but as long as it's not eyeballs and worms, I'm willing to try it."

Roxie grimaced. "Ew, Ma! I didn't need that in my head."

Trina laughed. "I'm glad you had a good night, Mimi. Do you want a refill on your drink? Hey, where's your glass?"

Willie started to look for it, then realized she'd left it downstairs. "Still on the table downstairs, I suspect."

Trina got up. "I'll get it. Won't take me a sec."

"Thanks, honey." As Trina left, Willie shook her head. "I love that girl. Never complains, never fusses, just a help all the time."

Roxie smiled. "She's good like that." Her smile waned. "You didn't say anything about the you-know-what, did you?"

Trina had already gone down the steps. There was no danger of her overhearing Willie. "The money? No, not a peep. I won't, either, I promise.

I'm not going to risk getting her hopes up like that."

Roxie nodded. "Good. I really hope it's real."

"So do I." Willie thought about Miguel. "I think I'd like to live in Diamond Beach. Wouldn't you?"

"Sure is nice." Roxie looked toward the windows —not that you could see much in the dark. "Can you imagine actually living on the beach? I mean, could that really happen?"

Willie was probably never going to stop smiling at this rate. "Why not? With that kind of money, anything is possible. And I think we *should* move. Trina could get a lot more money for what she does in a town like this. She could really make a name for herself. More so than in Port St. Rosa."

"I agree about that. You know," Roxie said, eyes narrowing. "We need to do a little research for her. See what the salons in town are like, what they charge, if there's any available space for her to open a place in, that sort of thing."

Willie thought about that. "You don't think that's putting the cart before the horse?"

"Maybe," Roxie said. "But if that money does come in, we'll be ahead of the game."

"That is true." Willie nodded. "All right. Let's do

it. We'll start tomorrow. But how are we going to distract Trina?"

Roxie stared at the television. "I'm not sure yet."

The front door opened as Trina returned. She walked into the living room, Willie's cup in hand. "Got it, Mimi."

"Thanks, honey. Just stick it in the dishwasher for me, will you?"

"Sure thing. You want anything else while I'm up?"

Willie glanced at Roxie, then back at Trina. "What do you say we make some popcorn and watch a movie? I could really go for some popcorn. With extra butter."

Trina grinned. "Are you in the mood for popcorn because of Miguel?"

"Hah!" Willie laughed. "I hadn't even thought about that, but maybe I am."

"Popcorn does sound good," Roxie said. "Maybe we were both influenced by those handsome men."

Shaking her head, Trina went into the kitchen and got out two bags of microwave popcorn, then a stick of butter from the fridge. "Well, now that you two have been talking about it, I want some, too. What movie are we going to watch?"

Willie looked at her granddaughter, at the young

woman she loved with all her heart. What a blessing that child was. "Your choice, honey. What do you feel like?"

"Something..." Trina bit her lip, a coy smile playing on her face. "Romantic. How about *Moonlight*? That one with Cher."

"You mean *Moonstruck*," Roxie said.

"That's the one," Trina said. She put the stick of butter in a glass measuring cup and stuck it in the microwave to melt.

"I'm in." Willie nodded enthusiastically. "That young Nic Cage is all right with me." She put her hand to her chest as she fluttered her eyelashes. "He's the most delicious Italian dish served in that whole movie."

"Ma!" Roxie laughed.

"What?" Willie said. "He is."

Trina snorted as the microwave beeped. She took the butter out and put the first bag of popcorn in but didn't start it yet. "Well, I'm putting on my jammies before we start."

"Same here," Willie said. She was ready for a nightgown and slippers. "I think I'll take off my face, too."

"Let's all get ready for bed, then meet back here," Roxie said.

"Deal," Trina said. "Then I'll make the popcorn."

They all departed for their respective bedrooms.

Willie took a nightgown from the dresser drawer. It was one Trina had given her a few years ago. It was sort of a medium purple printed with a pattern of coffee cups holding all kinds of different coffees.

She smiled as she changed into it. Then she said a little prayer the money really did come through and that she could use it to make Trina's dreams of owning her own salon a reality.

That girl deserved the world.

Chapter Six

*J*ules got to the Dolphin Club with about forty-five minutes to spare before she was supposed to go on. She had her guitar across her back and her purse and travel kit in one hand. She was about to check in at the hostess stand when Jesse walked up.

He greeted her with a big smile. "Hey, there you are."

She was surprised to see him. She figured she'd have to ask for him. "How did you know I was here?"

"I've been keeping an eye on the security cameras in the office." He laughed. "I am so glad you're here. I owe you big time."

She shrugged nonchalantly. "You haven't heard my set yet."

He shook his head. "I don't need to in order to

know you're going to be great. You look fantastic, too."

"Thanks." Her borrowed accessories were working, apparently. Points for Trina. "Where can I get set up and do a sound check?"

"Follow me." He took her through the club, which was pretty busy, to the special events venue. "This is all yours tonight."

She looked around. "It's really nice. Have you let the ticketholders know they're not going to see the act they paid for?"

He nodded. "We sent out a text and an email. So far we've only had about eight percent want refunds. I'm very happy with that. And we're going to sell any empty seats at the door, just in case."

"Are you?" She pulled out her phone. "I know it's late notice, but I'll post to my social media right now about some last-minute availability. You never know."

"No, that's great. Thank you."

As she finished up her post, an older man walked out from the side of the stage. He gave Jesse a nod. "Boss."

Jesse gestured to him. "Jules, this is Scotty Chamberlain. He's our sound and lighting guy. He'll get you taken care of and hooked into the system. Scotty, this is our saving grace, the beautiful and talented Julia Bloom."

Jules almost blushed. She switched her purse and travel kit to her other hand so she could shake the man's hand. "Nice to meet you, Scotty. Pleasure to work with you."

"You, too, Ms. Bloom."

"Please, call me Jules or I'll think my mother's in the room."

He laughed. "All right, Jules it is."

Jesse rubbed his hands together. "I'll let you get to it then."

Jules glanced at him. "Will you be here for the show?"

He nodded. "You bet. I'll be backstage. I wouldn't miss it."

She smiled. "See you there."

Scotty helped her get set up, mic'd up, and situated on stage. She liked to sit on a stool or pub-height chair, so he provided her with the latter. She sat and made sure she could get positioned comfortably. "This will work."

"Great." He ran through some lighting with her, finding what worked best.

After that, they did a quick sound check, then she put her guitar on the stand the club had provided and followed Scotty back to the dressing room.

"Here you go." He gestured to a small monitor on the wall by the door. "You'll be able to watch the stage activity and hear your introduction on this. So long as the sound is on." He tapped the screen and turned the volume up a couple of notches. "We're about fifteen minutes out. Doors will be opening right about now."

"Great, thank you." She put her bag down on the vanity table. It held a big mirror surrounded by lights. She'd take a quick look at her makeup and hair to be sure nothing was amiss, but otherwise, she was ready.

"You need anything, hit the intercom button."

"I'm sure I'll be fine. Thanks for all your help."

"Have a good show." He gave her a nod and left, closing the door.

Besides the vanity table, there was a big, comfortable-looking couch with a low, oval-shaped coffee table in front of it. On that was a fruit plate, another of cheese and crackers, and an arrangement of fresh flowers.

Next to the couch was a regular height table. On it was a large cooler with numerous kinds of bottled drinks, a Keurig coffee machine with a big basket of different kinds of K-cups, and a tea kettle, along with cups and a box that held a variety of regular and flavored teas. There was sugar, honey, artificial sweeteners, and powdered creamer, plus a bottle of half and half in the cooler.

She made a cup of herbal tea but used the Keurig, since she wanted to be quick. She added honey to it, because it was good for the throat, then let the cup sit a minute to cool enough to drink.

She paced while she waited, thinking about the songs she was going to do tonight. It was her standard small-venue set.

A countdown clock appeared on the monitor. Ten minutes to go.

She took her tea to the vanity table, flipped on the lights, and had a good look at herself. Other than a little more gloss, she was ready. She sipped her tea and waited for her introduction, watching the image of the closed curtains, behind which were her guitar in the stand and the empty chair.

She was nervous, but it wasn't stage fright so much as the low-key nerves of just wanting to do a good job and knowing she was about to face an audience who'd expected to see someone else tonight.

A crowd like that could be tough, although

considering they'd been offered a refund and had chosen to attend, she had hopes they'd be receptive.

A spotlight appeared on the curtains and the rest of the lights went down in the venue. Jesse's voice came over the speaker system. "Ladies and gentlemen, the Diamond Beach Dolphin Club is honored to present this evening's musical talent, here on short notice to fill in for Sam Mayfield."

Jules took a breath and walked into the side wing of the stage, where Jesse's voice could still be heard.

"She's an award-winning member of the Grand Ole Opry and a Florida native. She's also one of my favorite artists. Please join me in welcoming the talented Julia Bloom."

Applause filled the air. Jules walked out on stage as the curtains drew back. She nodded and smiled as she picked up her guitar and settled into her seat. "Thank you to the Dolphin Club for having me and a big thanks to all of you who decided to see me, even though I'm not Sam Mayfield."

A little bit of laughter rippled through the crowd.

She wanted to warm them up some more. "For those of you who aren't familiar with me or my music, I'm going to start off with something to help you get to know me. It's one of my biggest hits."

She started playing and, almost immediately, she

saw heads moving. She wasn't sure those folks recognized exactly what the tune was, but she knew when she started singing, they definitely would.

She took a measured breath as she leaned toward the mic. *"Big Red Kibble is the one for me. Makes my dog happy, as you can see—"*

The crowd erupted in applause and laughter.

Guitar nestled against her body, she held up her hands and smiled. "I don't only do jingles, I promise. Here's an actual song of mine you might know: *Country Girl.*"

Happy faces appeared in the first few rows that she could see. Good to know she had some fans out there. She repositioned her hands and strummed the intro, then began to sing.

"Bright lights, big city, country girl looking pretty. All she wants is a chance to sing in the town that made Elvis king. She's got those Memphis blues..."

Chapter Seven

Kat woke up earlier than usual without really knowing why. Couldn't be *that* early because bright sun was streaming through the shutters. She looked at the time. A few minutes after six.

She lay there for a little longer, staring up at the ceiling and thinking about the dream she'd had. She'd been so happy in the dream. She tried to hold onto that feeling but it was nearly half-gone and the last few bits of it were fast fading.

Why had a dream made her feel like that? And if that was really what being happy felt like, she had to have more of it. No matter what that meant for her life.

Maybe it was time for a much bigger change than she realized.

She squinted at the clock again. Might as well get

up. Being in bed wasn't going to accomplish anything. Even though it was comfy.

She'd stayed up last night after dinner, watching some television with her grandmother, but she'd been plenty tired. She'd tried to stay awake until Aunt Jules came home so Kat could hear all about her show at the Dolphin Club, but that hadn't happened. Kat's lids started drifting closed around eleven.

She yawned and decided to make the most of being up early and got dressed for a beach walk. Although, coffee before the walk seemed like a good idea. Otherwise, she might end up laying down on the beach and having a nap. She got out her sneakers, but just left them by the bed. She went out to the kitchen to start the coffee. Her mother was already out there.

"Morning," her mom said softly. She was in her robe and had the coffee pot under the tap, filling it with water. "I'm trying not to wake Grandma or Aunt Jules up."

"Right," Kat said. "I'm glad you're making coffee."

"I need some. But then I'm going for a power walk."

"I was going to do the same thing."

Her mom took the coffee pot over to the machine

and poured the water into the reservoir. "Do you want to join me?"

"I'd love to, yeah."

"Great." Her mom added a filter, scooped coffee into it, then hit the Brew button. "I need to get dressed."

"I need to get my shoes on. Meet you back here." Kat went to the bedroom, tied on her sneakers, then brushed her teeth. Not the best thing to do right before drinking coffee, but she didn't want to breathe her morning breath all over her mom on their walk, either.

She pulled her hair into a ponytail and slipped on a visor to keep the sun out of her eyes. She put her sunglasses on top of her head, so she'd remember to take them with her. Then she returned to the kitchen and got two mugs down from the cabinet before taking out the half and half.

Her mom showed up as the coffee maker was sputtering out the last few drops. They each filled their mugs, added sweetener and creamer, then stood there sipping until the caffeine kicked in.

Kat held her mug with both hands, enjoying the warmth coming through the ceramic. "Coffee is life."

Her mom let out a little snort. "No argument from me. How come you're up so early? I thought you were up late with Grandma watching murder shows."

"I was, sort of. I tried to stay up until Aunt Jules got back, but I didn't make it. Not sure why I woke up so early, but a walk seemed like the thing to do." There was something else, though. Something that had been on her mind since she'd woken up. "Do you ever wish you'd done something different with your life besides being a mom? Be honest—you won't hurt my feelings."

Her mom took another drink of her coffee, then set her mug on the counter. "Sometimes, yes. Which doesn't mean I regret having you at all. But I do wish I'd gotten to teach like I'd wanted to." A hint of a smile played across her mother's face. "I think I would have been good at it. I feel like I would have loved it. Now I'll never know."

"I'm sorry about that. The wondering, I mean. I bet you would have been a great teacher."

"Thanks." Her mom picked up her coffee again. "Why? Are you wishing you could do something different?"

"I don't know." But Kat was definitely wishing that. She just didn't know what that different thing might be. She drained the last of her coffee and put her mug next to the machine so she could refill it when they got back. "Ready to walk?"

Her mom set her cup alongside Kat's. "Yes. Back steps?"

"Right behind you."

Once they were out on the sand, side by side, Kat brought up the subject again. "I had a dream last night that made me happier than I think I've ever been in real life."

"Oh? What was it about the dream that made you feel that way?"

Kat shook her head. "I don't know."

"Yes, you do. Just tell me. I won't judge."

Kat took a breath. "In the dream, I was making jewelry. That was my job. I made pretty things with these gemstone beads and sea glass and shells and... It's dumb, I know."

"It's not dumb." Her mom gave her a look that Kat knew well. It said Kat had better not think it was dumb, either. "I bet there are lots of people who make a living doing just that. Especially in a town like this. Look at that shop in town. What's the name of that place?" She shook her head. "Tide Gems? Ocean Treasures? You know, the place that sells all that one-of-a-kind art and jewelry. Your grandmother would know."

Kat nodded. "I think you mean Tide and Treasure. I haven't been in that place in a while. Maybe I should go over there and see if any of it appeals to me."

"You definitely should. Maybe you could learn to make some simple pieces and see how that makes you feel."

The sand was nice and hard under Kat's feet. "Or if I'm even any good at it. I'm not creative. It's probably a du—"

"Kat."

"Well, Mom, it *might* be a dumb idea. I don't really feel any sort of major pull to make jewelry."

"But you are creative. I don't know why you'd think otherwise."

"Um, maybe because I'm an actuary? Being creative in my field of work gets you fired. It's pretty much the opposite of what you're supposed to do."

"I understand that, but it doesn't mean you don't have the ability to be creative."

Kat shrugged. "Maybe. I just felt so good this morning when I first woke up that I want to recapture that feeling."

"Makes sense. Who wouldn't?"

Her mom was breathing a little harder than usual but so was Kat. They both were obviously out of shape and in need of this kind of thing on a daily basis. Kat caught her breath before speaking. "We should do this every day."

"I agree."

"How much longer do you want to stay here?"

Her mom didn't answer right away. "I don't know. Truth is, I don't really want to leave. There are some memories here that only add to my feelings of betrayal, but I'm sure I'll feel that way when we get home, too. Might be worse there, for all I know."

"You can stay longer," Kat said. "You don't have a job to go back to. You could be here another month if you wanted."

"Not sure that's a smart idea. I should probably get back in a week or so and work on getting a job."

"What about Dad's insurance? And selling this place?"

Her mom let out a deep sigh and shook her head. "I found out that the attorney is also handling the life insurance, because he's the executor of the will, but that's all I know right now."

"Why?"

"Because...your father's lawyer is still trying to figure it all out. He said he needs a little time."

Kat frowned. "What's to figure out? Just read the will and tell us who gets what."

"I agree, but apparently, your father made changes right before he passed away and ... And I don't really know why there's a holdup. I'll call Mr. Kinnerman again when we get back and see if I can get an update. But until I know who's going to end up with the beach house and your father's life insurance, I can't do anything."

Kat considered that. "You think he left it to her?"

"I think it's possible he left some of it to her. I don't think he would have left us with nothing. At least..."

"At least you hope not. I hope not, too. That wouldn't be fair to you at all. Your entire life has been raising me and being Mrs. Bryan Thompson. If you don't get something for doing that, then you should change your name and go back to being Claire Bloom. I'll do it, too, if he's left you with nothing."

"Kat."

"I'm serious." Kat's anger over what her father had done was quickly returning. "If he screws you over like that, I don't want his name." She wasn't sure she wanted it now.

Her mom went silent for a little bit. "I've been thinking about going back to Bloom anyway."

Kat glanced over. "You should do it."

"Maybe. I don't know."

"Why wouldn't you?"

"Because it would mean having to explain to everyone why I was doing it. They think we had a perfectly wonderful marriage. Changing my name would be a pretty clear indicator that it wasn't."

"But that's the truth. He was lying to you. To me, too. All of that work he was supposedly doing was really just him spending time with his other family. Who cares if people know what he was really up to? It's not like it was your fault."

Her mother shrugged like she wasn't sure she agreed with that.

Kat decided to change the subject. "Danny Rojas and his dad are really nice."

Her mom smiled. "They are. That was fun last night, wasn't it?"

Kat nodded. "Are you going to help him with his new popcorn flavor?"

"If he really wants me to, sure."

"Cool." Kat liked the idea of her mom and Danny. Anyone who could make her mom smile was all right with her. "Maybe he'll ask you out on a date."

Her mom snorted. "Don't get ahead of yourself. We're just friends."

"For now." She gave her mom a little nudge with her elbow. "I'm going on a date tonight."

"What?" Her mom almost stumbled over a piece of driftwood. "You are?"

Kat nodded. "It's a double date, actually. He's a fireman. The one who told me about the sandcastle-building contest. And he's bringing a friend of his for Trina."

"What about Ray?"

"Ray told me if I wanted to see other people, he was okay with that."

Her mother looked stricken. "He said that?"

"I have the text to prove it."

"Wow." Her mom stared straight ahead. "Sometimes that man surprises even me. I know he wants to keep you happy, but dating other people seems like a bit much."

"Don't you think I need to see for myself if he's really the one?"

"Sure, but—"

"How else am I supposed to do that except by going out with other people?"

Her mom sighed. "I don't know. I guess that would be a way. I just would have thought that would be the kind of thing Ray would put his foot down about."

Kat sent a blast of breath through her nostrils. "Mom, Ray doesn't put his foot down about anything."

"No, I suppose he doesn't." She tugged at her T-shirt. "And this fireman, you met him at that sandcastle thing?"

"I met him the morning of that event on the beach. He handed me a flyer. But then I got to know him a bit better at the sandcastle-building contest, yes."

"He's nice?"

"He seems so. He's a surfer and a fireman. That's about all I know. And Trina's going with me, so it's not like I'm going by myself."

"How much protection do you think she's going to be?"

Kat laughed. "I don't know. I bet more than you think. Trina looks like she could throw a punch if she had to."

Her mom chuckled. "Maybe. Her mother sure does."

Chapter Eight

Roxie sat on the back porch and looked at the water while she drank her coffee. It was so quiet and peaceful at this time of the morning. She wasn't a super-early riser but being up at this hour had its benefits. A little alone time, out here in the fresh air, with the subtle scent of salt and sea drifting past was really nice.

The idea of never leaving this place felt like a dream. If it happened, it *would* be a dream come true, that much was for certain.

Coming to Double Diamond with Bryan had always felt that way to her, like a dream. Although maybe "gift" was a better word. Being here with him had always been such a special experience. It was a true escape. Not only had they been able to spend quality time together, but as an added bonus, this house was far nicer than the one they lived in. The location was infinitely better, too.

At home, sitting on her small lanai meant looking at her neighbor's fence. Roxie had planted a couple of palm trees along with some hibiscus and a few crotons to brighten things up, but a fence with plants in front of it was still a fence. They didn't even have a pool, which was fine. One less expense to worry about, and the community they lived in had one.

Roxie didn't need a pool to lay out by and she certainly wasn't going to put her hair in all that chlorinated water, but it was a nice way to cool off in the middle of a Florida summer.

Besides the fancy house and the incredible location, Diamond Beach now offered something that Port St. Rosa didn't—the chance for Trina to command top dollar for her services. Diamond Beach was well-named. There was a lot of money here.

No reason Trina shouldn't get a share of that.

Roxie smiled, thinking about what Trina's salon might look like it and how fun it would be to work there. All those wealthy women coming in. Big tippers, she imagined.

Maybe Trina would even have her own product line someday. Wouldn't that be something?

The sliding doors from the living room opened and Willie came out, still in her housecoat, a cup of coffee in her hand. "Morning, Rox."

"Morning, Ma. Trina up?"

Willie nodded as she shut the slider and came to sit by Roxie in a nearby chair. "I'm pretty sure I heard the shower." She sipped her coffee, then set it on the side table. "That was fun last night, wasn't it?"

"You mean the popcorn and the movie or dinner with the neighbors?"

"Both." Willie smiled. "But meeting Miguel was especially fun. Really helped take some of the hurt out of my heart about Zippy."

"I'm glad for that."

Willie let out a long, soft sigh. "Not all of it, mind you. But a good bit. Hard to believe he's really gone. And what he might have left me."

"I was just out here daydreaming about what Trina's salon might look like." Roxie smiled. "Getting ahead of things, I know, but I can't help myself."

"I don't blame you. It's fun to dream like that, isn't it? Especially when there's a real chance of it coming true. Not something we've had a lot of in this family. Dreams coming true, I mean." Wille picked up her cup again. "I used to feel that way about this place. First time we came here, I couldn't believe your husband had bought it. I was sure it was just a rental, but then we came back the next year and the year after that and, well, I had to believe eventually."

Roxie smiled. "This might be the best thing Bryan ever did. Outside of giving me Trina, I mean."

Willie nodded. "I'd agree with you on that. Trina first, then this place." She glanced over at her daughter. "He wasn't the worst husband you could have had. That's something."

Roxie nodded. "I did love him."

"I know you did, honey." Willie stretched her legs out so that she could rest her heels on the little rattan coffee table. "What's the plan for today? To start our recon for Trina? How are we going to keep her here?"

Roxie shook her head. "I don't know. Do you have any ideas?"

"We could say we're going to Winn-Dixie."

"Then we'd have to come home with groceries. Enough to justify the time away."

Willie seemed to give that some thought. "What if we tell her we're going to one of my grief meetings? I could say you're coming along because of Bryan."

"Might work. Unless she decides to come with us. And then if there's not really a meeting, she'll know we were up to something."

"Yeah, good point." Willie stared at Roxie. "You could come up with a few ideas, you know."

Roxie snickered. "If I had some, I would share them."

The slider opened again, and this time Trina came out, wearing her robe, her dry hair secured in a messy bun on top of her head, and a cup of coffee in her hand. She smelled like whatever sweet, fruity body wash she'd used. "Beautiful day, huh?"

Roxie and her mom both nodded. "Beautiful," Roxie said. "Any plans for it?"

Trina sat next to her mom on the sofa. "I was thinking I might go to the beach. Or maybe just lay by the pool." She grinned wide. "Either way, I want to work on my tan a little before my *date* tonight."

Roxie sat up. "Date? With who?"

"A guy named Miles, that's all I know," Trina said. "Kat set it up. She's going out with one of the firemen from the sandcastle-building contest and she got him to bring a friend for me so we can double date. Wasn't that nice?"

"Nice," Willie said, pointing her finger at Trina. "And smart. Better off not going alone these days."

"True," Trina said. "But I don't think that's why she did it. I think she wants me along so we can do something together. We're giving each other mini outfit makeovers. I'm spicing her up and she's toning me down."

"Down?" Roxie snorted. "You're fine just the way you are."

"I don't know, Ma," Trina said. "I'm not so sure about that." She sighed like the world rested on her shoulders. "I've never had a steady boyfriend, you know that. And I'd like one. Look at Kat. She's engaged. Or was. Either way, she at least knows what it takes to be in a committed relationship."

Willie leaned forward. "Are you lonely, honey?"

"Not lonely." Trina's smile was quick and easy. "But I'd love to have a boyfriend, Mimi. Someone to go out with. Someone to make a life with. You know how it is. If you didn't, you wouldn't have gotten married four times."

"True enough," Willie said. "But you don't know anything about this boy."

Trina shook her head. "Not much, no. I'm sure he'll be nice, though. I don't think Alex would bring someone who wasn't. He wouldn't want Kat getting mad at him. Oh, I do know that the guy is a paramedic. That's really good. Practically a doctor."

Roxie nodded. As a nurse, she approved of that. "Nothing wrong with someone in the medical field. Not at all."

"What did you say his name was?" Willie asked.

"Miles," Trina repeated.

Didn't sound like a very manly name to Roxie, but she wasn't about to say that out loud. Trina was excited and that was nice to see. Let her have her fun. And if this guy turned out to be a dud, there would always be a next one.

She looked at her daughter without turning her head, so it wasn't too obvious. Trina and Willie were talking about some reality TV show now, giving Roxie a chance to study her daughter. Trina was a beautiful girl, inside and out. She deserved someone who treated her like a queen.

Miles had better not think he was getting some kind of fast action with a tourist. She knew what locals could be like sometimes.

For a brief moment, she thought about following the young women on their date, but that didn't show a lot of trust in her daughter, and she didn't want Trina thinking anything like that.

But it was a mother's right to worry. At the same time, wouldn't it be something if Trina was about to meet the man of her dreams? What if this Miles was her knight in shining armor? Her prince on a white horse?

Roxie almost laughed at how quickly her thoughts had reversed themselves. That was a mother's prerogative, she supposed. She sipped her coffee, which needed to be refilled, and hoped that whatever happened tonight, Trina stayed safe.

Certainly with Kat there, the girls would be all right. But it wasn't just Trina's physical safety Roxie was worried about. She wanted her daughter to be safe emotionally, too. They'd all had their hearts broken enough lately.

Chapter Nine

Claire stepped out of the shower. The hot water felt good after the great walk she and Kat had just finished. She dried off, got dressed in her favorite white capri jeans but then got stuck on what top to wear. As she stared into her closet, her first thought was that her clothes were all so...boring.

There was that word again. And, boy, had she come to despise it. But as descriptions went, it wasn't too far off. Even her sundresses, an article of clothing that implied lightness and breeziness, seemed dull and lifeless.

She lived in Florida, for crying out loud. Where were the bright, happy colors? The tropical prints? The fun accessories and cute sandals and little straw purses?

What had she been thinking to clothe herself

this way? How had she gotten to such a bleak place in her life?

She knew how—by putting Bryan and Kat first. By worrying about them and not herself. But also by letting herself go until she no longer felt like she wanted to be seen.

That realization shook her. She exhaled, trying to flush the weight of that sudden understanding from her spirit. That era of her life was definitely over.

Unfortunately, she couldn't afford to go shopping. Not until she knew what was happening with Bryan's insurance and this house. With a sigh, she took out a gray and white striped top from her closet and pulled it on.

She looked at herself in the mirror. Didn't prisoners wear gray and white stripes?

Rolling her eyes at herself, she went back to the bathroom and did her best to recreate the hairstyle Trina had given her yesterday.

It wasn't too hard, but it would take getting used to, since it was a different way of doing things. She smiled suddenly. Wasn't that appropriate, though? From here on out, she *wanted* to do things differently. In fact, maybe that should be her new life motto. She spoke the words out loud. "Different is better."

Granted, that wasn't always going to be true, but it would certainly make her life more interesting. She went out to the kitchen. Her mom was getting a yogurt out of the fridge.

"Is that your breakfast?" Claire asked. "Because I was about to make some eggs. I was thinking about doing a frittata, actually."

"Oh?" Margo seemed to weigh that idea. The yogurt went back into the fridge. "That sounds lovely. Can I help?"

"If you want to chop some veggies, that would be great."

"I can do that. Which ones?"

"How about sundried tomatoes, a little onion, and mushrooms? I'll add some ham and cheese to that."

"Perfect." Her mom took an onion from the bowl in the center of the island, a knife from the knife block, then retrieved a cutting board from one of the cabinets. "Where's Kat?"

"Showering. Or maybe blow-drying her hair."

"I hope she maintains that new look."

"I'm sure she will. She's pretty fond of it." Claire got out a skillet that could also go into the oven. She drizzled some olive oil in and set it to medium-high heat. "You were right, you know."

"I was? About what?"

"About me being boring. I am. Or I was. I've decided that's not going to be me anymore. The hair was just the beginning. I'm going to take better care of myself from now on. I've already started by walking every morning. I'm going to keep that up, too. And I'm going to eat better. And dress better."

Her mother's brows rose ever so slightly.

Claire laughed. "Today's outfit doesn't count. None of them do until I can go shopping. My wardrobe is pitiful right now. Needs a revamp, but I can't really afford to do that until I know what's going on with everything else."

She looked at the time on the microwave. "As soon as it's nine, I'm calling the attorney again to get an update."

"Good for you," her mother said. "About all of it. If you'd like, I'd be more than happy to go shopping with you sometime."

"Thanks." She appreciated that, but her mother had more money than Claire did and her taste showed it. "I'll let you know."

The bedroom door opened, and a sleepy-eyed

Jules came out with Toby on his leash. "Please tell me there's coffee."

"There's coffee," Claire responded. "I'll have a cup waiting for you when you get back."

"You're a saint." Jules made her way to the elevator, Toby's nails click-clacking on the tiles like a woman in high heels.

"Late night?" Claire asked.

"Later than I intended." Jules smiled as the doors opened. "But a very good night."

The doors closed before Claire could ask any more questions. She looked at her mom. "What time did she get in?"

Margo shrugged. "I have no idea. I had my sleep mask on and my earplugs in, because I didn't want to be woken up."

Claire's phone beeped from the bedroom, making her realize it was still plugged into the charger. "Be right back."

She went into the bedroom and unplugged her phone, looking at the screen. Danny had texted her.

Just a simple *Good morning*.

She smiled as she typed, *Good morning to you*.

Almost instantly, three little dots appeared to let her know he was responding.

His text arrived. *Headed to Mrs. Butters around 10. Care to join me in my adventures?*

She sent back, *To make lemon popcorn?*

His response was a thumbs-up emoji.

Should she go? She had more than enough time to eat and be ready. Why not spend the day with Danny? It was certainly something new and different. She typed out, *I'd love to.*

Great. See you a few minutes before. I'll drive.

She put her phone in her back pocket and walked into the kitchen. Kat had joined them and was drinking coffee, her hair looking pretty close to perfect.

Margo had added the onions to the pan and was working on slicing the mushrooms. The oven had been set to three hundred and fifty degrees and was coming up to temp. Her mom glanced at her. "You look happy about something."

"I am," Claire said. "I'm going to help Danny work on that new flavor of popcorn today."

Kat grinned but said nothing.

Jules and Toby returned. Jules scooped Toby up and took him into the laundry room to wash and dry his feet. Claire immediately got to work on the coffee she'd promised her sister.

She had it ready well before Jules joined them in the kitchen.

Jules took hold of the cup and drank like it was her last hope for survival. Toby headed for the couch, no doubt in need of a nap to recover from his walk.

Claire laughed at her sister's pitiful state. "Are you going to make it? You have to tell us about last night. How did it go?"

Jules took her cup over to the counter that separated the kitchen from the dining room and hopped up on it, her feet dangling. "It went great. I just didn't intend for the evening to go that long. I don't regret it, just feeling my age a little more than usual this morning, I guess."

"Seriously?" Kat said. "We need more than, 'It went great.'"

"I agree," Claire said as she stirred the onions.

Jules drank more coffee. "The set went better than I expected. Even though those people didn't get to see the act they'd hoped for, they were very welcoming and responsive. Lots of great applause. No complaints and it was a lot of fun. It totally energized me to get to work on my next album. Then afterwards..."

She stopped to sip her coffee. Claire took out the

eggs, ham, and cheese, then got a big bowl to whip the eggs in.

As she started cracking eggs, Jules set her cup down and continued. "Afterwards, I hung out with Jesse for a bit in the club's office. He was thrilled with my performance and wants to book me for a show of my own. Anyway, we talked a lot and ended up going to get a late supper. Very late."

"Nice," Kat said.

Jules put her hand to her stomach. "Somehow that food is starting to smell good, although I don't know how I can be hungry."

Margo tipped the mushrooms into the pan with the onions and gave them a stir. Savory aromas filled the air.

Claire added salt and half and half to the eggs, then whisked some more until it was all blended. "What time did you get home?"

Jules shook her head. "One thirty? Maybe closer to two? Like I said, late. Might have to nap by the pool later. After I do some work on the song I'm writing."

Margo smiled. "That's nice to hear."

Jules nodded. "It's nice to be doing it."

Claire thought there was some extra meaning to that little exchange, but she was too busy with the frittata to try to figure out what it might be. She added the eggs to the pan along with the ham she'd just chopped up, a couple of big handfuls of shredded cheese, then the sundried tomato pieces, and mixed it all together.

A few minutes after that, the oven beeped that it was ready. She opened it and slid the pan in, then set the timer. "Breakfast will be ready in about twenty minutes, if you want to shower."

"Cool." Jules got off the counter. "I'll be back."

Margo started to clean up, but Claire shooed her away. "Go read or something. I've got this. Or Kat can help."

"All right." Her mom went to her chair.

Kat started putting things away.

Claire carried the cutting board and knife to the sink, smiling as she washed them up. She was going to spend the day with Danny. Such a simple thing, but her mood was light and buoyant.

Was the anticipation of spending time with the right person really all it took to be happy?

Chapter Ten

Trina finished her second cup of coffee. If she was at work, she'd be having another. As she planned to lounge by the pool, there was no need. That wasn't something she had to be alert for. Breakfast, however, was a different story. "Anyone making breakfast or are we on our own?"

Willie nodded. "I'm thinking of toasting an English muffin and having it with some butter and raspberry jam. Although, I wouldn't be opposed to a side of scrambled eggs if anyone's making some."

Trina smiled. "I can make some, Mimi."

Her mom laughed. "Pretty sure that's what she was going for."

"I don't mind," Trina said. "Scrambled eggs are easy. I can put an English muffin in the toaster for you, too, Mimi." She got up.

"Thanks, honey. Hang on a second."

"Sure. You want more coffee?"

"No," her grandmother said. "I was just thinking you should get your nails done for your date tonight. Your mom and I can drop you off, then she can run me over to the drugstore. I need to pick up a few things."

Trina held out her hands and looked at her nails. Doing hair was hard on a manicure, so she kept them short and painted them herself, as a rule. It was cheaper that way.

"I'll give you the money," her grandmother said. "My treat."

"Mimi, you don't have to do that."

"I want to."

Roxie nodded. "You should, Trina. Why not? It's not like you do it all the time."

Trina looked at her. "Which one, date or get my nails done?"

"Either," her mother answered.

She had a point, Trina thought. "Yeah, you're right. Okay, I guess I will."

"Good," Mimi said. "We'll go after breakfast, which means I better go get ready."

Trina headed for the sliding doors. "And I'll get to work on breakfast. Ma, are you going to eat eggs, too?"

"Sure. And an English muffin. I'm craving one, now."

"All right, I'm on it." Trina went inside and prepared to make the simple meal, pulling out the eggs, butter, English muffins, and jam.

She put a pan on the stove and added a good hunk of butter to melt. Then she split two muffins and put them in the four-slice toaster, which she had to get out from one of the bottom cabinets.

Just as she was adding the eggs to the pan, her mom and grandmother came in from the porch. They walked through the living room and went to their bedrooms to get ready for the day. When they came back, they were both dressed, hair done, makeup on.

And breakfast was ready.

They took their plates back out to the porch. The day was too beautiful not to eat out there.

Trina settled back into her seat. "Look at that sky. That blue is something else, isn't it?"

Her mom nodded. "It really is. Couldn't you just live here?"

Trina smiled. "Wouldn't that be something?"

Willie paused, one half of an English muffin glistening with raspberry jam almost to her mouth. "It would be. But does that mean you want to move here?"

She looked at her grandmother. "You mean like if we inherit this house?"

"Sure," Mimi said. "Like that."

"Well..." Trina hadn't truthfully considered it. Not seriously. It was too much of a fantasy, really. "I'd have to get a job here."

Her mom shook her head. "That wouldn't be hard for you. Any salon would be lucky to have you."

"Still, one of them would have to actually have a space for me. But that probably wouldn't be too hard." Trina thought a little more. "Could we afford this place? It has to be more expensive to live in a house this size."

"Probably," Mimi said. "But my social security would cover a lot of it. There's no mortgage here. Just utilities and insurance. The usual stuff."

"Right," Trina said. But it seemed to her that those things would be more expensive at the beach than they were back home.

"You'd make more," her mother volunteered.

Trina glanced in her direction. "You think?"

"Absolutely. Salons around here definitely charge more. Which means the stylists make more.

You know how it is at the beach. Or any place with tourists."

"True. Everything is more expensive. But that might make paying bills harder, too." Trina wasn't sure about such a move. Things at home weren't always easy, but they were comfortable.

"I could go back to work full-time," her mother said. "So that would help."

That surprised Trina. "You'd really want to do that?"

"To live in a place like this?" Roxie grinned. "Yes. I would definitely want to do that."

Trina glanced over at her grandmother. Both she and Trina's mom looked unusually happy. If moving here was what they wanted to do, she wasn't about to stand in their way. "I guess we could give it a try."

Her mother's smile fell a bit. "You don't sound convinced."

"I guess I'm just not sure. It's not something I ever really thought about seriously. Daydreamed about, but you know, that's just a fantasy."

Willie swallowed the bite of eggs she'd just taken. "What if your date tonight turns into something and he wants to see you again? That would be another reason to make Diamond Beach home."

Trina smiled at how cute her grandmother was.

"Maybe. But that's a lot of pressure to put on a first date, Mimi."

Willie waved her hand like that was nonsense. "He'll be smitten with you, you'll see."

Trina snorted. "Yeah, I don't know about that."

"Well," Mimi said. "He will if you get those nails done."

Trina rolled her eyes, but before she knew it, breakfast was done, and she was at the nail salon. A place called Fancy Nails. Looked nice enough.

Her grandmother had given her fifty bucks and told her to have fun, once Trina had been assured that the salon could take her immediately. Then her mom and grandmother had gone to the drugstore.

Trina stared at the racks and racks of polish, trying to decide. She had no idea what she was going to end up wearing tonight. She'd figured on her jean miniskirt with a zebra print T-shirt, but Kat would probably veto that.

Maybe a nice neutral hot pink? That could go with just about anything. Except Kat probably wouldn't think so and for reasons Trina couldn't really name, she wanted Kat to approve of whatever her nails ended up looking like.

Thinking like Kat was so hard.

Trina took the easy way out and texted her. *Getting my nails done. Hot pink okay?*

While she waited for Kat to answer, she picked up a bottle of glittery green. That was pretty sweet, too.

Her phone buzzed. She read Kat's answer. *Get a French. Can't go wrong with that.*

Hmm. A French manicure was nice, but it was awfully plain, too. She looked over at the young woman who was waiting to do Trina's nails. "Is there any way to make a French manicure more fancy?" She did have fifty bucks to spend, after all.

The young woman smiled. "You like glitter?"

Trina laughed. "I think I came to the right place."

Chapter Eleven

So far, they'd done a lot of looking without really finding much. Willie pointed up ahead to a tiny strip mall. Actually, it was too little to be a mall. It was only four stores. It wasn't even half a mall. There was a shiny black pickup in the parking lot, but no other cars. "How about that place."

"It looks abandoned," Roxie said.

"Which is probably why it's for *sale*," Willie said. They hadn't seen much else so far. Diamond Beach was a hot retail spot. "Maybe I could buy the whole thing."

"Yeah, and you'd have to fix it up, too."

"So?" She looked at her daughter. "If I could afford it, why not? Then I'd have rental income from the other three businesses."

"True, but you'd have to be sure those places were rented out. Not to mention hiring someone to get them into shape first." Roxie pulled into the parking lot. "That's going to be a lot of money, don't you think?"

"I'm about to have a lot of money. And who knows until we call the number on the sign and find out. Besides that, Miguel might know someone who can do the work. He's lived in Diamond Beach for a while. He's got to be pretty connected."

Roxie nodded. "True. I guess I'm just a little intimidated by what a big project it would be to take on, but if you get this money, you should do something with it that will make it work for you. Owning property would do that."

Willie was starting to get excited. This could be just the opportunity they needed. She stared through the window, her eyes narrowing in on the end unit. "Hey, that place looks like it might have already been a salon."

"Hard to tell with the glare on the windows, the signs taken down, and the paper on the windows." Roxie parked. "Let's get out and see if we can peek in."

Willie unlatched her seatbelt. The two of them got out and walked to the last store in the row.

Roxie put her hand up to shield her eyes and leaned in close to the window. "Ma, this was definitely a salon. There are three sinks lined up in the back."

Willie had her hand over her face like a visor, too. "And all those spots where mirrors must have been. Still needs a lot of work, but not nearly as much as if we were starting from scratch."

"I love the black and white checkerboard floor," Roxie said. "I think Trina would like that, as well."

Willie straightened, filled with so much energy she could barely stand still. "This is exciting."

Roxie exhaled, a little smile bending her mouth. "It is, but it makes me nervous, too."

"I know," Willie said. "I understand that, trust me. But think about what this could mean for Trina."

"Can I help you ladies?"

They both looked in the direction the voice had come from. A man walked toward them from the pickup truck. He was clean-cut and wearing jeans and a polo shirt with the words "Lewis Bros. Construction" over the breast. Seemed to be about Roxie's age. Maybe a little younger. Hard to tell with his tan.

Willie stepped forward. "Just having a peek. Thinking about the possibilities."

He nodded and seemed to take her seriously,

which Willie appreciated. "This used to be a great little shopping center."

Roxie joined her mom, coming to stand at her side. "What happened? Why'd it close down?"

"Owner passed away, and the family who inherited it didn't take care of it, tenants moved out, and the family put it up for sale as is." He glanced at the building. "Needs work now, unfortunately. There was some roof damage from the hurricane, which I've patched up as best I could, but besides that, things just weren't maintained the way they should have been."

Willie took another look at the former salon before giving him her full attention again. "You sound like you know a lot about this place."

He smiled. "I do, because I was the builder. Now the family just gives me a small stipend to keep an eye on the place, fix the most pressing things, and show the place to any potential buyers."

Roxie stuck her hand out. "I'm Roxie Thompson, by the way. This is my mom, Willie Pasternak."

He shook Roxie's hand, his smile warming up considerably. "I'm Ethan Lewis. Nice to meet you both. Are you considering buying the place?"

Willie took a quick look at her daughter, who seemed unusually occupied with Ethan's clear blue eyes. "We might be. Do you know what they're asking?"

Ethan stuck his thumbs in his belt. "Last I heard, they wanted one point six."

"Million?" Willie wanted to be sure. She didn't know much about buying real estate. She didn't want to misunderstand a single thing.

"Yes," Ethan answered. "But again, it's as is. There is definitely work that needs doing."

"Okay. What'll it take to get it presentable again?" If anyone knew, Willie figured it would be the man who'd built it.

"Honestly?" He scratched his head as he studied the building. "I'd say a couple hundred thousand on top of that. Probably why it hasn't had any serious offers in a while."

Willie wasn't fazed by any of the numbers he'd given her so far. Not with the sum that was potentially coming her way. "How much land?"

"I can't remember exactly, but I know there was a plan in place to expand with another strip of three stores and one pad in front that will take a stand-alone like a bank or a fast-food place. So enough for that and more parking, but again, I can't recall the actual lot size."

Roxie cleared her throat softly. "Maybe we could

get your number? In case we had any more questions?"

Ethan gave her a quick nod. "Sure."

Willie almost rolled her eyes, except that it was actually a good idea. "If we were to buy this place, would you be available to do the repairs and get things up to snuff?"

"I would," Ethan said. "I wish they'd pay me to do it now, but they don't want to put any more money into it." He dug out two cards from his back pocket and handed them each one. "There you go. You need anything, you just call me."

"Thank you. We'll do that," Roxie said. She tucked his card into her front pocket. "Maybe you should take down my number, in case you think of something we ought to know about this place."

He smiled. "All right."

She proceeded to give it to him, making sure that he spelled her name right in his contacts, too.

Willie had taken his card and tucked it in her fanny pack, but she wasn't quite done asking Ethan questions just yet, so when he looked up again, she said, "This place behind us looks like it was a salon. What were the other three stores?"

He pointed at the salon. "That was definitely a hairdressers, then the place next to it was a beach shop. You know, tourist stuff. T-shirts, postcards, sunscreen, beach towels, that kind of thing. Next to that was a card and gift shop. They sold a lot of candles. The other end unit was a pizza place for a while, but then they moved out. New people turned it into a fancy sit-down Italian restaurant and that didn't go so well."

"Too expensive?" Roxie asked.

He shook his head. "Not exactly. Diamond Beach can support higher prices. But the food wasn't so great. And the portions were small. Too small for Italian food, anyway. Nobody wants a kid-size plate of spaghetti for sixteen bucks."

Willie snorted. "For sixteen bucks, I can make enough spaghetti to feed an army."

"Exactly," Ethan said, chuckling. "Anyway, I have a few more properties I need to check on, but again, if you need anything else, just call. Or text." He was looking at Roxie. "My email's on the card, too."

Roxie, all smiles, nodded. "We'll be in touch. I hope your wife doesn't get jealous if there are two single women trying to reach you."

Ethan put his hands on his hips, eyes glittering with amusement. "I don't think she will. We've been divorced for six years."

"Well," Roxie said. "That's good to know. You have a wonderful day, Ethan."

"You, too, Roxie."

This time, Willie turned her head, pretending to be interested in the empty shop again so she could roll her eyes without either of them seeing her. That girl was shameless, but in truth, Willie was just as amused as Ethan appeared to be. He was a good-looking guy with his own business and what looked to be a brand-new pickup truck.

No surprise Roxie was attracted to him. And, of course, what man wouldn't be interested in a good-looking woman who didn't balk at the idea of spending close to two million dollars on a project that could potentially provide him with work, too?

And, yes, Ethan seemed like a nice guy, but Willie would do a little asking around. Namely, she'd see what Miguel had to say about him.

If nothing else, it was a reason to talk to Miguel again.

Chapter Twelve

Margo dressed impeccably for lunch. Brighton's Café required it. She wore one of three dresses she'd brought, a seersucker shirt dress with a white belt. She paired it with a white cardigan, white sandals, and blue button earrings.

She imagined Conrad would be similarly attired, but then again, she wasn't sure. Florida was so casual that it could be hard to predict what someone else thought was appropriate.

Didn't matter. She would have to use this lunch to explain her situation and that there was really no point in her continuing to attend the book club meetings, because she wouldn't be here for much longer.

She'd miss the loss of his friendship more, although that was such a ridiculous thought, she could barely stand herself. She'd only just met the man. Honestly, she needed to get her emotions under control.

The whole idea that she needed to be happy was, well, frankly, nonsense. She was fine. So what if she wasn't totally happy? She was healthy. She had her family. That was more than a lot of people had.

She picked up her purse and went to her grand-daughter's room. Kat was looking through her closet, probably trying to find the right outfit for her date this evening. "Do you mind if I take the car?"

Kat glanced over her shoulder, scrunching up her face. "I wouldn't, but I was going to get my nails done. Trina is, so I figured I'd better, too."

"You never get manicures." But Margo wasn't about to stand in the way of Kat's sudden interest in taking care of herself.

"I know, but..." Kat shrugged. "I thought I should."

"Well, I agree." Margo smiled. "Do you need a little money?"

Kat laughed. "Thanks, Grandma, but I can swing a manicure."

"All right, just checking. I'll see if Jules can let me use her Jeep again."

Kat nodded. "She's either upstairs or by the pool. Not sure where she ended up."

"I'll text her. You might need to keep an eye on Toby for a little bit."

"No problem." Kat squinted. "Where are you going, by the way? You're all dressed up."

"Lunch. With a friend." That was as much as Margo was willing to tell anyone. Especially since she was about to end things with Conrad. No point in dragging her family into it.

Kat pursed her lips and looked like she was about to ask who that friend might be.

Margo cut her off with a little half-truth. "I'll be late to meet Connie if I don't go now. See you later."

"Connie?" Kat looked disappointed.

Margo left, smirking to herself. She wasn't really going to be late. She just hadn't been sure how else to slip in Conrad's nickname. Not that she'd ever call him that. She stood in the kitchen and texted Jules. *Are you around? Can I borrow your car? Kat needs hers.*

Sure. Keys are in my purse. I'm by the pool working.

Hope all is going well. Margo didn't hear music, so Jules must be writing.

So far, yes. Thanks! You can take those books back to the library if you want. My creative block is GONE.

Margo smiled. *Glad to hear it.*

She went back to the bedroom, got the books, and the keys, then went downstairs. Jules was sitting on one of the chaises by the pool, head down, Toby asleep on the pool deck. Margo didn't interrupt.

She just went over and climbed into the Jules's Jeep. Margo didn't love the vehicle or driving it. Jeeps weren't the most sophisticated cars. More for tomboys and hippies, as far as she was concerned, but transportation was transportation.

She returned the books to the library, then took her time driving to the Hamilton Arms, the hotel that housed Brighton's Café. Years ago, she'd brought Jules, Claire, and Kat here for afternoon tea, which was a delightful event. She wondered if they still did it. She'd have to ask. Maybe she could bring them all back here one last time before they headed home.

She parked and walked in, admiring the gorgeous landscaping. As soon as she entered the lobby, the fragrant perfume of fresh flowers greeted her along with the reserved quiet of the space. Marble was everywhere. Tiling the floors, in columns on either side of the entrance, fronting the grand reception desk.

It gave the interior a majestic, Old World elegance that was generally lacking in new construction. She adored this place. It was no surprise to her that they did so many weddings here. The gardens on the property were just as beautiful.

She made her way through the lobby to the café, which sat at the right rear of the hotel to take advantage of the water views. The pool was, thankfully, to the left, cutting down on the noise and the need to see anyone in their swimsuit.

She walked into the café and smiled at the man at the door.

He nodded at her. "Good afternoon, ma'am. One for lunch?"

"No, I'm joining Conrad Ballard. I don't know if he's here yet."

The man smiled. "He is. Right this way."

She followed him and they arrived at a cozy little table by the window. The view was wonderful and a thoughtful awning outside kept the sun from blazing in.

Conrad stood. "Margo. How nice to see you again."

"You, too, Conrad."

The host pulled out her chair for her and she sat. "Do you eat here often?"

Conrad smiled. "Just when I'm trying to impress someone."

She laughed. "Well, mission accomplished."

"Good." He picked up his menu, a single laminated page, but kept his eyes on her. "You look lovely, by the way."

"Thank you. So do you." He did, too. He was in pale blue slacks and a short-sleeved white shirt with embroidery down either side of the button placket. Tropical without being gaudy, the way so many of those shirts were. She approved.

She glanced over her menu and made her decision quickly. The shrimp salad would do nicely. A scoop of freshly made shrimp salad over a bed of mixed greens accompanied by the chef's selection of fruits and vegetables. She set the menu aside.

"Would you like a glass of wine?"

She would have, but not while driving. "I'd better not. I've borrowed my daughter's car. Don't want to take any chances."

"I understand." He went back to perusing his menu.

That gave her a moment to study him and wonder what he'd say when she told him she wouldn't be able to see him again. Of course, that implied he'd *want* to see her again. She felt like that was a distinct possibility.

He looked up. "Do you know what you're getting?"

She nodded. "The shrimp salad. What about you?"

"The grouper sandwich." He put his menu down. "I have to confess something."

"Oh?" She leaned in, intrigued. "What's that?"

"It's been a long time since I've been on a date."

She laughed. "Is that what this is?"

"Isn't it?"

She nodded. "I suppose so."

"Is that all right?" He sat back slightly. "You don't look like you agree."

"No, I do. It *is* a date. And I haven't been on one in a very long time, either. Probably longer than you, I'd venture to say. But..." She exhaled, not quite ready to tell him the truth. They hadn't even ordered yet. She hated to drop such bleak news so early.

"But what? Was I wrong in thinking there was a spark of something between us?"

"No, you weren't wrong." She smiled tightly. This wasn't going how she'd imagined it. "It's just that I realized something yesterday after I got home."

Their server arrived just then, a young man named Ernesto. He brought them glasses of ice water. "Good afternoon. Are you ready to order?"

"Yes," Margo answered. "I'll have the shrimp salad and an iced tea, no lemon."

"Grouper sandwich with sweet potato fries," Conrad said next. "And water is fine for me."

"Very good." Ernesto took their menus and left.

Conrad looked at her expectantly. "What did you realize?"

"That as enjoyable as book club was, as was then spending time with you, it's rather pointless."

His face fell. "Why is that?"

"Because I don't live here. And I'll be going home soon. Back to Landry. It's not like I'm going to drive three hours just to come to book club."

"Why not?" he said. "You're welcome to stay in my guest room. No strings attached, of course."

Her instinct was to respond that she wasn't that kind of woman, but he'd said no strings attached and, besides that, he didn't strike her as being the sort of man who'd offer her a room in the hopes of more nefarious activities. She smiled. "That's very kind of you, but that's quite a drive for me."

He held her gaze for the moment, his eyes narrowing slightly. "And you're not interested enough in book club, or in me, I suppose, to make the effort."

"No, that's not what I meant." She sighed in frustration. "Conrad, I am twice widowed. I am not the carefree young woman I once was."

He nodded. "I get that. You're guarded and a little prickly and cautious."

"I am *not* prickly."

He laughed. "Margo, you are a living human cactus. But I get it. Pain does that to a person. Makes them shut down and close themselves off and do just about anything to keep from getting hurt again. Saw it in my fellow Marines who'd faced the horrors of combat. It's a defense mechanism."

They both fell quiet as Ernesto returned with her iced tea and a small glass caddy with a variety of sweetener options in it.

She took out a green packet, tore the top off, tipped the contents into her tea, and stirred the drink.

"If I offended you, I didn't mean to," Conrad said. "I'm a plain talker. Not everyone appreciates that."

"It's fine. You didn't say anything that wasn't true." She sighed. Why was life so hard?

"Why did you come to book club?"

She took a sip of her tea before looking at him. "Because a friend of mine suggested it as a way of finding happiness. She said I needed to get out more and be around people, but I see now that—"

"So did it?"

"Did it what?"

"Help you find happiness? Did book club make you happy?"

She couldn't lie. What was the point. "Yes, it did, but—"

"Did lunch with me make you happy?"

Warmth spread through her, a warmth she had no business feeling. "This isn't about that."

"I think it's exactly about that. What are you afraid of? Why isn't it worth making an effort to feel something good?"

She couldn't answer him. She didn't want to. She stared at the ice cubes in her glass.

"You're afraid to get hurt again." His words were a statement, not a question.

She looked at him. "What's wrong with that? What's wrong with wanting to protect myself?"

"Nothing, so long as you aren't also losing yourself in the process."

"I'm fine."

He let a moment of silence go by. "If you were fine, you wouldn't have been trying to find happiness."

She turned her head so she could look out the window. The sky and water were both so blue, the sun so bright. It looked like the perfect day.

His hand covered hers, causing her to let out a

little gasp at the sudden contact. "What would it take to make you reconsider? Because I'd love a shot at making you happy."

She stared at his hand on hers. It was so nice to be touched. To be wanted. This was worth risking heartache for, wasn't it? She'd be a fool not to. She closed her eyes for a moment before meeting his gaze. "Just be patient with me."

He nodded and gave her hand a little squeeze. "I can do that."

Chapter Thirteen

Jules read through the lyrics she'd written one more time, nodding her head at the way the words sounded, the rhythm of them. She was thrilled with how the song had come out, although it was nothing like anything she'd done before, and she could already hear snippets of the music in her head. She knew how she wanted it to sound. Now she just needed to work on that part. She looked over the edge of the chaise. "I think this is going to be a good one, Toby, my man."

Toby lifted his head, ears twitching at the sound of his name.

Jules was ready to work on that music. But first, she had to take care of Toby. She closed her notebook and picked up his leash. "Do you have to go potty? How about one more try before we go upstairs?"

She actually planned on leaving him on the second floor so he could nap on the couch if he wanted. He wasn't always the biggest fan of her working out a song on her guitar. He seemed to regard it more as noise than music. She took him to a grassy spot, but after a quick tinkle, it was clear he wasn't going to do anything else. "All right, let's go."

She gathered her things and got them both on the elevator. At the second floor, she led Toby out and unleashed him so he could scamper free. "Kat? You here?"

Kat came out of the bedroom, but only halfway out. "Yep."

"Just dropping Toby off before I go upstairs to work on some music."

Kat looked at Toby but not at her aunt. "Okay."

Jules hesitated. This morning at breakfast, she'd thought everything was fine. Of course, she'd been half-asleep from her late night. And now that it was just the two of them, Kat was definitely being short with her again. She studied her niece. "Everything okay?"

"Sure." Kat started back to her room.

Jules sighed. "Then why have you been sort of weird around me lately?"

Kat went still. "I just have a lot on my mind."

"Yeah, I'm not buying that." Jules took a few steps toward her. "Did I do something to upset you?"

"No." Kat huffed out a breath. "It's nothing, I swear. Look, I...just read some stuff in your notebook that I shouldn't have. Sorry. But it was strange."

"Stuff?" Jules didn't understand. "What kind of stuff?"

Kat shot her a look. "All that stuff about cutting someone with a knife and a bleeding heart and aching bones and a deep grave. It was creepy and weird, all right? Like murdery weird."

Jules thought a minute, then burst into laughter. "So you read my songwriting notes? Kat, that's how I create. I write out all the phrases and wordplay that I can think of around a particular idea and let it take shape on the page. It helps me find what works and what doesn't. That's all that was. The starting point to a new song I'm working on."

Kat stared at her. "For real?"

"Yes. I guess songwriting is weird and creepy sometimes, but I swear I'm not planning on murdering anyone. Cross my heart and hope to ... Well, never mind that, but it was all just about a song. That's it. Although you've maybe watched too many episodes of *Forensic Files* with Grandma."

Kat snorted. "Yeah, maybe. I'm sorry for thinking it was something strange. I had no right to read your notebook anyway. I'm sorry about that, too."

"No, you didn't have the right, but it's not like I spill my secrets in there. Just song ideas. We cool, then?"

Kat's smile was sheepish. "Yeah, of course, we're cool. Thanks for not thinking I'm an idiot."

"Well, let's not go that far." Jules winked at her and laughed. "You need me, I'm upstairs."

Kat nodded, smiling. "I'm going out in a little bit to get my nails done. Grandma's out with some friend of hers, Connie, and Mom is with Danny at Mrs. Butter's helping him figure out what lemon popcorn should taste like. No clue what the downstairs crew is doing."

"Thanks for the update." She didn't mention she was meeting Jesse at the club again tonight, this time for dinner.

She hung Toby's leash on a hook in the laundry room, then grabbed her guitar from the bedroom and took the circular steps up to the third floor. She stood on the rooftop deck for a moment, just having a look. The expanse of blue before her was stunning. It never got old.

Too bad this wasn't her everyday view. Wouldn't that be something?

Spending time with Jesse was making her think more and more about being here. Which wasn't to say she was about to move for a man she'd just met. But Landry didn't have anything that compared to the Dolphin Club.

She had daydreams of being able to pop in there and try out new songs. That would be pretty cool. And there was no question that her current residence was way too big. It had been great when the boys were young and had friends over all the time, but now? It was five thousand square feet that echoed with emptiness.

She frowned. It wasn't like the boys had just moved out, but maybe living in that big house all alone had something to do with the creative block she'd been going through. Everything there felt sort of forgotten, in a way. Like it was part of her past.

Could Diamond Beach be her future? Toby sure loved it here and since he was the only man who was a part of her daily life, she wanted to consider his needs, too.

If she moved to Diamond Beach, she wouldn't

get a house again, she didn't think. A really nice condo on the beach would be perfect, so long as her neighbors didn't mind her music. It would be less maintenance, too, which would be nice not to worry about.

She could easily go on tour if she only had a condo to think about.

The frothy white edge of the waves looked like ruffles from up here. She smiled and turned to go inside.

Her phone buzzed as she shut the door behind her. She pulled it from her back pocket and looked at the screen, answering right away. "Cash! It's so nice to hear from you. How are you, sweetheart?"

"Hi, Mom."

She knew instantly from his voice that something was wrong. "Are you okay?"

A brief silence preceded his answer. "No."

When he didn't say anything else, she prodded him. "What's wrong?"

"You have to promise not to say anything to Dad. Not yet anyway. I'm not ready to talk to him."

"Sweetheart, I won't say a word. I don't talk to your father very much these days."

"Yeah, I guess him getting remarried wasn't your favorite thing."

She laughed softly. "He's remarried twice since we split. I promise you, it really doesn't bother me." Her first husband and the father of her two boys was Lars Harrison, bass guitar player for the band Alchemy. He was constantly being linked with some new woman, all of them younger than him and most of them models.

Jules really didn't have the time or attention span to keep up.

"Well, good, I guess."

She waited. "I'm not going to judge you, whatever it is. If that's what you're worried about."

Cash sighed. "I'm just no good at this, Mom."

She sat on the couch in the living room of the third floor. Across from her was the small kitchenette. Light gleamed off the chrome handle of the toaster oven. "No good at what?"

He sniffed. "At...*music*."

Cash was in L.A., doing his best to get discovered. But this was a hard business. She knew that better than most. "That's just not true. You have a great voice and you've been playing guitar since—"

"Mom, you don't have to lie to me. I know I'm not that good. And now I know why. It's because I really don't want to do this. I just never had the heart to tell you or Dad, because I knew you'd be disappointed in me. But I just can't anymore. I can't."

Her heart ached for him. "Oh, honey, if you think for one second that I'd be disappointed in you because you didn't want to pursue music, then I'm so sorry I've made you feel that way. I don't care what you do, I just want you to be happy." She wasn't sure if Lars would agree, but she'd done most of the parenting. It didn't matter to her what he thought.

Cash sniffed again. "Really?"

"One hundred percent. I don't care if you want to be a sock salesman."

He laughed, a sound like cool water. "I don't think that's a thing, Mom."

"Well, someone's got to sell socks. What would you rather do?"

Another sigh. "That's just the thing. I don't have a clue. I know whatever it is, I'm not going to find it here in L.A. This town is...plastic and gross and the people are so fake."

She nodded. "I can understand that."

"I want to come home."

She hadn't been expecting that, but it made her smile. Maybe not the best circumstances, but she'd be happy to have one of her boys around. "Great. When do you want to come?"

"Um...tomorrow?"

"Really? I mean, that's great, but I'm actually at Diamond Beach with Grandma and your Aunt Claire and Kat. I can leave early, though. I have my own car."

"Are you there because of Uncle Bryan?"

"Yes." Neither of her boys had been able to come to the funeral because of the timing. Jules hadn't minded. Wasn't like they'd known Bryan that well. None of them had, apparently. "Aunt Claire wanted to take one last trip here before she has to sell this place." When the boys had been younger, they'd come here, too. But that had been close to ten years ago for both of them.

"Could I come there? I don't want to cut your time short. And it would be nice to be around family. I haven't seen Kat in ages. You said she's there, right?"

"Yep. It would be great to have you here." She'd explain about his uncle having a second family after he got here. It wasn't something he needed to know about now anyway.

"Okay. I'll get a rental car and drive over when I land. Can you text me the address?"

"Sure. But can you afford a rental car?"

"I have some money saved up. Doesn't matter what it costs. I just want to get to where you are."

"I'll help you with the bill." She was really smiling now. "What time do you think you'll get in?"

"Maybe by two or three tomorrow? My flight is pretty early."

"Sounds good. I can't wait to see you. I'm sorry things didn't work out the way you'd hoped, but sometimes life turns you in a new direction when you least expect it. Don't worry about anything, okay? We'll figure this out together."

"Thanks, Mom. I love you."

"I love you, too."

Chapter Fourteen

Kat knew the nail place she wanted to try but when she parked and headed for the shop, she was surprised to see Trina sitting on the bench outside. "Is this where you went?"

Trina grinned. "Great minds, huh?"

"What are you doing sitting out here?"

"Just waiting on my mom and Mimi to pick me up. They're on their way."

"Oh." Kat glanced at Trina's nails. They were hot pink with glittery silver tips. "I thought you were getting a French manicure?"

"This *is* a French manicure. Just the super-fancy version."

Kat rolled her eyes but laughed softly. "You really can't help yourself, can you?"

Trina shrugged. "I am who I am and I like what I like."

"I see that." A car pulled up to the curb. Kat turned to see Roxie behind the wheel and Willie in the passenger seat.

Willie put the window down. "Do you need a ride, too?"

Kat shook her head. "I just got here. Thanks, though." She gave them a smile and a wave.

Trina got up, putting her purse strap over her shoulder. "I'll see you back at the house. I guess we'll work on our outfits then."

"Sounds good." Kat went inside.

The woman at the reception desk greeted her and Kat asked for a manicure and a pedicure. She wasn't sure what shoes she was wearing tonight, but she wanted the insurance of a fresh pedicure, just in case.

"Number three chair," the woman said. "After you pick a color."

"Okay, thanks." It didn't take Kat long. She went for the sort of thing she always did, choosing a soft, neutral pink called Iced Blush for both her pedicure and manicure. Easier that way, she thought. Plus, matching was classy.

She settled into the third pedicure seat, adjusted

it, turned on the massage function, then slipped off her flipflops and put her feet into the hot water that was already filling the basin. She pulled out her phone and saw a text.

It was from Ray. *Just checking in. Hope all is well and that you're okay. Miss you.*

She smiled. That was nice. *Everything is fine. Doing all right. How's work?* She sort of missed him, but it felt disingenuous to say it, so she didn't.

He didn't text back right away, so she figured he'd probably sent the first message while between patients.

She played a matching game on her phone while the technician worked on her toenails. A new message alert popped up. Probably Ray. She finished her game before checking it.

Except it wasn't from Ray. It was Dwayne Margolis, her boss at the actuary firm.

If you're available, please call me at your earliest convenience.

She frowned. That didn't sound good. Especially when he knew she was out on compassionate leave. She turned off the massage part of the chair before dialing his number. The feature made too much of a hum and there was no way he wouldn't hear it.

"Dwayne Margolis, how can I help?"

"Dwayne, it's Kat. I just got your text." She held her hand over her mouth to keep out any other noises. She didn't think he'd figure out she was getting her nails done, but then again, that was a conversation she didn't want to have.

"Hi, Kat. How are you doing? I'm so sorry to bother you. I know this is a tough time for you right now." Dwayne was in his fifties, had two kids in college, and a wife who didn't work but liked to shop.

"It is, but I'm doing okay. My mom is taking it pretty hard."

"It" being the discovery of her father's other secret family, but Kat wasn't about to tell Dwayne that. She really hoped no one back home found out.

"I'm sure she is. I appreciate you calling me. I wouldn't have asked if it wasn't important, but the leadership board from Omar Industries needs to speed up their timeline. They're coming in tomorrow, which I realize is incredibly short notice, but you're the lead on that account."

She blinked, wondering if she really understood what he was asking. "Are you saying you want me to be there for the meeting?"

"Would it be possible? These guys are not Zoomcall guys. They're face to face." He was tapping a pen or something on the desktop. "You know that."

She did. She'd met with them twice already for that reason. "We're not really ready to go over results yet. We're still a month out."

"I know that, and I've explained that to them. They really just want a status update. They're about to spend a lot of money on this deal and they need reassurance that it's all still making sense."

And for that, he wanted her to drive three hours. She couldn't believe it, except that she could. Some clients were just more hands-on than others. Omar Industries was one of those. As much as she didn't want to go, she needed her job. More than that, she wanted to be reviewed favorably when the next round of promotions came up.

"You really think I need to be there?" She could guess the answer to that question. He wouldn't have asked her to call otherwise.

"Yes, I do. I'm sorry. If I could do anything about it, I would, but these guys are just needier than most."

They were also a big account. Probably the biggest the firm had. Saying no would be very bad for her career. She closed her eyes and tried not to let the frustration she was feeling into her voice. "What time is the meeting?"

"Not until one, which should give you plenty of time to get here and then get back to your family. I promise I won't let the meeting go more than an hour."

If she did this, Dwayne would owe her. He had to know that. She sighed in a way that she hoped sounded grief-stricken. She didn't want to overplay things, but at the same time, her boss needed to know this wasn't the best timing. "All right. I can do it. Maybe...maybe it'll be a good distraction."

"That's a great attitude, Kat. I know it'll be hard, but I really appreciate it. I won't forget it, either. I promise you that."

"All right. Thanks. I'll see you tomorrow, I guess."

"Great. Have a good evening."

She hung up. She planned on a having a great evening. But tomorrow wasn't going to be nearly as much fun. At least she could swing by the house and make sure everything was okay there. Maybe grab another pair of shorts.

Ray's response to her last text came in. *Work is busy!! I've moved a few patients around but still have one Friday morning. Could return to beach house after that, though. How are you feeling about us?*

She leaned back and stared at the ceiling. That really wasn't a question she wanted to answer right now.

In fact, she didn't even plan on telling him she was coming back to work for the day. He'd want to meet for a meal or something and she just didn't have it in her. Besides, that would mean she wouldn't get back to Diamond Beach until late.

No, it was better if she just went to work, did the meeting, then came straight back. She twirled a piece of hair through her fingers.

Her hair! It was completely different. How was she going to explain that? She couldn't say she'd had it done for the funeral. Dwayne had been there. He'd know that wasn't true.

Maybe she could just say her aunt had encouraged her to go to the salon as a way to cheer herself up?

Or maybe she was overthinking it. Men didn't really notice stuff like hair anyway. She could pull it back and it wouldn't look that much different.

She was worrying for nothing. She sent Ray a quick answer that she hoped would be the end of it. *Feeling about the same.*

She wondered if that would still be true after her date with Alex tonight.

Chapter Fifteen

At first, the smell of popcorn and sugar had been overwhelming. Not in a bad way, Claire thought, but enough that her mouth wouldn't stop watering. Now, thankfully, she'd gotten used to it. The smell was still incredible, but she didn't need to swallow every couple of seconds.

Danny was working on the third batch of lemon-flavored glaze, mixing corn syrup and sugar and flavorings, along with a little food dye to really bring the color to life. They'd already tried one with actual lemon zest, but the heat of the process had turned it bitter. "This will be the one. I can feel it."

"Maybe," she said. "The last one was really close."

"Fingers crossed." He took the sunny yellow mix he'd made and hand-tossed a fresh batch of popcorn into it. The kernels turned a bright, buttery yellow as the flavoring coated them. Then he spread the popcorn out on a large sheet tray to dry. He smiled at her. "I'm really glad you came with me to help."

She smiled back. She'd been smiling a lot today. "I'm sure you could have figured it out without me."

"I don't know. To be honest, I'm not that great at flavors. That was really my dad's thing. My daughter's kind of taken over in that department now. In fact, she's the one who came up with the cotton candy popcorn. That stuff has developed a cult following."

Claire had tasted it when they'd first arrived. Danny had had her taste all the available flavors so she would understand the level of intensity he was going for. "It's good you have her working in the business, then."

He nodded. "It's very good." He gave the popcorn a gentle mixing with two flat, stainless-steel scrapers, lifting and folding the pieces in a way that was obviously done to keep them as whole as possible. He set the scrapers aside. "All right, let's give this a taste and see what we think."

She reached over and took a piece as he did the same. She chewed, trying to be as thoughtful about what she was tasting as she could be.

He shrugged. "The color's spot-on. The lemon flavor is really good. But what do you think?"

"It is good. The salt is right. And the lemon flavor is strong and nicely tart. Like good lemonade." Maybe too tart in large quantities? She shook her head as she tried to analyze it more. "But it's lacking something. Sorry. I know that's not what you want to hear."

"No, I want the truth." He ate another piece. "And I agree with you. What do you think it needs?"

She didn't know much about popcorn, but she knew enough about baking to understand what made a dish rise above its competition. Why one cookie was better than another or why a certain pie disappeared faster than the one next to it. "It needs texture. The crunch of the popcorn is one texture, for sure, but it's still missing that extra something. Lemon squares are cool and creamy. You're never going to reproduce that in popcorn. But you might be able to add a different element."

She looked around, finding just the thing. She went over to the large container, helped herself to a small scoop using the metal scoop already inside and returned. She used her fingers to lightly sprinkled granulated sugar over the tray of lemon popcorn. "Stir it once."

Danny did as she asked.

She added another light sprinkling of sugar. "Try it now."

He picked up a few pieces and popped them in his mouth. A few chews and he smiled. "You're some kind of genius." He tossed a couple more pieces in his mouth. "That is exactly what it needed. A little more sweetness to balance the tartness and that different kind of crunch. It's almost like lemon kettle corn. Sweet, salty, tart. This is exactly it."

She tried a piece herself. "It is really tasty. It's very refreshing, which is not something I'd ever have thought about popcorn." She actually couldn't stop smiling. "We make a good team."

"We make a great team. Thank you for your help today." He leaned in and kissed her, catching her off guard.

She inhaled, caught her breath, and...kissed him back. He tasted of sugar and lemon and she knew she would forever associate that flavor with him.

It was a short kiss. When he pulled away, he winked at her. "Now to see if we can recreate this in a large batch. That's the real test."

She did her best to form meaningful words, but his kiss was still fizzing through her head. "What, um, can I, uh, do to help?"

"Be ready with that sugar. There's going to be a lot of sprinkling to do. We'll get a shaker to do it when we put the flavor into production."

In a haze of sugar and bliss, Claire worked as Danny's assistant while he started one of the cooker-coaters, the big machines that actually made the different kinds of glazed popcorn. The popcorn itself was made in giant copper poppers.

Danny worked carefully, pouring each ingredient in according to the proper order, adding a fresh batch of just-popped popcorn near the end. He was making an enormous amount. Enough to fill a bathtub, it seemed to her.

When he dumped the popcorn onto the cooling table and started stirring and lifting with big stainless-steel paddles, she got busy sprinkling sugar over it all.

Finally, he declared the first official batch of Summer Lemon popcorn done. He scooped some into a paper bucket. "Let's go see what the employees think."

They took the bucket through to the retail front of the shop. There were three employees working—an older woman named Ruth, a young man named Teddy, and a young woman named Kelly.

There were a few customers in the shop, too, but

they were all still browsing the racks and shelves. Besides popcorn, Mrs. Butter's sold popcorn-themed items such as banks, salt and pepper shakers, T-shirts, stuffed animals, gift baskets.

Danny portioned out the popcorn into small paper dishes and passed them out to each employee. "Give me your honest opinion."

Kelly was the first to chime in. "This is, like, so good. I love it, boss. Tastes like summer."

Danny smiled and Claire felt a small amount of relief. After all, if his employees hated it, he only had her to blame.

Teddy nodded. "Yeah, I'd eat a bucket or two of this."

Ruth smiled. "Reminds me of a lemon square."

Danny looked euphoric. "That's exactly what we were going for. That was the inspiration."

Claire pressed her hands together as Danny chuckled. He nudged her with his elbow. "Looks like we did it."

"You did it," she said. "I just tasted it."

"That's not true, it was a team effort. You helped a lot." He nodded at his employees. "Thanks, gang. This is going to be our new flavor, Summer Lemon." He glanced at Claire. "So long as my daughter, Ivelisse, approves."

Ruth looked over from where she'd gone to help a customer. "She'll love it, Danny. I don't think you have to worry about that."

Claire wasn't so sure. What would Danny's daughter think about a strange woman in the kitchen with her father? She might not like it. "When are you going to share it with her?"

He looked at his watch. "Soon. She's due here in the next twenty minutes. I asked her to come by this morning before I picked you up."

Claire hadn't been expecting to meet his daughter today. "Oh. That's wonderful," Claire lied. Why was she so nervous about this? It wasn't like she and Danny were dating. Okay, so she'd kissed him. And he'd kissed her back. Twice.

But that wasn't a reason to get nervous. Kissing Danny was good.

His daughter not liking Claire? Now *that* was a reason to be nervous. The minutes seemed to spin by in a whirlwind of time and before Claire knew it, his daughter was walking through the front door, the little bell overhead jangling to announce her arrival.

Ivelisse was a gorgeous woman with big brown eyes and the kind of easy beauty that required very little makeup.

Thankfully, she was as kind as she was beautiful.

She gave Claire a big smile, stretching out her hand. "Hi. You must be Claire. I've heard so much about you."

Claire swallowed and shook the woman's hand. "It's a pleasure to meet you. Your father speaks highly of you."

Ivelisse glanced at her dad. "I pay him to do that."

They all laughed, then Danny presented her with a sample of the new flavor. Ivelisse selected a couple of pieces of the lemon popcorn and put it in her mouth. A moment after she started chewing, she nodded. "You've got a winner on your hands. Let's get this stuff into production."

Chapter Sixteen

Trina wasn't surprised that Kat had come home with the same blah color on her fingernails and toenails. It was pretty much what Trina had expected her to do. But that was okay. Trina was going to jazz her up. "All right, let's see what you've got to work with."

Kat opened the closet doors and Trina took a look. Wasn't much in there. A few sundresses and a couple of pairs of pants. Probably capris.

Trina went through them. Her hand landed on a pair of slim black pants. "Hey, what are these?"

"Oh, nothing. I don't know why I even brought those. I was too sad about my dad to pack properly."

Trina pulled them out and took them off the hanger. The black pants looked like they'd hit just below the knee. What Mimi would call clam diggers. "I have a top that would be perfect with these."

"I'm not wearing those."

"Why not?"

"Because they're really tight and they're sort of... they show off too much."

Trina smiled. "They sound perfect. I'll go get the top that I'm thinking about. Be right back."

She tossed the pants on the bed and ran down-stairs, grabbed the top from her closet and came back up. She held it out to Kat. "Here. Go try this on with the pants."

Kat's brows rose. "I don't think—"

"You want to give Alex a reason to look at you, right? You want to look pretty and sexy and all that?"

"I guess."

"You guess?"

Kat sighed and took the top. She went into the bathroom to change. She called out to Trina with the door closed. "This top needs a strapless bra. I don't have one."

"Just go without. Your boobs aren't that big."

"Thanks."

Trina giggled. "Hey, you should be happy about that. Smaller boobs stay perkier longer."

A few moments later, the bathroom door opened, and Kat came out.

"Wow," Trina whispered. "You look like Sandy from Grease when she goes to the dark side."

The top Trina had brought Kat was a black, off-the-shoulder peasant blouse with an embroidered white floral design on the front and around the ruffle that made up the neckline. It was close to the body, matching the silhouette of Kat's trim black pants.

"I don't know..." Kat went to the mirrored closet door to have a better look.

"Black sandals with some hot pink accessories and you'll have heads turning wherever we go."

"Yeah, but maybe not for the right reasons," Kat said. She turned one way, then the other. "And I don't have any hot pink accessories."

"Well," Trina said. "I do. I've got the earrings, the bracelets, and a cute little purse you can borrow. And if you don't think you look hot, you're nuts. Go ask someone else."

"All right, I will." Kat grabbed her phone off the bed and sent a quick text. "I asked Aunt Jules to come down." She tossed the phone back on the bed and crossed her arms. "What about your outfit?"

"I'm wearing a cute sundress and sandals. Very simple."

"Sure. I'll believe it when I see it. Go get changed and let me have a look."

Trina hesitated. "I have another option, too." The sundress had been a last-minute decision. "I could do my jean skirt and a top."

"Hmm. Which do you think is less loud?"

"The jean skirt and top." Trina wasn't sure which top, though. The black with the beaded trim maybe? Then she and Kat would be in the same colors. She could even wear her hot pink wedge flipflops for some extra color. Although that might be too matchy-matchy.

"Then put on the jean skirt and top."

"Okay, I'll be right back." Trina ran downstairs again and changed. She went with turquoise flipflops that had turquoise rhinestones on the straps and added some turquoise jewelry. Then she grabbed the hot pink accessories she'd mentioned to Kat and took them back upstairs with her.

Aunt Jules was in Kat's bedroom when Trina returned. She was eager to hear what Jules thought.

"What's the verdict?" Trina asked.

Jules was smiling. "I don't think Kat has ever looked sexier. Seriously. I didn't think she was capable."

"Come on," Kat said.

"I mean it." Jules shook her head. "With the new hair and these clothes, you've leveled up. I've always thought you were a beautiful girl, but you never did much with it. Frankly, I had no idea you had that kind of body under there."

"Aunt Jules." Kat looked stunned.

Trina beamed and held out the earrings, bracelets, and purse she'd brought up. "These are to go with the outfit, too."

"Perfect," Jules said. "You look great, too, Trina. But then, you always look nice."

"Thanks. Kat hasn't approved this outfit yet."

"It's fine," Kat said. "Not what I would have put you in but it'll do."

"Then what would you change?" Trina was willing to do something different if that's what Kat wanted. Mostly because she still planned on putting lashes on Kat and Trina was pretty sure that was going to be a battle.

Kat shrugged one bare shoulder. "That skirt is a little short."

Aunt Jules crossed her arms. "She's got the legs for it."

Trina could have hugged her.

"Okay," Kat said. "Never mind. It's a cute outfit. I'm not going to change any of it."

Trina said, "Thanks. But what about your outfit? Do you really not see how great you look?"

Kat took a breath and glanced into the mirror again. "It doesn't look like me. I'm still getting used to the hair. Now, seeing myself in something like this...it's like there's a stranger looking back at me. A hot stranger, but it's still weird."

Jules snorted. "Wait until Ray sees you like this. Maybe I should send him a pic."

"No." Kat turned suddenly. "Please don't. I'm not ready for that."

"I won't," Jules said. "But he'll see it eventually. The hair anyway."

"Yeah, I know." Kat exhaled. "I have to go home tomorrow for a meeting at work with some really needy clients and I'm not even telling him I'm going to be around. He'll want to get together and I'm just not there yet. I know it's weird, but I don't know how else to explain it."

"You're going back to Landry?" Jules asked.

Kat nodded. "Yeah. I don't want to but I'm the lead on this account. And I don't want my boss mad at me."

Trina frowned. "He knows your dad just died, right? He shouldn't be asking you to come in."

Kat nodded. "I agree. But I need this job. And I could really use a promotion. Besides, it's what Dad would have done. You can't deny that."

"Nope," Jules said. "You're right about that."

Trina blinked. That was the first time she'd heard Kat say just Dad. Not *my* dad. Like she'd suddenly accepted that her father was also Trina's father. Like Kat was acknowledging their sisterhood. Trina's entire being warmed.

"Hey," Jules said. "Do you think you could bring your cousin back with you? Long story, but Cash is flying in tomorrow. He didn't know I was here. He was planning on renting a car and driving over but if you're going to be there..."

Kat smiled. "Cash is coming in from L.A.? Cool. Yeah, I can definitely bring him. Tell him to text me his deets."

"I will," Jules said. "Thank you."

The prospect of meeting a cousin thrilled Trina. "Cash is your son?"

"Yep," Jules answered. "I haven't told him about you yet. I figured that was a conversation best had in person."

Trina laughed. "Yeah, probably. But it's super cool that I'm going to meet a new cousin! I can't wait."

Kat was looking at herself in the mirror again. "I'll fill him in on the ride over."

"Sounds good," Jules said. Toby trotted in, whining. "That's my cue to leave you hot chicks to finish getting ready for your big double date. Have fun."

Chapter Seventeen

Kat felt like she was having an out-of-body experience. How did she look like this? She looked like those glamorous girls who posted aspirational pictures on Instagram. She looked good. Better than good. She looked hot.

She'd even let Trina put some tiny false eyelashes on her, along with more makeup than she usually wore, but Kat had to admit...it worked.

She'd never felt this pretty in her life. It was kind of awesome. But that also made her feel shallow. She'd been so concerned that she was doing something worthwhile with her life and now, all of a sudden, being pretty made her happy?

What did that say about her? She didn't know. She wasn't sure she knew who she was right now. Dressed like this, looking like this, about to go out with a man who wasn't Ray. A man who might be able to make her feel something she'd never felt with Ray.

It was like the old Kat Thompson had died along with her father. She was probably in denial about something and desperately needed therapy.

Well, that wasn't going to happen tonight, was it?

Right now, she was driving herself and Trina to the restaurant to meet Alex and Miles for dinner. Her hands were sweating a little. She was genuinely nervous. Would there be fireworks with Alex? Butterflies?

Wait. Was she already having butterflies? Her stomach definitely felt...flitty.

She let out a long, slow breath to try to calm down. Regardless of how she felt about Alex or being pretty, she owed Trina for helping her. "Thank you, Trina. I really mean it. I never would have looked like this if not for you. I feel a little weird, but I also know I look far better than I would have if left to my own devices."

Trina smiled. "You're welcome. I was happy to do it."

"I know you were. That's kind of amazing about you. You really like helping people, don't you?"

"I do. I love it. Making people feel better about themselves is just the best thing ever. It makes me feel good."

Kat pulled into the parking lot of the Flying Fish. She hoped Alex had made a reservation. It looked crowded. She parked and turned off the car. They were a few minutes early.

"You okay?" Trina asked. "You seem nervous."

"I am a little nervous, but it's more than that. I'm struggling a bit. Mostly with how I feel right now."

"Meaning?"

"Meaning I love how I look. I never thought I could look like this. But at the same time, it makes me feel shallow that I care so much. Like, why does it matter what I look like so long as I'm doing something to make an impact on the world in a positive way?"

Trina unhooked her seatbelt. "Why can't you do both? I take a lot of pride in how I look, but I also put a ton of work into making other people feel good."

Kat thought about that and nodded. "I suppose I could do both. I can definitely work on my image. Although, I can't do much about my job. Being an actuary pays pretty well, but I'm not really helping people. Well, I am, but I'm only helping them make decisions about how to make more money. It's not exactly the most philanthropic of careers."

Trina shrugged. "Sounds to me like your job is the problem, not the way you look. You just need to do something different. What would you rather be doing for work? What would make you feel like you were making a difference?"

Kat had never once considered that. It hit her with an impact she hadn't anticipated. "I...I don't know."

"Then you need to figure it out. Maybe you could start by volunteering. There are all kinds of things you could do. Animal rescue, working with kids, helping out at a women's shelter, or a food pantry—"

"Maybe I could tutor?" Kat thought about that. "I like kids and I'm really good in math."

"For real?" Trina laughed. "I can't do math without a calculator. That's pretty cool that you're good at it."

"I work with numbers all the time. They're like a second language to me."

"I bet there are a lot of charity organizations that could use someone with good math skills. Seriously."

Kat stared at the restaurant. "I've never thought about that. I bet there are." She smiled at Trina. "Thanks. I love the idea of helping out a charity and putting my existing skills to work. It feels really doable."

"You're welcome." Trina tipped her head toward the building. "You ready to go in?"

Kat nodded. "You nervous about meeting Miles?"

"Nah," Trina said. "He's either going to like me or he's not. I can't do anything but be myself."

Kat shook her head. "You're sort of amazing, you know that? I don't love what my dad did, but having you as a half-sister might actually make up for it."

Trina's mouth opened but she didn't say anything. She blinked really hard and stared up at the ceiling. Then she sniffed.

"Are you crying?"

"I'm trying not to," she squeaked out.

Kat laughed. "Hey, I didn't mean to do that to you."

Trina pressed her fingers into the corners of her eyes. "It's the nicest thing you've ever said to me. I'm really happy to have you for a sister. You know that, right?"

"I do." Kat put her hand on the door handle. "Let's go find our dates."

Together, they walked in. The restaurant was busy. Alex and another guy were at the hostess stand, checking in. Alex was in khaki shorts and a Hawaiian shirt. The guy she assumed was Miles was in dark jeans and black bowling-style shirt.

Kat and Trina went up and stood behind them, grinning. Kat cleared her throat. "Good evening, boys."

Alex turned around first. His eyes widened, his mouth came open, and he just blinked at her. "K-Kat?"

She laughed. "Yes, it's me. Were you not sure?"

"I just, no, it's totally you. I've just never seen you dressed up." His grin went ear to ear. "No, it's definitely cool. You look hot."

That was not a word she'd ever been called by a man before. She felt like the sun was radiating through her body. "Thanks. You remember my sister, Trina?"

Alex tore his gaze away from Kat to nod at Trina. "Yeah, definitely. How are you?"

"Great," Trina said.

Alex gestured to the guy next to him. "This is my buddy, Miles. He's on the paramedic crew."

Trina smiled up at Miles. He was a little taller than Alex and more muscular, with dark hair that nearly touched his shoulders and deep, soulful eyes. He had tattoos on both arms and a day or two's worth of stubble on his face. His right wrist sported three bracelets, one leather, one silver chain links, one of polished black beads. If Alex looked like a surfer, Miles looked like a nightclub bouncer who spent his time off in the gym.

He dipped his head at her. "Hey. Nice to meet you."

"Nice to meet you, too." She stuck her hand out. "I'm Trina."

Miles took Trina's hand and kissed her knuckles.

Kat almost laughed, but only because Trina looked like she might melt into the floor. That's when Kat noticed one of the young women working at the hostess stand arrive with menus in her hands.

The young woman smiled at them. "Your table is ready. If you'd like to follow me."

Alex put his hand on the small of Kat's back and tiny electric sparks zipped through her. Kat breathed through her mouth. The proof she'd wanted had arrived. She was sure she'd never had sparks coursing through her because of Ray.

It was a weird moment. Happy and sad, but like a new door had been opened at the same time. This was what it should feel like with a man, wasn't it?

That tingling, so-excited-you-can't-stop-smiling anticipation of what was going to happen next.

At that very second, she knew that she and Ray weren't going to get back together. They both deserved more. They both deserved *this*.

Although maybe Ray felt this way about her already? It was worth talking about. Even if she didn't really want to.

They followed the hostess to their table, a booth in the back corner.

Miles stood aside, letting Trina in first. Alex did the same for Kat, which put her across from Trina. They exchanged quick glances, both of which seemed to tell the other that things were starting off well.

Kat truly hoped Miles was a good guy and that Trina had a great night. She hoped they both did, really. It was high time they had some fun.

But more than that, Kat wanted tonight to be the start of a new beginning for her. Yes, she needed to talk to Ray and tell him she'd made a decision about them. It wouldn't be a fun conversation, but she hoped he'd understand.

She wanted nothing but the best for him. And for herself.

And now, after talking to Trina, Kat realized she

had a path to follow. Volunteering at a charity seemed like exactly what she needed to do.

The idea filled her with happiness and a real sense of purpose. Life felt livable again in a way it hadn't since her dad had passed.

How amazing was that?

Chapter Eighteen

S ince Willie had gone next door to talk to Miguel, Roxie decided she might as well take her makeup off and put her nightgown on before fixing herself some dinner. Then she'd pour herself a little glass of wine and maybe sit on the back deck and watch the sun set. If Willie still wasn't back, she'd find a movie to watch or something.

It was a rare night that neither Willie nor Trina were around. Maybe she'd do a face mask, too. There was never a bad time for some pampering.

Her phone buzzed with a text from a number she didn't recognize. Curious, she opened up the message.

Hi, it's Ethan from earlier today. I was wondering if you'd like to go out for a bite to eat? If you haven't eaten already. If I'm being too forward, just say the word.

Roxie smiled. And started typing. *The only word I have for you is yes.*

Ethan was a good-looking guy. He had his own business. Why wouldn't she say yes? After all, she hadn't made sure her number was in his phone just because Willie might buy that strip mall.

Great, came Ethan's reply. *Skipjack's?*

She knew the place. It was a little hole in the wall about a block from the beach in between a surf shop and a bike rental place. *Sure. What time?*

Twenty minutes?

See you then. She texted Willie next. *Meeting Ethan for a bite at Skipjack's. Don't plan on being gone too long.*

She didn't, either. She had no intention of sitting there all night, getting sloshed. That was just dumb, especially when she'd only just met the man. It was just going to be a quick meal. Maybe she'd have a glass of wine, but no more. And she'd be home in two hours. She'd make sure he knew that, too.

Just because she looked like a good time didn't mean she was easy or lacked common sense. This was her first foray into the world of dating since losing Bryan, and while she was still grieving, his betrayal had changed a lot about how she felt.

He probably wouldn't like her going out with

someone else so soon after his passing, but bigamists didn't really get to be bothered by things like that. "Sorry, Bry. You only have yourself to blame."

But being home in two hours wasn't only Roxie being cautious. She wanted to be there when Trina got back so she could hear all about the date. Trina would either be happy and glowing, or sad and bummed out.

Either way, Roxie would be there to listen.

She freshened up her makeup, though if Ethan had waited another five minutes to text her, she would have had to put on a whole new face. She changed from leggings into jeans and added a little leopard cardigan over her black tank top.

Her phone chimed. She looked to see Willie had texted back. *Have fun. See if you can learn anything new about that property.*

Roxie laughed. Her mother was all fired up about that place, but the day had pretty much come and gone without a deposit appearing in Willie's bank account. Roxie realized that didn't necessarily mean the money from Zippy wasn't coming, but it didn't reassure her, either.

Willie was putting a lot of stock in that dough. Maybe too much. If it didn't show up, she was going to be pretty disappointed.

They all would be. But Willie was counting chickens before the eggs had hatched. Never a good thing.

Roxie grabbed Trina's car keys. She already knew her daughter wouldn't mind her taking the car. When they were at the beach, whoever's car they'd come in became communal property. Roxie would give her some gas money, too.

She drove to Skipjack's and found a parking spot on the street. She locked up the car and went in. The little restaurant was nautically themed with porthole windows, lengths of thick rope, and lots of brass, all against a backdrop of knotty pine. Everywhere.

Ethan was standing at the end of the bar closest to the door. "Hey. You came."

He'd put on a collared shirt. He looked nice. "I said I would, so here I am. Is this your usual hangout?"

"I guess you could call it that. A friend of mine from high school owns it."

"You've been in Diamond Beach a while then."

He nodded. "I have. Whatever that's worth. You want to grab a booth?"

"Sure. I should tell you now I can't be out too long. I have my mom to look after." That wasn't the complete truth, but it was a good enough reason to leave whenever she needed to.

"Okay, I understand. I appreciate you coming out."

They settled into a booth against the far wall, opposite the bar and in the dining area of the restaurant. A server came over to them, bringing menus and glasses of water.

Roxie glanced at the menu. It was typical tourist food. Fried baskets of shrimp, fish, or chicken fingers with fries, sandwiches, burgers, a couple of salads. The entrees looked better. Lots of seafood dishes. She looked up at him. "Since you're here all the time, what do you recommend?"

"Do you like seafood?" He chuckled. "I guess I should have asked you that before you got here."

She smiled. "No, I do. You're good there."

"Well, in that case, the seafood sampler is great. John, that's my friend who owns the place, gets all the seafood as fresh and local as he can. I know this looks like a tourist trap, but the food is better than you'd expect."

"Yeah?" She looked at the menu with a new eye. Maybe she'd been too quick to judge. "I think the seafood sampler might be too much food for me."

"What about the Florida lobster tails with the filet mignon?"

She looked at that item. It was the most expensive thing on the menu, so he wouldn't be suggesting it if he couldn't afford it. She nodded. "Okay. That sounds great."

He put his menu down. "I'm going to get it, too."

The server returned, they ordered, both requesting their steaks medium rare and neither of them getting a drink other than water, then they were left alone again.

He made a curious smile. "Thank you for not thinking I was a creep for texting you."

She laughed. "I'm glad you did. It would have been a letdown otherwise after all that work I did to make sure you had my number."

He chuckled softly. "I have to say I appreciate a woman who knows when not to be subtle." His grin faltered slightly. "So are you and your mom really interested in that strip mall? Or was there something else going on?"

"You found us out. We were just laying a trap for any eligible men that might be in the area."

He snorted. "Okay, right, dumb question. It's just going to be a lot of work, that's all."

"You mean getting the shopping center up to code?"

"No, it's not that bad. It's really mostly superficial. It just went so long without proper maintenance and then it's been sitting. Looks dated now. But even cosmetic work can take time."

"How long do you think? To do whatever needs to be done?"

He stared at his water glass. "Two to three months, maybe. Some of it's hard to judge, because it depends on what work gets done. Like would you want the minimum done to get it ready and open, or do you want to give the place a new, fresh look? It all comes down to decisions."

She nodded. "If it was your place, what would you do?" She hadn't anticipated getting information about the strip mall from him, but this seemed like some valuable insight. Her mom would be happy.

"If it was my place and I had the funds, I'd give it a new façade. It's got a bit of a bad rep. Making it look new would erase a lot of that. Giving it a fresh face could get possible tenants excited, too."

"Would that be hard to do?"

"No, not really. Again, it's all about decisions. Personally, I'd do a fake front with some metal roofs, paint the stucco so that each store front looked like it was a separate shop. Like a little village."

"Like the place down the street."

"Yep. That shopping center is always busy. Tourists love it, because it's quaint and looks beachy."

"It also has three times as many shops."

"But the property you looked at could have more, too. Granted, that would be a much bigger job, requiring plans and permitting and all of that. But it could."

"Definitely worth thinking about."

Their food arrived and it did look good. Their meals also came with bibs, which both of them found funny.

Ethan tied his on. "I hope you don't think less of me for wearing this, but I know my limitations when it comes to dipping anything in melted butter."

She picked her bib up and unfolded it. "Tell you what, I'll wear mine, too. In solidarity."

"Thanks."

"Looks really good." She'd ordered a baked potato and coleslaw as her sides. She added butter to the baked potato, then cut into her steak. It was perfectly cooked. She took a bite of it, then tasted the coleslaw. "This *is* really good."

His mouth turned up in a little half-smile. "My sister makes the coleslaw."

"Your sister works here?"

Ethan leaned his head to one side. "Well, she's married to John, so..."

"You didn't mention that."

He shrugged. "I didn't want you to feel like you had to like this place on account of it sort of being in the family."

She sipped her water. "I do like it. I have to admit, I thought it was kind of a tourist trap like you said at first, but this meal is changing my mind."

"Good." He cut off a piece of lobster and speared it with his fork. "I keep telling John he needs to update the place. It's looked this way since the '90s, but he says there's no need to fix what's not broken."

"I can see that."

"Yeah, but all of this wood? I mean, it's all right, but imagine this place with a coat of white paint and some beadboard. Still beachy, still nautical, but cleaner and more modern. He could probably charge more."

She smiled at him, another slice of steak already on the end of her fork. "You like making things better, don't you?"

"I suppose I do. I can't help it. It's my thing. My

area in the business is handling remodels. I guess I can't leave my work at the office."

"Nothing wrong with that. Especially if you love it."

"What do you do?"

"I'm a nurse. Mostly in palliative and hospice care."

His brows lifted. "That's admirable. Hard work. In all kinds of ways."

"It can be." She ate the bite of steak. "You said you were divorced, right?"

He nodded, looking less than happy. "Right. Things ended badly, but I came out of it with two great kids."

"Can I ask why it didn't go well or is that none of my business?"

He hesitated. "She met someone else." A shadow seemed to come over his face and she thought maybe she shouldn't have asked. "Someone who should have known better. It was...a mess. The kids were younger then and they really struggled. Ultimately, they chose to stay with me."

"Wow." Roxie felt for him, but she was glad he'd gotten the kids.

"If it wasn't for my family, my parents, my brothers and my sister, I don't know what we would have done." He laughed but the sound was bitter-sweet. "Anyway, those kids are all grown up now and pretty well-adjusted, I'm happy to say."

"I'm glad. Family is important."

"It's everything. Although sometimes, even family can put you through it." He looked at her. "How about you? Ever been married?"

Her smile was slow and probably a little sad. "That's both a long and a short story. But I'll give you the short version first. I'm a widow."

His eyes rounded. "I'm sorry."

She shrugged. "I am, too. But let me tell you the long version..."

Chapter Nineteen

*W*illie giggled, unable to help herself. She blamed the rum. Miguel was making drinks with coconut milk and pineapple on the back porch of his house. Pina coladas, but not frozen, so she wasn't sure if they were still called that. Didn't matter, because they were delicious. She was on her second one. "These taste like dessert."

He nodded. "They are sweet. But you're sweeter."

Willie laughed again. It was so nice to laugh. And so nice to be wooed. She was pretty sure that's what Miguel was doing. Wooing her. Bringing her out here to the cozy screened porch. Making drinks. How could she not be wooed? The sun was sinking down behind the watery horizon, painting the sky in the most gorgeous shades of pink and orange. "Are we still going to that restaurant you mentioned?"

He brought his drink over and sat down on the

couch beside her. Close enough to touch, but he didn't. "Yes, tomorrow night, if that works for you."

"It does."

"Good. I made the reservation. We will have *mofongo* and you'll see how good it is. I'm going to call an Uber to drive us. You know what that is?"

"An Uber? Sure. It's like a new version of a taxi."

"That's right." He smiled at her. "You're a smart woman. I like that. So many at our age cut themselves off from the world. You're not like that."

"I have help," Willie said. "My daughter and my granddaughter. They keep me connected."

"Yes, my son and my grandchildren do the same for me. It's wonderful to have family near, isn't it?"

"It is." She'd be lost without Roxie and Trina. They were such a blessing to her.

Miguel held his glass out to her. "To you and the new happiness you've brought into my life."

She grinned. She was definitely being wooed. She clinked her glass against his. "To us."

His brows lifted in a mischievous sort of way. "I think I am in trouble with you." He laughed. "And I am not even bothered by it."

"I might be trouble." Willie sipped her drink. "But at least I'm not hiding it. You already know I've had four husbands." They'd had a long talk at dinner the other night and shared all sorts of things about their pasts.

Miguel seemed to ponder that. "Maybe I'll be number five."

She giggled. "Maybe you will be, if you play your cards right." She knew that wasn't true. There was no way she was getting married again. But spending time with a nice man like Miguel? Now that was something she was more than willing to do.

He sighed in a sort of happy, contented way. Then he sat up a little and frowned. "You came over here to talk to me about something."

"That's right, I did. But you distracted me with drinks."

"My deepest apologies. I am all yours. What would you like to discuss?"

"I have some questions for you, actually. What do you know about Lewis Brothers Construction? Have you heard of them? Are they trustworthy?"

"Yes, very," he said. "They've been in Diamond Beach a long time. As long as I have. Maybe longer. They have an impeccable reputation in town. I've met a few of them—the father and one or two of the brothers—at the Chamber of Commerce meetings. Good men."

"That's nice to hear."

"Are you doing some remodeling?"

Willie liked to keep her cards close to her vest but telling him a little information wouldn't hurt. "I'm looking at a possible investment property. But it would need some work and one of the companies that might do it would be Lewis Brothers. I talked to Ethan Lewis already, actually."

Miguel looked at her with a new light in his eyes. "Buying a property here? Does that mean you'd be making Diamond Beach your permanent home?"

She nodded slowly. "It would."

He put a hand to his chest. "This is great news."

"It hasn't happened yet." And as the money had yet to arrive in her account, it wasn't a guarantee. "It might not. But I believe in planning ahead."

"What kind of investment property? A house?"

"No." She hesitated, feeling like she was getting into deeper waters. But what did it matter if Miguel knew? She doubted very highly he would care enough to tell anyone. She wasn't going to give him any specifics, though. "It would be a business. But I shouldn't really say more than that. It's such early days that I don't want to jinx anything."

"I understand." He held up one hand as if to reassure her. "I won't ask anything else. But I will say that I am impressed with you. Buying a business at our age is no small feat. You are fearless, Willie. You are...an inspiration."

She had to smile. "Thanks. But I wouldn't be working there, you silly goose. I am definitely retired. It would be for my daughter and grand-daughter."

"Even so." He swiped his hand through the air like her fearlessness wasn't up for debate. He tossed back the last of his drink. "We must celebrate this good news. We need music."

He got up and turned on the little radio on the side table. Latin music with a bouncy beat came on.

Willie bobbed her head. It reminded her of the music that had played in one of the clubs she'd been to in her youth, a club in Miami called Club Tropica. It was a sort of jazzy, big band sound with pulsing drums and a seductive bass beat.

Miguel swayed to the rhythm, moving his hips in a way that Willie hadn't seen a lot of men his age do. Or even men half his age. He held out his hand to her. "Come. Dance with me."

"I don't know how to do that."

"Salsa is easy." He wiggled his fingers. "Don't be afraid. I will teach you."

She took his hand. She hadn't danced in ages.

He positioned her beside him so that they were

both facing in the same direction. "Look how simple. You just start with your right foot, walk forward, then rock your hips and walk back."

She did her best, then shook her head. "My hips don't work like yours."

"You did fine. But we can do a simple side-to-side." He turned her so that she was facing him and held both of her hands.

That was nice. His hands were soft and warm.

He stepped one foot out to the side, then bought it back in and stepped the other foot out. "Now you try it with me, to the music."

She followed his feet. The side-stepping was easier. And dancing with Miguel was fun, helped along by the music that seemed to give her new energy.

He taught her a few more simple steps and after several minutes, they both collapsed back onto the couch, happy and laughing and a little worn out.

She drank the last of the drink he'd made her and let out a very contented sigh. "I haven't had that much fun in ages."

He looked over, smiling. "Well, then, we will have to do it again very soon."

Chapter Twenty

Margo was only half-watching the police investigation show playing on the television. She was being distracted by the pictures Conrad was texting her. Memes, he called them. She wasn't sure how that was pronounced.

To her, they just looked like cute or funny pictures with clever sayings on them. She especially liked the last one he'd sent of a sweet little kitten winking with the phrase, "*Hi, Cutie!*" over top of it.

This must be what flirting was like these days. She ought not to like it, but oddly, she found it amusing. And a little sweet. As if Conrad was going out of his way to make her smile.

It was working.

Just like he'd convinced her not to give up on the possibility of them just because she lived three hours away.

There was still no reason to believe a relationship of that nature could work or last for any significant length of time. But he'd been so insistent on how easy it would be to make things work, so persuasive about the good times they could have together, and had flattered her with all of his talk about what a special woman she was, that she'd given in.

Now, she had to laugh a little. She'd been swayed by a man for whom words were a sort of currency. It was no wonder she'd succumbed to his charms. It was proof of his talents. And charm. Conrad was most definitely charming.

And handsome.

She shook her head. She was acting like a besotted schoolgirl. All because, what, a man had paid five minutes of attention to her?

She supposed that just proved how fragile the female psyche was. Especially one as battered and bruised as hers.

Well, it wouldn't hurt to indulge herself a little. But there was no point in getting completely swept away, because she would be leaving. They all would. It was just a matter of when.

The elevator hummed and, a few moments later,

Claire stepped out, two shopping bags in one hand, a large one and a small one.

Margo narrowed her eyes in disbelief. "Where did you come from? I thought you were already in bed."

Claire laughed. "Nope. Just getting home. I was with Danny."

"So you were with him all day?"

She nodded. "Yep." She lifted one shoulder in a loose, fluid movement that told Margo her daughter had allowed herself a little more wine than usual. "Didn't plan on it, but it just happened."

Margo gestured to the couch near her chair. "Come sit and tell me all about it."

Claire seemed surprised. "Really?"

"Yes. You must have had an interesting time to be gone all day."

Claire nodded and seemed to disappear into a memory for a second. "Yeah," she said softly. "We did."

She held a finger up. "But first, how about a cup of decaf? Doesn't that sound nice?"

Margo shook her head. "I have a cup of tea right here." It was nearly gone and mostly cold, but she was more interested in what Claire had been doing than getting something new to drink.

"Tea sounds nice," Claire said. "Maybe I'll have a cup of that instead."

Margo gave in. "Put the kettle on. I'll have another cup."

Claire went into the kitchen, put her purse and her shopping bags on the counter, then got the kettle out, filled it with filtered water. She cranked a burner to high and set the kettle on it. Then, she took out a cup and selected a tea bag to go in it.

Margo joined her, taking one of the blackberry herbal tea bags for herself. With a little cream in it, the tea tasted like a summer tart she'd once had in England. She'd been reminded of that trip earlier today during her conversation with Conrad.

They'd talked about *everything*. He didn't seem to care what the topic was, just that they were together.

"Mom?"

"Hmm?" Margo glanced over, aware she'd been wool-gathering.

"I asked if you wanted sugar or the green stuff."

"The green."

Claire handed her a little packet. "You seemed lost in thought for a bit there. Something on your mind?"

"No." *Someone, yes.* "All right, come tell me about your day."

They took their cups back to the living room, Margo returning to her chair, Claire getting situated on the couch.

Claire looked toward the bedroom. "Is Jules here?"

"No. She went out for dinner."

"By herself?" Claire's face showed no small amount of amusement at that idea.

"No, with the owner of the Dolphin Club. I guess he wanted to talk to her about doing another show there."

"Oh, that's nice."

Once again, Margo narrowed her eyes. Was Claire deliberately stalling? "So, come on. Out with it. How was your day?"

Claire's face lit up in a big smile. "It was really nice. I got to meet Danny's daughter, Ivelisse. Isn't that a pretty name? She's gorgeous, too. Enough that she could be a model. Granted, she's probably too old, but you'd never know it to look at her."

Margo nodded. "Where did you meet her?"

"At Mrs. Butter's. She came in to taste the new flavor." Claire sipped her tea, still smiling. "Summer Lemon, he's calling it." She let out a little gasp. "I completely forgot. I brought some home for everyone to try."

She put her cup on the coffee table and went into the kitchen, pulling a clear plastic sleeve out of the shopping bag. It was filled with buttery yellow popcorn. She brought it over, opening it as she came.

She held it out to Margo. "Here. Try it."

"I don't know..."

"Mom, seriously? I helped invent this flavor. You have to try it."

Margo took a piece and ate it. It was surprisingly good. "That is very lemony. And not in an artificial way, as I imagined."

Claire sat back down and put the bag on the counter. "I told them over dinner that if they really want to expand on that flavor, they should drizzle it with white chocolate and add some toasted almond slivers. And guess what? Ivelisse loved that idea. She wants to run a few tests to see how it comes out. Their crunches—that's the popcorn mixes that have extra things added, like nuts or those tiny M&M's and some kind of chocolate drizzle—are big sellers, so Ivelisse is always looking for new ideas. She said they might even do it as limited summer edition thing."

Margo pursed her lips. She wasn't sure how her daughter had managed to breathe during all of that.

Claire was clearly excited by the day she'd had. "So you went to dinner with Ivelisse?"

"And Danny. We went to this place called Churro's, which sounds like a touristy Mexican place, but it was really good. You should have seen the size of the bowl the guacamole came in. It was like this, I swear." She held her hands in front of her like she was holding a basketball.

Margo had never seen her daughter in this kind of mood. Chatty and animated, her eyes lit as if from within. Margo stared as a realization came to her. Claire *was* happy.

"Sounds like you had a great day."

Claire picked up her tea and took a sip. "I did. Danny is just so much fun to be around. He's really smart and Ivelisse obviously adores him, and why wouldn't she? He's given her such a great opportunity at Mrs. Butter's."

Claire sighed and sat back. "I know it's crazy, but wouldn't it be something if we could stay here? How nice would it be to have the Rojas for our permanent neighbors?"

Margo didn't say anything, just sat quietly, afraid she might accidentally ruin the mood. She'd suggested they make the beach house their new home just a few days ago and Claire had vehemently turned her down. Had she really had a change of heart this quickly?

There seemed to be only one way that might be possible. She was falling for Danny. But why wouldn't she be? A handsome man was not only paying attention to her, but he'd gone out of his way to help her with some tasks that needed doing.

In a very brief period of time, Danny had already proven himself to be cut from much better cloth than Bryan had been. Not such a hard thing to accomplish, given that Bryan had been absent more than he'd been present.

The cheating low-life.

Claire looked over. "You don't think so?"

Apparently, being quiet was not an option. "I think they're lovely people. They'd be great neighbors."

Claire sat up. "But what about staying here? In Diamond Beach? You said you wanted to. That you'd be willing to sell your house and move in with us here. Do you still feel that way?"

More than ever. But Margo was hesitant, too. It was such a big decision. Wasn't it? "Of course I do, but you said it would be too expensive."

Claire nodded. "I did say that, because I thought it would be." She smiled. "Danny already said he'd give me a job. In fact, he told me they've been thinking about opening another location. Not sure where yet, but they want to expand into some other types of sweets, so it would almost be like a test kitchen."

"Does you wanting to stay here mean you've heard something from the attorney, then?"

Claire frowned. "No. He was out of the office. The best his receptionist could tell me was that he'd call me when he returned. I just thought...I don't know, that we could make it work here somehow."

Margo didn't want to hope for something more than she had a right to, so she just nodded thought-fully. "Yes, maybe we could."

Chapter Twenty-one

*J*ules woke up with a lightness in her soul. She stretched and smiled. It was a wonderful feeling, that sense that everything was good and bright and going the way it was supposed to. Cash would be arriving today. It had been far too long since she'd seen her son.

And even if he was coming here because he was in a bad place, she felt sure that she could help him turn things around.

Then, of course, there was the wonderful dinner she'd had with Jesse last night. She'd gone to bed with a smile on her face, so it was no wonder she'd woken up with one.

Toby lifted his head. He was sprawled on the foot of the bed, near the right side.

Jules nodded at him, not wanting to say anything that might wake her mom up. She slipped out of bed, changed into leggings and a big T-shirt, pulled her hair through the opening of a ball cap, which she secured on her head, then grabbed sunglasses. She picked Toby up, put him on the floor, and opened the door.

Toby trotted out. Jules followed. The house was quiet, but it was early. No coffee had been made yet, a pretty good sign she was the first one up. She got Toby's leash from the laundry room and they took the elevator to the ground floor.

She inhaled as she walked out. The air was clean and fresh and held just the right amount of salty tang. The low roar of distant waves called to her. Toby was headed to a patch of grass along the side of the house. She followed him, letting him do his business. When he was done, she cleaned it up, depositing the bag in one of the garbage bins.

"What do you think, Tobes? How about a quick walk on the beach?"

If his little tail wagged any harder, he might achieve lift-off.

She grinned. "Beach it is, then."

She took him for a quick walk, but she didn't stay out too long. She wanted to eat and get upstairs to finish working on the song she was writing. She was so close to being done and once Cash got here, her time would be his.

Plus, he'd be staying upstairs, making it harder for her to use that space as her personal creative lab.

Once she and Toby were back inside, she washed his feet in the sink, dried them on an old towel kept for that purpose, then got him some breakfast. He was more than happy to eat after his little romp.

She started a pot of coffee. While she was doing that, her mother came out. "Morning, Mom. I hope I didn't wake you."

"No. Coffee smells good. How was your dinner last night?"

"Nice," Jules answered. She pondered making breakfast, but with Kat and Claire still in bed, she wasn't sure. Maybe she'd make some just for herself and her mom. "Oatmeal?"

"Only if you're making some for yourself."

"I am. With raisins and brown sugar."

"Sounds good." Her mom nodded and went to the cabinet and got two cups out.

Jules got to work on the oatmeal. She measured out the water, the oats, and a little salt then added the raisins, brown sugar, and a few shakes of cinnamon.

Kat wandered out. "Hey, is there coffee?"

Jules nodded. "Morning to you, too."

Kat chuckled. "Sorry, morning." She rubbed at her face. "We had a late night."

"We?" Margo asked. "Does that mean your date went well?"

Kat headed for the coffee maker. "It did. After dinner, we went to this place called Gray Beards. It's kind of a surfer bar. They had a guy playing guitar and singing oldies. We danced and played darts and had a really good time. After that, we went for a walk on the beach."

Jules smiled. "Sounds like fun. What time do you have to leave for Landry today?"

Margo made a face. "You're going to Landry? Why, Kat?"

"Ugh." Kat rolled her eyes. "I have to be there for a meeting. I mean, I shouldn't have to be, but these clients are just needy. It's all right, though. Cash is coming back with me."

This time, Margo looked at Jules. "Cash is here?"

"He will be," Jules answered as she gave the oatmeal a stir.

"No one tells me anything," her mother said.

Kat sipped the coffee she'd fixed for herself. "Grandma, you were gone most of the day and then Trina and I left and we just didn't see each other."

Margo went to get coffee, too. "I thought Cash was in L.A."

"He was," Jules said. "He's struggling a bit. He just needs some time with family, I think. He'll be fine." She hoped that was true. He had sounded so desperate on the phone. She hated to think of either of her boys in any kind of pain, regardless of whether that was emotional, physical, or otherwise.

"I'm sorry to hear that," her mother said. She filled a second cup with coffee for Jules. "A little time at the beach seems to cure a lot of ills, though."

Jules nodded. "Yes, it does."

Claire came out of her room, dressed in capri leggings, a T-shirt, a sunhat, and sneakers. Her sunglasses were hooked on the neck of her T-shirt.

"Morning," Jules said.

"Morning, family. Look at all these beautiful faces."

Jules's brows rose, but she said nothing about Claire's unusually chipper mood. "Oatmeal?"

"No, thanks," Claire said. "I'm going to get my power walk in, then I'll make myself some eggs. Trying to cut back on carbs."

Their mother snorted. "You were eating popcorn last night."

"Just a few pieces," Claire said. "You should all

try some. It's the flavor I helped Danny create yesterday. Summer Lemon. It's in that bag over there."

Kat went to the bag Claire had indicated and opened it up. "I'll try some." She popped a few pieces into her mouth. "Hey, that's pretty good." She nodded. "The Summer Lemon name fits."

"Thanks." Claire smiled. "How was your date?"

Kat got a slightly dreamy look on her face. "It was fantastic. I can't lie. I didn't know dates could be like that."

Claire didn't seem convinced. "It wasn't weird having Trina along?"

"Not at all." Kat ate another piece of popcorn. "You know, I'm starting to think that having a half-sister isn't such a bad thing."

Claire shrugged. "I guess not."

"Hey," Jules said. "Your half-sister is in the room, you know."

Claire snickered. "I know. But Kat and Trina are a different situation. They didn't grow up together like we did. You and I are more like full sisters." She put her sunglasses on. "I'm going to make a quick run to Publix after I have breakfast. When I get back, I'm going to need the kitchen."

"What for?" Jules asked out of curiosity. "What are you making?"

Claire smiled mysteriously. "I just have an idea I want to try out." She headed for the sliding doors. "See you later."

"What's gotten into her?" Jules asked of no one in particular.

Margo got a funny little look on her face. "Danny Rojas, that's what."

Chapter Twenty-two

Trina put her robe on and went to get coffee, yawning as she walked into the big room that housed the galley kitchen and the main living area. She'd slept in a little later than usual, but she'd had a busy night. Her mom and Mimi were sitting outside, already drinking coffee, so she fixed her own cup and went outside, too.

They stopped talking the second she pushed the door open. "Hey."

"Hello, there," her mom said. "How was your date?"

Trina grinned and sat on the couch beside her mom. "I really like him. He's very sweet."

Her grandmother nodded. "Good. We need to meet him."

"Mimi, we've only been on one date." Which

Trina had thoroughly enjoyed. "Although we will be going on another."

Her mom smiled. A brighter smile than usual. "That's really good, Trina. Is his schedule flexible?"

An odd question, but Trina answered anyway. "Not super flexible. He's a paramedic, so he's kind of important, you know? He works a forty-eight-hour shift, then has two days off. But he said he wants to spend his next day off with me. Maybe going to the beach or something."

She didn't want to oversell how much she liked Miles, but she liked him a lot. He was just so great. They'd talked about all kinds of things. Work. Life. Their interests. Their dreams. They'd danced and played darts, beating Kat and Alex three games to two. Afterwards, they'd walked on the beach.

And held hands.

He'd kissed her goodnight, too, which had also been amazing, but holding hands like that had been more than Trina could put into words. She hadn't realized how much she enjoyed that, because she hadn't done it with anyone in such a long time.

Mimi nodded. "It's good to see you smiling, my girl. I have a question to ask you. It's a big question, so if you don't feel ready, you just say so."

Trina had no idea what her grandmother was up

to. Which was pretty standard, actually. She smiled. "I'll do my best to answer. Hard to know if I'm ready until I know what the question is, though."

"True," her grandmother said. She took a breath. "How would you feel about making Diamond Beach your permanent home? It would be for all of us, of course, but I want to know how you'd feel about it."

After her date with Miles, all she could think about was when she'd get to see him again. Living in Diamond Beach would definitely make that easier. "I would love to live to here, but how would we do that?"

Mimi grinned at Trina's mother, who grinned right back. "You tell her. It's your news."

Mimi sipped her coffee, then put the cup aside. "You know that my last husband died. Zippy."

"I do know. I'm so sorry." Trina's grandmother had just told her about his passing the other day. She'd been so upset. Trina hated to see her grandmother grieving but with the loss of Trina's dad, she understood better than ever how important it was to acknowledge all those feelings.

"Well, there's a little more that I didn't tell you. Zippy, a man of incredible generosity, left me some money."

"That's great, Mimi." Trina had only met Zippy

once. He had a very nice house and a very cool pool. She couldn't imagine selling his property had raised enough cash for them to start a new life here. But then, what did she know about real estate prices in Las Vegas?

Her grandmother started laughing. "I didn't know if I should believe it or not, but I checked my bank account this morning. And the money is there."

"Okay." Trina glanced at her mom. Roxie was biting her bottom lip like she was trying to keep herself from going mental. Something was up.

Mimi leaned in closer and spoke softly. "Trina, it's a *lot* of money. Enough that I'm going to buy you your own salon. We've already got a place picked out. We'd like to show it to you after we eat breakfast and get ourselves ready. If you're interested."

Trina's mouth came open and her chest felt tight. She wasn't sure if she was breathing or not. Her whole body tingled with an odd kind of numbness. This couldn't be a joke, could it? Her grandmother would never pull a trick like this.

She looked at her mom again. Her mom nodded.

Trina tried to breathe again. "Mimi, is this for real?"

"Trina, my girl, it's as real as feathers on a hen."

"I can't believe it." Trina shook her head, attempting to process the news. Then a new thought occurred to her. "Mimi, you can't spend all of your money on me."

Her grandmother barked out a laugh. "My dearest girl. I'm not spending it all, I promise." She hooked her finger toward her for Trina to come closer.

Trina leaned in.

"It's seven and a half million dollars."

Trina blinked. "Did you say…"

"I did." Mimi nodded. "So what do you think? Want to go have a look at your new salon later today?"

"Yes," Trina breathed. "I still can't believe it."

"Let it sink in while you get ready," her mother said. "Your grandmother and I will make breakfast so you can shower first, but we're not leaving until eleven. After we look at the shop, we'll go get some lunch."

Trina got up. "This is really real."

"Really real," her grandmother repeated.

"Holy cow." Trina felt a little numb and tingly but she made herself move toward the door. She stopped suddenly as the weight of what was happening hit her. She looked at her grandmother.

"Mimi." Tears flowed before she could get another word out.

She sank to her knees in front of her grandmother's chair and hugged her. Arms wrapped around her from two sides as her mother joined. "I don't know how to say thank you. This is too big of a thing. Thank you isn't enough."

Her grandmother kissed her head and patted her hair, tears of her own wetting her cheeks. "You do more than enough for me every day. You don't need to say anything else. Having you as a granddaughter is reward enough." She managed a smile. "I'm so happy I can do this for you. You don't even know."

Trina nodded and smiled up at her grandmother. "I'll never be able to repay you. I know you're not asking me to, but this is overwhelming."

Her grandmother's hands cupped Trina's cheeks. "I know, sweetheart. But it's exciting, too, don't you think?"

"The most exciting." Trina kissed her grandmother's face.

Next to her, her mother got to her feet. "We're not making a big breakfast, since we're going out for lunch after we meet with Ethan."

Trina got up. "Who's Ethan?"

"Ethan is the man who built the strip mall," her mother explained. "He's going to show it to us."

Her grandmother made a funny little face. "He's also the man your mother went to dinner with last night."

"Mom had a date? Wait, a strip mall?" Trina's brows jumped. She wanted to know about the date, but her curiosity about the new shop got the best of her. "Just how big of a place is this?"

Her grandmother laughed. "Go get ready and you'll see for yourself soon enough."

Trina showered, then came back out in her robe to eat, her hair wrapped up in a towel. Her mom and grandmother were in the kitchen, making breakfast sandwiches, one of Trina's favorite things.

After breakfast, she fixed her hair and put on some makeup. She wanted to look as nice as possible. Like someone worthy of owning her own salon.

Her outfit was a pair of cute, cuffed capri jeans, a white and lime green polka dot T-shirt with tied sleeves, and white crystal-covered flipflops. She added some jewelry before coming back out to the living room. "I'm ready."

Her mom smiled. "Your grandmother's still working on her face but I'm sure she won't be too much longer. If you don't mind, I'll drive, since I know where we're going."

"Works for me," Trina said. "You still have my keys anyway."

"They're in the bowl," her mom said, meaning the one on the small foyer table.

"Let's hit it," her grandmother said as she came out of her room.

About twenty minutes later, they were pulling into the parking lot of a small strip mall. Trina couldn't believe her grandmother might actually buy the whole thing, just so Trina could have her own salon. It was enough to make her start crying again. She didn't. But she could have.

They parked and got out.

A man did the same, exiting the only other vehicle in the parking lot, a shiny black pickup truck. He waved at them. "Ladies. Roxie."

Trina's mom waved back with a big smile. "Hiya, Ethan. Thanks for meeting us."

"Happy to do it." He looked at Trina. "You must be the new salon owner."

Trina let out a little gasp. Hearing him say those words sent a shiver through her. "Maybe."

He shook her hand. "Hopefully, you like it." He

nodded to her grandmother. "Good to see you again, ma'am."

"Oh, please," she said. "Call me Willie."

He led them to the storefront on the end and unlocked it with a big set of keys, then he pushed the door open and got out of the way. "There you go."

Trina stepped inside first. She didn't go far. She wanted to take it all in so she could remember this moment for the rest of her life. She took a breath, imagining she could smell shampoo and conditioner and bleach and hairspray. "I love the floor."

"I knew you would," her mom said.

"But," her grandmother started. "All of this can change. Whatever you want it to look like, Ethan and his crew can make it happen. Isn't that right, Ethan?"

He nodded. "The only hindrance is money."

Her grandmother lifted her chin. "Thank the good Lord and a man named Zippy, that's not a hindrance anymore."

Trina walked through the rest of the salon like she was in a dream. She could see the physical space before her but in her mind, she was already redesigning it into the image of the salon she'd had in her head since graduating beauty school. She looked at the bathroom, the storage room, the employee breakroom that also housed the hookups for the washer and dryer, then came back out to where her family was waiting.

Her mom was chatting softly with Ethan but looked up expectantly. "What do you think?"

"Just a second." Trina clasped her hands together in front of her and prayed this wasn't a dream she was about to wake up from. "Mimi, you're sure about this? Sure that you want to do this?"

"I've never been so sure about anything in my life, and I've said 'I do' four times. Do you like it?"

Trina nodded. "I love it."

Her grandmother looked at Ethan. "Call the owners. I want to make an offer."

Chapter Twenty-three

Claire left as soon as she could for Publix, knowing that Kat would need her car for the drive back to Landry. She practically ran through the store, concentrating on the baking aisle. She filled the cart with everything on her list, getting duplicates of some things so she could experiment all she wanted.

Baking was a science and creating recipes from scratch sometimes meant things went wrong. She wanted to be prepared.

Not just with ingredients, but she got plenty of foil pans too, so her creations could be easily distributed without her having to worry about getting dishes back.

She would make small test batches, carefully recording what went into each one. Some might not work, but she was all right with that. All she needed was one or two of them hit the mark she was aiming for.

She got home and hauled everything upstairs in two trips on the elevator, then began to organize herself. First thing she did was get the two big bags of popcorn Danny had given her to take home and experiment with.

For her purposes, she felt it was important to use Mrs. Butter's popcorn. He'd given her a bag of the regular salted and a bag of the kettle corn.

Next, she grouped her ingredients according to the different recipes she planned on making. To start with, she wanted to try three variations of her idea.

Then she fixed herself another cup of coffee, put some soft background music on the stereo, and got to work. She'd never been so energized about baking. For once it wasn't about what Kat needed for school or making something for a church function or because someone was sick, or brand new to the neighborhood, or had just had a baby, or any of the other various reasons she used to bake.

This time, it was all about her and her skills. She was challenging herself to come up with something new and interesting. Something Danny would be impressed with.

Sure, he'd offered her a job, but part of her felt

like he'd done that maybe not because he pitied her, exactly, but there was an element of pity there. She was certain of it.

She wanted him to need her because of what she could do for him and his business.

To that end, she melted butter, measured popcorn, portioned out other ingredients, diced dried fruit, greased a couple of foil pans, and stirred pan after pan until she had her three test batches.

She made room for them in the fridge, so they'd cool faster. She was eager to taste them and see how close she'd come to what she'd imagined.

While she was waiting for them to cool, she cleaned up, handwashing a lot of her tools so that she'd be prepared to remake anything that had failed.

Her mother came back from a walk on the beach. She'd taken Toby, which Claire found surprising, as that wasn't something her mother liked to do. She didn't have anything against the little dog, she just made it plain that she didn't want to be responsible for him.

"I suppose I should wash his feet," she said.

Claire wiped her hands on a towel. "I can do it."

A look of disbelief came over her mother's face. "Are you sure?"

"Yep. Happy to." Claire needed the distraction. She came over and smiled at Toby. "Did you have a good time on your walk?"

Her mother rolled her eyes. "He chased every seagull within a fifty-yard radius. He's relentless."

Claire laughed. "That's good. He'll probably sleep the rest of the day." She scooped him up and took him into the laundry room.

When she set Toby free and came back out, her mother was nowhere to be found. Claire peeked into the bedroom and found her. "Everything okay?"

"Yes. Why?"

Claire shrugged. "You're not sitting on the couch watching your shows."

"I have an engagement this afternoon."

Claire moved back a step. "You're going out? You know Kat's leaving, so her car won't be here."

"I know. My friend, Connie, is picking me up."

Connie? Who was Connie? And how had her mother made a friend? Claire couldn't imagine, but she was happy for her mom all the same. It was high time she had a girlfriend to pal around with. "Where are you going?"

"To the Maritime Art Museum. We'll probably get a bite to eat afterwards, so you don't have to worry about me for dinner."

"All right. Have fun."

"Thank you."

Strains of guitar music filtered down from upstairs. They were muted, but Claire could just pick out a snippet of the tune. Seemed catchy. She hoped Jules was having a good day up there.

She made herself a quick lunch of ham and cheese rollups with a couple of celery sticks filled with peanut butter. Afterwards, she went into the bedroom and laid on the bed to read some more of the book she'd almost finished last night.

She kept stopping to check the time, though. She was eager to sample her creations.

After she finished the last few pages, she went to the fridge and pulled the pans out. They seemed cool enough to her.

She flipped the first one over onto a cutting board and used a long knife to make squares. She tasted the first one. It was a ton of carbs, so she only took a small bite.

She smiled. It was good. Really good. It was better than she'd expected, actually. She hadn't been sure her idea would work.

On to the second one. It was fantastic. Chewy and crunchy and sweet and full of tropical flavors.

Lastly, she sliced the third one and tested it.

Also very good, but it needed the final touch. A drizzle of chocolate. She melted down some of the chocolate chips she'd bought, spooned the chocolate into a plastic bag, then cut the tip off and decorated the squares with a nice back and forth pattern.

Since the bars were cool, the chocolate hardened up nicely.

The only thing left to do was take them next door to Danny to sample. She smiled and blew out a breath. She was nervously excited, but eager to see what he'd think.

She sent him a text. *Are you home? I have something I want to show you. If you're available.*

Yep, he responded. *Come on over.*

10 mins.

She put a handful of the squares back into each baking tin and put their lids on, then packed them all in a shopping tote. A quick check in the mirror to make sure she was presentable and not sporting a smudge of chocolate or marshmallow anywhere and she was out the door.

He opened his door as she was walking over, greeting her with a big smile. "What have you got for me?"

"A little something I whipped up." She was being

coy on purpose. She knew she had something good and wanted to build up some curiosity in him, too.

"Baked goods?" he asked as she came through the door.

"Sort of." She looked around. "Your house is really nice." Deeper blues and bright whites with pops of yellow, green and red gave it a vibrant, tropical feel that was also masculine.

"Thanks. Is it my imagination or are you stalling?"

She laughed. "Let's go into the kitchen."

"Right this way." He led her in.

"Wow. I love it." The blue cabinets and white quartz countertops weren't something she'd ever have pictured but they looked sharp. Like something out of a magazine. She set her bag on the counter. "Did you do this yourself?"

"I did."

"Very impressive." She got the three pans out. "I hope you think these are just as impressive." She turned toward him. "You know how you gave me those bags of popcorn to experiment with?"

He nodded, glancing at the pans. "Yes."

"Well, I did some experimenting. And I think I came up with something that could work at your shops." She took the lid off the first pan and pushed it toward him. "These are popcorn bars. Like Rice Krispie Treats but made with popcorn. This one in particular is made with your kettle corn. I've been thinking of them as popcorn crispies, but you could call them anything you wanted."

He stared into the pan. "I didn't even know you could do that with popcorn."

"Neither did I, until today. Try one." She held her breath as he picked one up.

He bit into it and chewed. "Are you kidding me?"

She exhaled, unsure how to interpret that. "I don't know."

"This is incredible. This is our popcorn?"

She nodded, smiling.

"I can't believe this. It's perfect. These will fly out of the shops." He pointed at the other pans. "What else have you got?"

"Two variations on that same bar." She took the lid off the second and slid it toward him. "This is the tropical crispy bar. It's made with the plain popcorn and loaded with shredded coconut, bits of dried mango and pineapple, and white chocolate chips. It *could* have a white chocolate drizzle instead of the chips, though."

"That sounds amazing." He pointed to the third pan. "And that one?"

She pulled off the lid. "Classic peanut butter cup. Peanut butter base drizzled with a medium dark chocolate."

He shook his head as he picked up one of the tropical bars and tasted it. He closed his eyes as he chewed. "This bar is...I don't even have words for how good it is."

She grinned.

He tried the peanut butter one. "Mmm. You're right that this is a classic. The salt and the sweet. This is a winner, too." He looked at her. "Claire, you're amazing. You just came up with these?"

She nodded. "I have some other flavor combo ideas, too. Like toffee bits, peanuts, and a butterscotch drizzle. Or kettle corn with dried cherries and dark chocolate. Or you could put a big square of a plain crispy bar on a stick, dip it in chocolate to coat it, then sprinkle the chocolate with crushed Oreo pieces or rainbow sprinkles or anything really."

"Those all sound good." He was looking at the squares in the pans. "These are amazing. Plus, you made those lemon squares, which were some of the best things I've ever eaten. What else do you make?"

She shrugged one shoulder. "All kinds of things. Cakes. Cupcakes. Pies. Cookies. Oh, I do this one cookie with orange zest and white chocolate chips.

It's like a creamsicle in a cookie. Kat always loved it when she was little."

He blinked like he was trying to take it all in.

She wasn't sure what his response was going to be. Maybe she'd said too much. "So what do you think? I can give you my recipes. Do you want the bars for Mrs. Butter's?"

He took a deep breath. "No."

She wasn't sure she'd heard him right. "No?"

"Claire, your flavors and ideas are next level." He picked up another tropical bar. "I'd love to have these bars in the stores, but I have another idea. Something bigger. Something my dad and I have been talking about for a while now, but never did anything about. Until now. I want to open a Mrs. Butter's Bakery. And I want you to be my partner."

Chapter Twenty-four

*R*oxie lifted her glass of Diet Coke with a sense of pride that felt brand new. "Here's to the new owner of the Beachview Shopping Center."

Ethan was seated across from her, next to Willie. They'd invited him along to lunch at Digger's Diner, which Roxie was glad about. She liked him very much. He raised his cup of coffee and clinked it against her glass. "Congratulations, Willie."

Trina brought her glass of iced tea up to meet their beverages. "You're the best, Mimi."

Willie smiled and lifted her tomato juice to complete the toast. "Thank you. But remember, we only have a verbal agreement right now. I'll feel better when it's official."

Ethan sipped his coffee. "It won't take them long. They're happy to make the sale, I promise you."

Willie nodded. "That much was apparent in their willingness to negotiate. I'm happy about that."

Roxie was filled with so much happiness, she could barely contain it. "How soon can you get started on the renovations, Ethan?"

"As soon as the contract is signed. Well..." He smiled. "Sooner, really. We can work on the preliminary stuff anytime." He glanced at Trina. "Do you know how you'd like the salon to look?"

She nodded. "I have a pretty good idea. I love the floor, so I'd like to keep that. For the rest, I want to go white and bright with accents of black, gold, and hot pink. But not too crazy. I want the hair to shine when my clients look in the mirror, not the décor around them."

He folded his hands on top of his menu. "I'll do whatever you want. You'll need to go to the lighting supply store to pick out lights. Well, you'll need to pick out everything. Paint colors. Chairs. Some kind of cabinet for each station. Mirrors. Art, if you want some."

Trina looked excited. "I can't believe this is happening."

"Believe it, my girl," Willie said. "Looks like we have some shopping to do." She perused her menu for a bit, then glanced at Ethan. "I want to get those other stores ready for renters as soon as possible, too, but Trina's shop comes first."

"I understand."

Their server, a young man wearing a nametag that said "Troy," came over to take their orders.

"Blueberry pancakes," Trina said. "With a side of bacon. I know that's not lunch food, but it's what I want."

"Sounds good to me," Willie said. "But I want whipped cream on mine."

"Oh, me, too," Trina added.

Troy looked at Roxie. "And for you?"

"Chicken Caesar salad, please. Hold the croutons."

He turned to Ethan last. "What would you like?"

"Jalapeno cheeseburger with fries."

"Sweet potato or regular?"

"Regular."

Troy collected their menus and went off to put their orders in.

Roxie looked at Ethan. "How soon do you need Trina to pick all that stuff out?"

"The sooner everything is picked out and ordered, the better. Then I can get started right away," he answered. "I can give you the name and address of the lighting place I prefer. They can order anything they don't have in stock from their books, and if you give them my name, they'll give you my builder discount."

She looked at Trina. "Maybe we should go there after lunch and at least have a look around."

Trina nodded. "Sure. If Mimi's up for it."

"Let's do it," her grandmother said.

"Thanks," Roxie said to Ethan. "Any suppliers you want us to use, just let us know. Maybe…you could come over to the house sometime and we could go over it all."

He smiled, holding her eye contact. "Whenever you want me, I'll make time. Just call."

"I'll do that."

Willie finished the last of her tomato juice. Roxie knew her mother would have preferred a Bloody Mary. Willie patted the table in front of Trina. "What about those sinks? Aren't they kind of old? And shouldn't you have four of them? Three doesn't seem like enough."

Trina laughed. "Mimi, you seem to think I'm going to be really busy."

"You are, which is why it all needs to look perfect. I'm going to hire someone to do advertising for the shop once it's open. I'm going to get one of those planes that flies banners by the beach and everything. We'll do a big open house and invite lots of local businesspeople in. Say, maybe you should join the Chamber of Commerce. Get to know people."

Ethan nodded at Trina. "That's a great idea. I'm a member. I could bring you to the next meeting as a guest, if you want."

Trina looked at Roxie. "Would you come with me? I wouldn't know what to do at a meeting like that."

"Sure," Roxie said. "But I've never been to one, either." She turned back to Ethan. "What are they like?"

"Lots of networking. Nothing to be afraid of. Everyone there is a business owner and the whole goal is to help each other's businesses succeed and grow."

"How about that," Trina said. "Sounds exactly like the kind of thing I should do."

Troy came back to refill Ethan's coffee cup.

Ethan pushed his cup closer to the end of the table. "You will have to pay dues and you may be asked to serve on a committee, but I promise, it's all worth it."

"I'm in," Trina said.

Roxie loved the idea of networking. "Could I join, too?"

"Will you be working at the salon?" Ethan asked.

"Yes," Trina said before Roxie could answer. "If she wants to." She looked at Roxie. "I'd love to have you as the salon manager. I know you could do it. And I really want someone I trust keeping an eye on things."

"Whatever you need, I'm there." Roxie was happy to be included.

"As a senior-level employee, you can definitely join," Ethan said. He glanced at Willie. "Will you be joining?"

"Heck, no," she said. "I'm not working at the salon just for that."

He laughed. "But you'll be the owner of the Beachview Shopping Center. That qualifies you."

Willie blinked like she hadn't considered that. "Then maybe I will. After all, I know Miguel is a member."

"Miguel Rojas?" Ethan asked.

She nodded. "That's him. You know him?"

"Sure, I know him, his son, Danny, and Danny's daughter, Ivelisse. They're all members."

Willie grinned. "I'm definitely joining. That'll give Miguel and I more chances to hang out."

Troy returned carrying a tray loaded with their food. He carefully put a plate in front of each of them.

Trina's blueberry pancakes looked and smelled delicious, but Roxie had a new reason for watching her figure, and he was sitting across from her. She couldn't help but want to keep trim with such an interesting prospect in her life.

Ethan picked up his burger, which also looked and smelled heavenly. "Do you have a name for your shop?"

Trina nodded. "I'm thinking A Cut Above. How's that sound?"

Roxie could barely contain her pride. She put her arm around her daughter. "It sounds perfect, because that's exactly what you are."

Chapter Twenty-five

*L*istening to podcasts had made the drive
back to Landry go by pretty quickly, but
the meeting with Omar Industries felt like
it took an eternity. Kat had never been so glad for
anything to come to an end as she was that meeting.

She made enough small talk to exit gracefully
and went straight to her car.

She exhaled in relief. She was tired of fake smiling. Tired of pretending like she cared about any of
their business decisions. She wished being a beach
bum was a career path, because she could have
easily switched.

After her amazing date with Alex last night and
discovering that he spent one Saturday a month
working with at-risk youth, she was more determined than ever to find a way to volunteer some of
her time.

She didn't know what it would be yet, but he'd promised to help her. She headed for the airport to pick up her cousin, Cash. It would be nice to see him.

The other thing she'd discovered on her date was how much guilt she was harboring concerning her relationship with Ray. He'd given her so many good years—which wasn't to say she hadn't done the same for him—she felt like she was letting him down now.

Not much she could do about that feeling, though. The changes in her life weren't about to magically disappear. She had to see them through. Ray deserved a face-to-face meeting so she could tell him everything in person. If he wanted to keep seeing her, she supposed she was okay with that. So long as he understood that she wasn't ready to get back into a committed relationship.

Not until she figured out what to do with her life. Although at least that was becoming clearer.

Cash texted not long after she pulled into the cell phone lot at the airport where people went to wait on their arrivals.

Here! Gate C. Thanks!

She texted back. *On my way!*

She found him right where he said he'd be, his guitar case in one hand and a big rolling duffel bag in the other. He looked very L.A. in his skinny jeans, shaggy hair, and leather jacket with a rock band tee underneath. He seemed super fit, too, but she supposed that was also an L.A. thing. Tans and muscles.

She pulled up and hopped out. "Hey, Cash!"

"Hey, Kitty Kat. How are you?"

She grinned at the old nickname and gave him a hug. He was as muscley as he looked. Maybe she'd hook him up with Alex. He might like to learn to surf. Or maybe he already knew how? "I'm all right. How are you?"

He sighed as he hugged her back. "Hopefully better soon."

"Yeah? Things not good in L.A.?" She opened her trunk for his stuff.

He hoisted the duffel in first. "They're all right, I guess, but I just need to figure some stuff out."

She barked out a laugh. "Well, I can understand that. Maybe we can figure it out together. I just need to run by the house first and pick up a few things, then we'll be on our way to the beach."

"Sounds good. Maybe I can raid your fridge a little? I haven't eaten anything yet today. Super early flight."

"You're welcome to anything you find, but the

pantry will probably be a better bet. We cleaned out the fridge. We can always pick up some fast food, too. Come on."

The house was only twenty minutes from the airport and on the way to Diamond Beach, so things had worked out pretty well, logistically. She and Cash chatted the whole way.

He told her all about how L.A. was such a hard place to live, then shared his realization that music wasn't the right choice for him and how much he worried about his dad's reaction to that decision.

She sympathized. Having a famous rock star for a dad was a pretty big shadow to live under. Aunt Jules wasn't exactly a nobody, either. Kat definitely understood some of what Cash must be feeling.

She told him all about losing her dad, finding out about his second family, and how she was now questioning everything she thought she knew.

As it turned out, they had a lot of the same things going on.

She pulled into the driveway of the house. "I'm really glad you're here. I haven't seen you since you went to L.A. and I realize now just how much I've missed you."

He smiled. "You always were the big sister I never wanted."

She laughed and playfully punched his arm. "Brat. Well, now you're going to have a second one."

"Yeah, how about that. That's wild, man."

She parked the car and unhooked her seatbelt. "Come on. Let's find you something to eat."

"Great." They got out and went inside after she unlocked the door. Cash went toward the kitchen, and she went up the steps to her bedroom to grab a few more wardrobe options.

There was music playing. Had she or her mom left something on? They must have, but she didn't remember doing it. Maybe it was the alarm on her mom's clock radio.

She opened the bedroom door and gasped. Ray was in her bed with another woman. Heidi, one of his nurses. And they *weren't* sleeping.

Because of the music, neither Ray nor Heidi noticed her. Kat screamed. "What are you doing?!"

Ray jumped and hit his head on the headboard. Heidi yanked the covers over herself, leaving Ray exposed. He grabbed at the covers, too, but Heidi had a better grip and his hands slipped, causing him to fall off the side of the bed.

He put a hand up. "It's not what it looks like."

Kat stared in horror. "Are you serious right now? It's exactly what it looks like. You're both naked in *my* bed. Why aren't you at your place?" She held her hands up as if she could shield herself from what she was seeing and shook her head. "You know what? I don't need an explanation. I know what you're doing."

Heidi shook her head. "It wasn't my idea."

"Oh, shut up," Kat snarled. She had a feeling she knew why Ray was here. This place was closer to his office than his apartment.

Cash came bounding up the stairs. "What was that?" He looked into the bedroom. "Oh. Dang." He shook his head. "Not a good look, Ray."

Ray frowned. "Cash?"

Kat was angry enough that she thought she might have suddenly developed the supernatural ability to shoot laser beams out of her eyes. She tried it and failed, sadly. "Get out of my house. Now."

"Kat," Ray pleaded. "I can explain."

"No, you really can't." She shook her head.

Heidi scrambled for her clothes, trying to get dressed while still under the covers.

"Please," Ray said. "Just give me a chance. You broke up with me."

"That's not what happened." Kat crossed her arms. She was seething inside. It hurt, too, realizing she'd given so many years of her life to a man who'd done the same thing her father had. Cheated. "Hurry up before I call the police and tell them there are two naked intruders in my house."

Ray found his scrub pants and tugged them on, then got to his feet.

"Faster," Kat said. "Or I'll get Cash to throw you out just like you are."

"Have a little mercy," Ray said. "I have a reputation, you know. The least you could have done was texted that you were coming back."

"Mercy?" The nerve. Kat lunged forward, but Cash caught her arm. Ray jerked back and bumped into the dresser, almost falling over.

Heidi, now back in her scrubs, slipped out from under the covers. "I'm really sorry," she said as she ran past Kat and down the steps.

Ray found the rest of his things and followed behind her.

Kat stood in his way, her hand out. "Not so fast."

Ray looked confused. "What?"

"The house key. Because you are never, ever coming back here." And to think she'd felt guilty. What an idiot she'd been.

Cash stood shoulder to shoulder with her. "You do and you'll have me to deal with."

Ray glanced up at Cash, who was at least four

inches taller and fifty pounds heavier. He nervously worked the key off his key ring and dropped it in Kat's hand. "Maybe I can call you tomorrow and we can—"

"No." Kat glared at him. "I never want to speak to you again."

Cash stepped back into the hall so Ray could get by.

He scampered down the steps after Heidi, the door slamming behind him.

Kat swallowed, a wave of hurt washing over her. "I can't believe that just happened."

Cash looked at her. "Are you okay?"

She shook her head and burst into tears. "No, I'm not."

Chapter Twenty-six

Margo and Conrad took their time wandering through the Maritime Art Museum, reading all the placards, discussing the most remarkable pieces, and even watching a presentation on watercolor painting.

"That was interesting," she told Conrad as they strolled through the final gallery. "I thought the use of color was especially nice."

"It was," he agreed. "Thinking about picking up a brush? Taking a crack at something yourself?"

"Oh, no. I don't have the slightest bit of artistic talent in me."

He frowned. "I highly doubt that. Plus, you're an intelligent woman. I'm sure you could pick it up in no time."

She wasn't sure intelligence and creativity necessarily went together. "Have you ever tried it?"

"Not watercolors, but I've tried my hand at painting." He smiled. "Enough to know that I do my best work with words. Have you ever tried writing?"

"Since school? No. Nothing more than letters to friends. Although..." She stopped talking and shook her head. There really wasn't anything more she wanted to share.

"Although what? Come on, finish what you were going to say."

It wasn't in her nature to disclose such closely held thoughts. Especially not when it came to things that were really just daydreams. But Conrad was proving himself over and over again to be a safe place for such conversations. "I will confess that I've always wondered if I could write a book."

"So why don't you?"

"At my age?"

"What does age have to do with it? Words don't age. Good stories don't, either. I say go for it."

"You say that about everything." He was so encouraging. In that, he reminded her of her late husbands. They'd both been that way, too.

"Because I don't think anyone should put limitations on themselves. What's the downside to attempting to write a book?"

She shrugged. "I wouldn't know the first thing

about such an endeavor. Where to start. How to write something that long. Any of it."

He smiled. "I don't think that's true. I already know you're an avid reader. I believe reading as much as you do has implanted the basics of how to craft a story in your subconscious. I'll go a step further: I think you already have a story in mind."

She glared at him because, somehow, he knew too much. "What makes you say that?"

"That's just who you are. You pay attention to things, and you internalize anything you might think is important. Am I right?"

She exhaled. He wasn't wrong. "I still wouldn't know how to start."

"What genre would you write? If you were going to write."

They headed for the gift shop but stopped by a display outside of it. A giant anchor covered in tiny mosaic tiles. It was beautiful.

Reluctantly, she answered as she studied the intricate patterns covering the metal surface. "Something with a murder." She smiled a bit. "I feel like that's something I could write competently about."

All those shows she'd watched had definitely left their mark.

He cut his eyes at her, but they gleamed with mischief. "Should that concern me?"

Her smile inched further toward her cheeks. "Have *you* ever thought about writing a book?"

He nodded. "Often. I've started a few but always gotten stuck." His eyes narrowed in thought, his gaze on the anchor. "Maybe we should write one together."

The idea sparked something inside her. "Are you being serious?"

He turned away from the anchor to face her. "I am. Are you interested?"

"Maybe. Would it be a murder mystery? Or some kind of thriller?" She'd had an idea about a woman whose husbands kept dying and was suspected of being a black widow, but the murders were actually being committed by her twin sister, luring the men to their deaths easily, because they believed she was the innocent twin.

"Either one. I'm game." He smiled. "Tell me your idea."

Her stomach rumbled with a most unladylike noise before she could answer.

He laughed. "How about you tell me over an early dinner?"

"Deal," she said. "But not before I stroll through the gift shop."

She'd had such an enjoyable day, she bought a small woodblock print of an anchor as a memento. Then she and Conrad found a restaurant nearby, a place called Molly's Seafood Grill.

They went inside, got a table, and ordered. The broiled seafood platter for him, the broiled scallops for her.

Then she told him her idea, expounding on it like she'd never done before, but the very act of speaking the idea out loud made it expand. She could see subplots and red herrings and twists she'd never dreamed of previously.

When she was done, their meals halfway gone, she felt as though she'd just given birth. Not physically, but metaphorically. Which she supposed was something a lot of writers must feel. Not that she was a writer.

But the thought had taken on an authenticity she'd never felt before. Like it wasn't just possible, it was imminent.

"The only problem," she said. "Is that I don't know who the hero is. There has to be a hero. A detective maybe? The police officer assigned to the case? An FBI agent? I really don't know."

"Is he the love interest?"

She nodded. "Yes, I think he is. I think he should help the heroine save herself, though. Not be the sole reason she survives. The two of them, working together."

"All right. How about a retired Marine?"

She grinned. "You would say that."

"We're a very heroic bunch."

"I'd agree with that. How does this retired Marine come into her life?"

Conrad sat back, clearly thinking. "He's her... next-door neighbor and realizes something's wrong. Or maybe he's a private detective?" Conrad paused, thinking. "Maybe he meets the sister and somehow knows it's not the heroine? He can tell them apart when most people can't."

"Oh, I like that."

Conrad smiled. "I like you and I like this idea and I want us to write it. I have a friend who's a published author. I'm sure I could talk him into having a look at it when we're done. Just to see what he thinks."

"You're serious about this, aren't you?" To be honest, there'd been a trill of excitement running through her ever since they'd starting talking about it.

"Very serious. What do you say?"

She was losing her mind to think writing a book was really going to happen, wasn't she? And yet, a new kind of energy had taken hold of her. It was the sort of thing she couldn't ignore. "I say...yes."

Chapter Twenty-seven

*A*s the arrival of Kat and Cash got closer, Jules found it impossible to concentrate on anything but her son walking into the house. She checked the time, filled with anticipation. She would have loved to put the finishing touches on her song, but Cash came first. She couldn't wait to see him and put her arms around him.

Truth was, she'd missed him more than she realized. She missed Fen, too, but he was in a serious relationship and had his own life. Cash was her baby, and even as a little boy, Fen had never needed her the way Cash had. He'd been much more independent. More like his father. Nothing wrong with that. So long as he didn't become *too* much like his father. But he and his brother were very different people.

When the soft whirr of the elevator announced

its arrival, even Toby joined her in waiting for it open. He'd clearly sensed her excitement, even if he didn't know what was happening. He would soon enough. He loved Cash.

The doors opened and her son walked out. He dropped his duffel bag then set his guitar next to it. "Hi, Mom."

She grinned and wrapped him in a hug. "Hi, honey."

She held him tight as Toby danced around their legs, letting out little yips of doggy joy. "It's so good to see you."

"You, too, Mom." He backed away, his smile one of happiness, but there was something darker in his eyes. He scooped Toby up, giving the dog some love as he slanted his gaze toward his cousin, getting off the elevator behind him. "Kat is...not good."

"I'm fine," Kat mumbled.

But Kat's eyes were red, and she looked miserable. Jules was instantly concerned. "What's wrong? Are you okay? Did something happen to the car?"

Kat sniffed and shook her head. Her chin wobbled like she might start crying. "I caught Ray cheating on me. At our house. *In my bed*."

Jules's jaw unhinged in disbelief. "What?"

Cash nodded as he scratched Toby's head. "I saw

it, too. He had one of his nurses with him. Some chick named Heidi."

"Oh, Kat, honey." Jules embraced her. "Are you okay?"

"Y-yes and n-no," Kat stammered. She rubbed at her eyes when Jules let her go, looking very much like she was trying not to break down. "I'm kind of a mess. I just need to talk to my mom."

"She's still over at Danny's. Grandma's out, too. But I'll text your mom for you." Jules pulled her phone out. Claire really ought to know about this.

"No, it's all right." Kat sniffed and rubbed at her face. "I think I'll take a hot shower. Might make me feel better. I can talk to her when she gets home."

"Are you sure? You can talk to me, too, you know."

Kat managed a smile. "I know. And I will when I'm ready. But you need to catch up with your son. I'll be all right. It's just going to take a minute to deal with...all of it." She blew out a breath and looked away. "There are some images in my head I could really do without."

"I'm sure," Jules said. She could only imagine. Actually, she didn't need to imagine. She'd seen some of those same images herself, featuring both of her exes. "If you need me, I'm here. Anytime. I mean that."

Kat gave her a quick nod, then headed for the bedroom. Jules let her go, watching after her for a moment. The poor thing must be gutted. Even if Kat wasn't ready to marry Ray just yet, they'd been together for longer than some people stayed married.

That kind of betrayal after so many years had to be a blow. It had been for Jules. Her heart went out to Kat. Then Jules got angry, thinking about how they'd considered Ray family. Treated him as such.

He was dead to her now.

She turned to look at Cash again. He'd put Toby down and the little dog was staring up at him like Superman had just arrived. Jules understood exactly how he felt. She cupped Cash's face in her hands. "I have to say it again: It's so good to see you."

He laughed. "You, too."

She let him go. "Are you hungry? Thirsty?"

"Nah. I grabbed some food at Kat's." His brows lifted as he glanced toward Kat's room. "Ray was butt naked. So was the woman with him. Kat saw it all. She was *mad*. Like, I've never seen her that mad."

"I bet."

"She's really hurt, too. She was crying and everything." He shook his head, frowning. "I guess you figured that out. Anyway, I drove for about an hour until we stopped for gas so she could get herself together."

"I'm glad you were there." What a good guy he was. It made her proud. "I'm sure it helped to have your support."

He nodded. "She told him to get out, but I was willing to throw him out if he didn't. I would have, too." His gaze hardened with anger. "What a jerk. Kat didn't deserve that. Nobody does, but wow, they were supposed to get married."

Jules smiled. It was so sweet to see him protective of his cousin. "No, she didn't deserve that." She wanted to hug him again, but she didn't want to overdo it. She'd hug him some more later. "How are you doing?"

He shrugged. "I'm dealing. It helped to talk to Kat. She's going through some similar stuff, you know? I mean about not knowing exactly what she should be doing with her life, not the thing with Ray."

"Right."

"I actually wouldn't mind getting settled in and taking a shower myself. Kind of a long day, you know?"

"I'm sure. Big travel day. The upstairs is all you. You remember where everything is? Towels and stuff?"

"I'll figure it out." He smiled. "I can't believe how long it's been since I've been here, but I'm glad I came. I think this is exactly what I needed. I feel better already."

She was glad to hear that. "Good. When you want to talk, just let me know. I'll be right here. And we can do whatever you want tonight. Go out to dinner. Walk on the beach. Sit by the pool. Anything."

"Cool. Thanks. If it's all right with you, I'd be happy to stay in and chill. I don't need anything fancy for dinner, either. I'd be good with a sandwich. Or two. I'll eat anything, really. I'm not gonna be picky."

"You just let me know. I can order pizza, too."

He grinned. "That doesn't sound awful. Maybe later we can take that walk on the beach. I'm sure Tobes would like that."

"He would. You go shower. We'll figure it out when you come back down."

"All right. Hey—I want to meet my new cousin, too. Trina." He grinned. "Kat filled me in on all the stuff with Uncle Bryan on the way here."

Jules nodded. "We'll make that happen. I know she's looking forward to meeting you, too."

"Cool." He bent down to give Toby one more rub on the head, grabbed his duffel bag and guitar, then used his thumb to call the elevator. The doors opened and he stepped on. "See you in a bit."

She nodded, her heart full. Was there a mother who didn't feel more complete when her child was under the same roof?

She said a quick prayer of thankfulness, then picked Toby up and kissed his face. "Our boy is home. I don't know how long we'll get to keep him, but we'll just enjoy him while he's here, huh?"

Toby licked her face, making her laugh. She danced around with him, softly singing, "Our boy is home, our boy is home."

Just then, the elevator started whirring again. It arrived, the doors opened, and Claire stepped out, looking about as happy as Jules had ever seen her. Her smile expanded when she saw Jules. "You are not going to believe what I have to tell you."

Jules snorted softly as she put Toby down. "That makes two of us."

Chapter Twenty-eight

illie felt high. Or what she imagined high felt like. She'd never indulged in the medical marijuana like some of her senior friends. Not that she was against it for the glaucoma and such, but she was secretly a little afraid of it. She didn't want to end up naked and dancing on a table. She had enough of a reputation already.

She preferred a natural high. Or the kind that came from a gin and tonic. But today, being with Trina and seeing how happy that child was, had put Willie on a whole new plane of happiness.

It wasn't about to end, either. Trina was over the moon and Willie was right there with her, soaking up all the love and appreciation her granddaughter was giving her. Roxie was happy, too, of course, but some of that was because of Ethan.

Willie had no problem with that. Ethan seemed

like a good man. Her only concern was that things not go badly between him and Roxie and cause them to lose their best hope for getting the strip mall renovated in a timely fashion.

Maybe she should say something to Roxie about it, but her daughter had to know that was a possibility, didn't she?

Roxie and Trina were currently sitting in the living room working on a look book for the salon. Willie was in the bedroom, changing into something a bit dressier for her dinner with Miguel.

Part of her wished she wasn't going, so she could stay home and enjoy all the talk about the new salon, but there would be plenty of that to come. And a night out with Miguel wasn't something she wanted to miss, either.

After lunch today, they'd said goodbye to Ethan, then gone to the lighting place, where they'd gotten a bunch of catalogs to take home and look through. After the lighting place, they'd gone to Walmart so Trina could buy a binder. She wanted to keep all of her ideas for the salon in one place, along with anything else that might have to do with the renovation.

Willie was all for that. Organization was a good thing. She'd never been great at it, but Trina seemed to have picked up a recessive gene somewhere. Maybe her father? Hard to say. Willie hadn't known him that well.

Then again, none of them had.

Willie assessed her available outfits. She'd looked up the flag of Puerto Rico, just to refresh her memory. She wanted to wear something that honored Miguel's native country. Fortunately, she'd brought what was typically her Fourth of July outfit with her.

A bright blue terrycloth jogging set with capri-length pants and a matching jacket. Under it, she typically wore a white T-shirt emblazoned with a red rhinestone star. Not exactly the Puerto Rican flag, but she felt sure Miguel would appreciate it all the same.

She added a blue bracelet with white stars on it and some dangly silver star earrings and she was ready.

She checked her lipstick in the mirror before going out to the living room. "All right, my girls. I'm off to meet Miguel. The Uber he ordered will be here soon to pick us up for dinner. I want to hear all about your plans when I get home, all right?"

Trina jumped up and gave her grandmother a

hug. "I hope you have a great time. I promise we'll fill you in on anything we decide."

"Good."

"Yeah, have fun, Ma," Roxie said. "You look great."

"Thanks. I plan on it." Willie headed for the elevator. In her fanny pack, she had some tissues, some hand sanitizer, forty bucks in cash, her lipstick, and her phone. She was set for the night.

Once on the ground floor, she turned to walk to the end of the driveway. Miguel was already there.

He waved at her, coming toward her a few steps. He was in tan pants and a pale green shirt she'd recently learned was called a *guayabera*, a loose dress shirt with matching sets of pleats on either side of the button placket. His had matching breast pockets as well.

She smiled. "You look very handsome."

"You look very sparkly." He grinned. "You are dressed in the colors of my country's flag."

"I know. I did it on purpose. I hope that was okay."

He touched his heart. "I love it."

A silver sedan pulled up behind him. Miguel glanced at it. "Our ride is here." He opened the door for her and helped her in, then went around to the other side and joined her in the back seat.

He leaned forward. "You know we are going to Papi's, right?"

The driver, a young man, smiled. "Si, senor."

Miguel laughed softly and the two exchanged words in Spanish that Willie couldn't understand. She didn't mind, though. She felt oddly proud of the man beside her and his ability to communicate in more than one language.

When Miguel sat back, he was still smiling. "The young man is from Guatemala, but he's been here two years. And he knows where the restaurant is. He said it's one of his favorites."

"That's always good to hear. You're going to help me order, right?"

Miguel took her hand. "You have nothing to worry about."

When they got to Papi's, they were ushered right in, and Miguel was treated like a celebrity. Clearly, they knew who he was, and he'd been here more times than he'd let on. It amused Willie that he'd been so sly about it.

The interior was bathed in soft, golden lights, giving the rich colors a jewel-like quality. Stucco walls and a terracotta floor felt authentic, although

Willie wasn't sure if they were. In the background, music played that reminded her of the station she and Miguel had danced to. And the smells from the kitchen, smokey and flavorful, made her mouth water.

They were given a cozy corner booth lit by a flickering candle in a pretty glass holder. From their vantage point, they could see most of the restaurant, including a small garden courtyard with a fountain and hanging lights.

"This is very romantic," Willie commented. "I like it a lot."

Miguel smiled. "I'm glad you approve. But wait until you taste the food."

A server, an older man in a shirt very similar to Miguel's, brought them glasses of water and menus. "Good evening. Welcome to Papi's. I'm Hector, and I'll be taking care of you. Can I start you off with some drinks?"

"Pina colada," Willie said. Why not? She wasn't driving. But she didn't plan on having more than one. She wanted to keep her wits about her, especially because she wanted to stay awake long enough when she got home to hear what the girls had come up with for the salon.

Miguel nodded. "Make that two."

"Very good," Hector said. "I'll be right back."

Willie glanced at her menu but in the dim light it was hard to read. She dug her phone out and turned on the flashlight, directing it at the page. She still couldn't make much sense of it, as a lot of it was in Spanish. She looked over the top of it at Miguel. "Okay, what should I order?"

"Do you trust me?"

That was a rather deep question, but she figured he meant about the food. "I do."

"Is there anything you don't like?"

She thought. "Not really. But if you get me a plate of something weird like pig snouts or goat brains, I want the option to veto."

He laughed. "I was thinking I would order *mofongo* for us to share, but that's really a side dish. A very delicious side dish, but there should be more to a meal. I thought I would get you some *arroz con gandules y lechon*."

"Can you translate that?"

He nodded. "It's roast pork with rice and pigeon peas." He closed his eyes for a moment and sighed. "The food of my childhood."

She definitely wanted to try that. "Perfect." She closed her menu and pushed it to the edge of the table. "Thank you for bringing me here. I'm really enjoying it."

"Thank you for being willing to come."

"Who wouldn't want to experience something new?"

He snorted. "You would be surprised."

"Sounds like you have a story about that."

Hector returned with their drinks, tall glasses filled with creamy yellow slush topped with a fresh piece of pineapple and a little umbrella. "Are you ready to order?"

Miguel took care of it, telling Hector exactly what they wanted, all in Spanish, of course.

Hector nodded and smiled. "Very good, sir." Then he left them alone.

Miguel picked up his glass. "To a wonderful night with a wonderful woman."

Willie gently knocked her glass against his. "Thank you."

They each took a sip. She thought it very good, although maybe the one Miguel had made for her had been a little bit better. "Now, tell me who didn't want to try something new."

Miguel shook his head. "It was a year or so ago. A woman I thought was someone worth getting to know.

But she wasn't interested in who I was or where I came from." He laughed softly. "I must confess, I thought you would be that way, too, at first. I'm afraid I painted all women with the same brush after her. But you? You're not like that at all. As I've said, you're fearless. I love it."

She smiled. "You're not exactly afraid of things, either."

"Life is too short."

"Yes, it is." Something she was becoming more and more aware of every day. "Why did that woman want to go out with you if she didn't want to know you?"

He pursed his lips. "I am ashamed to say it."

"Say what?" Willie wasn't sure what he was getting at.

Miguel sighed. "She was interested in my money."

It was Willie's turn to laugh. "I promise you, that's not something I'm remotely concerned with."

"No?"

She shook her head. "I have my own money." Thanks to Zippy. She leaned in. "In fact, you remember that investment property I was telling you about?"

He nodded.

"Well, today, I made an offer on it and it was accepted. All that's left to do is sign the paperwork."

His mouth came open and he lifted his glass again. "Congratulations! Now we have even more reason to celebrate."

She couldn't agree more.

Chapter Twenty-nine

Claire, her heart heavy with the news Jules had told her, knocked on Kat's door.

From the other side, came her daughter's quiet, "Come in."

She opened the door. Kat was sitting on the bed. Only the reading lamp on her nightstand was lit, casting most of the room in shadows. Her knees were pulled up, her arms wrapped around them. Claire's heart ached for her daughter even more. "Your aunt told me what happened. I'm so sorry, sweetheart."

Kat sniffed. "Thanks. I can't believe he did that, Mom."

Claire came in, shut the door behind her, then went and sat on the same side as Kat at the foot of the bed. "I can't, either."

Kat didn't make eye contact, just stared past her

knees at some unknown spot. "Makes some other things make sense, though, you know? Why he was always so willing to go along with whatever I wanted. Why he was in no rush to get married. Why he didn't care if I wanted to see other people." She shook her head. "First Dad, now Ray."

"You deserve better, sweetheart."

Kat was silent a moment, then she looked up, her eyes a little red, but also full of determination. "I want better, Mom. And I already know I can have it. This was a real wake-up call. I was stupidly feeling guilty about going out with Alex, even though Ray had told me it wasn't a big deal. That guilt is *gone*."

"As it should be." Claire was proud of Kat for not wallowing. A certain amount of hurt and self-pity was to be expected, but Claire had never imagined her daughter would come through a thing like this with so much resolve. That was new.

"Alex has already shown me that I can do better when it comes to relationships. Trina has shown me that I do better when it comes to myself. Talking to Cash made me realize that what I think I should be doing and what I should actually be doing are probably two different things." Kat picked at the seam of her jeans. "It's past time for a change."

Claire smiled. "Good for you."

Kat crossed her legs. "I mean it, too. I'm going to change my life. I want to...do something different. Something more meaningful. I don't know what yet, and I probably won't until I start looking, but I want to work for a charity or a foundation or a non-profit. Some kind of place that helps people." She frowned and shook her head. "The people I work for now? They don't need my help. And none of them do anything with their money to make the world better."

"You do sound determined."

"I am. Are you going to be mad at me if I quit my job?"

Claire shook her head. "Why would I be mad at you? It's your life. And if you want to make it count, then by all means, you do what you feel led to do. There might be one little problem, though."

Kat's brows knit together. "What's that?"

"What are you going to live off of until you find a job?"

Kat sighed. "I don't know. I'm kind of hoping I can find something pretty quick so there won't be too much of a gap."

"Does that mean you plan on returning to Landry soon?"

Kat made a horrified face. "Mom, I don't ever

want to go back there. For one thing, I don't think I can sleep in that bed again. Not after what I saw going on there. For another, I don't want to live in a place where everyone's going to find out what Ray was doing. I'm sure it wasn't the first time. And it's humiliating."

Claire could only nod. She completely understood.

Kat's mouth bent, like she was about to cry. "For all I know, everyone already knew."

"I don't think that's true." Claire took a breath. "But I know how you're feeling. If I had the option to never go back there, I would take it without a second thought."

"What do you mean 'if'? Why can't we stay? Sell the Landry house and stay here."

Claire's soft exhale sounded more dire than she'd meant it to. "It all comes down to money, sweetheart. This place is expensive. And I don't just mean Diamond Beach. I mean this house. Maintaining it. Paying the bills that come with it. Now, your grandmother did offer to help, but I still don't know if this house is going to be an option."

"You mean because of Dad also being married to Roxie?"

Claire nodded. "The attorney who's the executor

of the will hasn't been very forthcoming with information. I tried to reach him again today, but he was out of the office. I'm frustrated beyond belief but there's not much I can do until he tells me what the will says."

Kat groaned. "Dad really screwed us over, didn't he?"

"I don't know yet."

"Men," Kat muttered. "Why are some of them such wastes of space?"

Claire thought about Danny and about the new reason he'd given her to stay. "I promise you, they aren't all that way." She patted Kat's hand. "Look, if it turns out that I get the house, then I'm willing to sit down and do some hard numbers to see if we can make it work."

Kat straightened a little. "Yeah?"

Claire nodded. Then she smiled. "I made some popcorn bars for Danny Rojas to try today, and he liked them so much, he offered me a job. A good job. A career, really. He wants to start a Mrs. Butter's Bakery, and he wants me to be his partner in it. He's willing to give me a stake in exchange for me developing the recipes and helping to run the place. It would be my decision as to what the menu is, too."

"Mom! That's amazing. You really are the best

baker I know. Where would the bakery be? Here in
Diamond Beach?"

"I don't know yet. He doesn't have a location. But
I'm sure it would be close enough to drive to. The
only problem is until that place is up and running, I
still wouldn't have an income." She didn't expect
Danny to pay her for sitting around and coming up
with recipes. "Unless I work at one of the popcorn
shops, which I could do. Danny said as much."

Kat reached out and grabbed her mom's hand.
"Listen, I have money saved up. Money in my
wedding fund. I will gladly put that toward us
making a new life here."

Claire shook her head. "I can't ask you to do
that."

"You're not asking. I'm offering. And if Grandma's
really serious about pitching in, then we should be
okay. I mean, things might be a little tight, but we
can always rent out the first floor, can't we?"

Claire took a breath. "Yes. We'd probably need to
install some sort of real door at the interior steps,
but yes, that would help." She couldn't shake the
worry that she was *not* going to get this place,
though.

"Then we'll do that. We'd recoup the money
pretty quickly if we started renting it out right away.

And then once we're making enough, we won't have to do that anymore. In fact, Grandma could move downstairs and have her own space all to herself that way."

Claire nodded, thinking while she listened. "Maybe Danny could help with the door. He's very handy. He's a real do-it-yourselfer."

"Never hurts to ask." Kat squeezed Claire's hand. "We can do this, Mom. I'm starting tomorrow to look for a job that means something. I'm not wasting any more time. I'd suggest you start calling the attorney every day. Maybe twice a day, until you find out what the heck is going on."

Claire nodded. "I will call him again first thing tomorrow." She felt better having talked to her daughter, but her intention had been to make her daughter feel better, not the other way around.

"Good."

"Are you sure you're okay?"

Kat took a breath. "No, I'm not okay. I'm hurt and I'm mad and I'm still a bit in shock. But I'll get over it. Just like I'll get over Ray." She shrugged. "What I know is I'm moving on. Like you should be doing. We have to look to the future, Mom. We need to figure out what makes us happy, then do that."

Claire smiled. "When did you get so insightful?"

"When I realized that there was more to life than just me. I've been kind of selfish in my choices. I'm sorry about that." Kat sniffed again. "I want to do better."

"I don't think you've been selfish."

Kat shrugged one shoulder. "I could have helped you more around the house. I could have seen the sacrifices you made for me. I could have spent more time with you. I want that to be different going forward."

"You had your own life, Kat. I never expected you to give that up for me."

Kat hesitated. "You like Danny Rojas a lot, don't you?"

Claire smiled. It was impossible not to. "I do. He's not just a kind man, he's a good listener and he understands what I'm going through. He's been through it. Although not with a secret family attached, but still. He's been a great help to me in so many ways."

"Well, I approve of whatever's going on there. Just so you know. Do you think...maybe you and Danny would want to go out to dinner with me and Alex? Or would that be weird?"

Claire laughed. "That would not be weird. And I think Danny would love to do that. I'll ask him tomorrow, okay?" She was thrilled her daughter had even suggested such a thing.

"Okay," Kat said. "I know it's early, but I think I'm just going to chill in here for the rest of the night. Maybe read a little. Today wore me out."

"I'm sure it did." Claire got up and hugged her daughter. They really needed to do more of that. "I love you. And I'm proud of you."

"Thanks, Mom. I love you, too. And I'm thrilled that Danny has recognized your talents."

Claire grinned. That made two of them.

Chapter Thirty

*R*oxie got up early, earlier than she intended, and went for a walk on the beach. She had so much energy built up from yesterday, it was the only way she could think of to put it to use. The beach was beautiful. The water and sky the most perfect shades of blue.

She even threw in some walking lunges, using the sand for extra resistance, and was pleased to get her heart rate up. When she got back, she did pushups and squats out on the deck, then went inside, still full of energy but ready for coffee.

Her mother was sitting on the couch, speaking softly on the phone. "Mm-hmm. That's right. We can go over today. Be happy to. Okay. I'll text you."

While her mother finished up the call, Roxie got coffee going. She took out some eggs, too, figuring she might as well make breakfast for all of them.

Her mother hung up. "You're not going to believe this, but I might have rented one of the strip mall's stores."

Roxie turned, completely surprised. "That's fantastic. How on Earth did you manage that?"

"Last night at dinner, I told Miguel about buying the strip mall. As it turns out, his son is looking for a new location, because he wants to expand the business."

Roxie shook her head. "You didn't say anything about that when you got home."

"I wasn't sure anything would come of it. Miguel wasn't, either. But he promised to talk to his son and see what he thought. They know the location. They want to look at the units available. Do you think you could get Ethan to meet us over there again today?"

"I'll text him right now." She pulled her phone out of the pocket of her leggings. "It would be great to have a renter already lined up."

Willie smiled. "It would be, but I'm not worried about having empty spots."

"I am, a little. I don't want you to spend all of that money and then have the place sit vacant." She texted Ethan. *Can we get in to see the other units today? We might have a renter. They want to see what's available.*

"It won't," Willie assured her. "You'll see."

Trina joined them, her salon binder in her hands. "Hey, Ma. Hey, Mimi. Coffee smells good."

"It'll be ready in a couple minutes," Roxie told her.

Willie grinned at Trina. "How would you feel about having a bakery as one of the other tenants in the shopping center?"

"A bakery? That would be cool. Especially if they served coffee. I would love having a place nearby to get a mocha latte."

Roxie groaned. "You had to say that, didn't you? Now I want one." She laughed. "But you make a good point. I hadn't thought about that." She looked at her mother. "And you didn't say it was a bakery."

Willie nodded. "That's what they want to open. A brand-new store. Mrs. Butter's Bakery."

Trina sat at the counter. "Hang on. You're talking about the neighbors, right? They own the Mrs. Butter's stores. But those places sell popcorn."

"I know," Willie said. "But that's why this is brand new. They want to diversify. Apparently, they'll still have popcorn and popcorn treats, but also other baked goods."

"Huh." Trina thought a minute. "Sounds good.

Like I said, as long as they serve coffee, I'll be a customer."

The coffee sputtered out the last few drops. Roxie filled three mugs and got out the creamers. "What do you want in yours, Ma?"

"Sugar and the vanilla creamer."

Roxie fixed the coffee and took it over to her mom, then she fixed her own. One less sugar than usual and only a splash of creamer. As she took her first sip, her phone vibrated.

She took it out again and looked at the screen. "Ethan answered. He asked what time do they want to see it."

"Miguel told me they can go anytime this morning," Willie answered. "They're eager."

"You think an hour would be enough time for them?" Roxie asked.

Willie nodded. "I'm sure they'd make it work."

Trina looked up from her binder. "Can I go again, too? I want to have another look."

"Of course," Roxie said.

"Thanks." Trina smiled. "I want to take some pictures with my phone. I should have done that yesterday, but I was so overwhelmed it never occurred to me."

"Good idea." Roxie texted Ethan back. *An hour okay?*

Yes, he answered. *See you then.* He signed off with a smiley face.

She smiled before putting her phone back in her pocket, then she returned the eggs and creamer to the fridge. They could eat later. "All right, let's get moving. We're meeting Ethan at the shopping center in an hour. Ma, let Miguel know."

Willie held up her phone. "Already done." She picked up her coffee and carried it out with her.

Roxie and Trina followed, also taking their coffees.

Somehow, the three of them managed to get showered, dressed, made up and out the door in time. Roxie hadn't washed her hair, just judiciously applied some dry shampoo.

Ethan was waiting for them when they pulled into the shopping center parking lot. Less than half a minute later, Danny and his dad arrived. Claire was with them.

Roxie hadn't been expecting that. Were she and Danny that much of an item now?

The three of them got out of the car, each of them holding to-go cups of coffee bearing the Java Jams logo. They must have stopped on the way. She was a little miffed. She would have loved to stop for coffee, too, but she didn't think they'd have time.

Miguel greeted Willie with a kiss on the cheek.

Roxie offered Claire a tight smile. "Morning. Didn't expect to see you here."

Claire nodded. "I could say the same thing. How are you involved in this?"

Roxie lifted her chin slightly, proud of the answer she was able to give to that question. "My mother is the landlord."

"Your mother owns this whole center?"

Roxie nodded. "She just bought it. Trina's new salon is going in that end unit." She pointed to where Ethan was unlocking the door for her daughter.

Claire glanced over, then back at Roxie. Her eyes narrowed. "Then you plan on staying in Diamond Beach."

Roxie could practically see the wheels turning in Claire's head. "That's right, we do."

Claire took a breath and seemed to be searching for words. "Have you...heard from the attorney?"

"No. Have you?"

Claire shook her head. "No. I've been trying to get ahold of him, though. Do you plan on staying at the beach house?"

"Roxie?" Ethan called. "Which one do you want me to unlock first?"

Roxie smiled. His timing was perfect. "That's up to Danny and his dad." She looked at them. "The very end unit was once a restaurant. Maybe that might have the best setup for a bakery. Doesn't matter to us, though. You can look at all of them."

Danny, who was talking with Willie and his father, nodded. "I'm happy to start at the end." He gestured to Claire. "Come on, let's see what we think."

Claire started toward him. Roxie followed. Why was Danny so interested in Claire's opinion?

Trina stayed behind in the salon while the rest of them trooped into the former Italian restaurant. The signs of that previous life were evident in the abandoned tables, red walls, and the ornate scrollwork of the crown molding. Roxie swore she could still smell a hint of garlic in the place, too.

Danny went directly through the doors that led to the kitchen. Everyone followed him. He stood in the midst of the remaining equipment, hands on his hips, and turned slowly to take it all in. He nodded. "Plenty of room in here for what we'll need."

He looked toward Claire. "What do you think?"

"I think I want to look at the front of the store

again."

They all headed back out front. Claire and Danny stood side by side, discussing where things would go. Display cases. The sales counter. A seating area for customers who wanted to eat in.

Finally, Danny looked over at Roxie and Willie. "This space has a lot of promise, but since we're here, we might as well look at the other two."

They all walked next door. Roxie took the opportunity to join Claire, since Danny was talking to his father. "Are you and Danny going out? You seem...close."

Claire kept her eyes on the building. "You want to know why I'm here, don't you?"

Roxie hadn't anticipated such a direct response, but she was all for putting things out in the open. "It had crossed my mind."

Claire finally looked at her as Ethan unlocked the door. "Danny and I are opening the bakery together. I'm his partner. And the Director of Product Development."

Roxie stared at Claire. At her self-assured smile and the amusement in her eyes. Then Roxie realized something.

Claire had every intention of staying in Diamond Beach, too.

Chapter Thirty-one

Standing in the middle of the kitchen, Margo hugged her grandson, who'd just come downstairs. "My word, you've gotten big."

Cash laughed as he hugged her back. "Grandma, I'm twenty-six. I've been full grown for a while now."

"You've still gotten bigger." She let him go to take a better look at him. "You've been working out. You've put on muscle."

He grinned. "Yeah, I have. Thanks." He nodded at Jules, flexing ever so slightly. "See? Grandma noticed."

Jules rolled her eyes. "Yeah, yeah."

Margo smiled. It was wonderful to have Cash visit. She and Conrad were going to work on their book today, but all she'd promised Conrad was that she'd text him when she was ready. She'd anticipated spending some time with her grandson. "What are your plans today?"

Cash shrugged. "I want to get some beach time. That's really about it. I'm still trying to get used to the time change, so there might be napping on the beach, too."

Margo nodded. "Toby will be glad to participate in that."

Jules laughed. "That's for sure." She took her cup to the coffee maker. "Should we make some breakfast?"

Margo nodded. "I'm sure Cash is hungry."

"Yeah, I could eat a horse. Or some pancakes. Maybe with some bacon. A couple of fried eggs wouldn't hurt, either."

Margo had forgotten how much young men ate. "Set the table," she said. "Your mom and I will get breakfast."

She looked at Jules. "Let me go check on Kat." She'd heard all about Ray's philandering ways when she'd returned home from her day out with Conrad, but Margo had yet to see her granddaughter. Kat had sequestered herself in her room. Understandably.

"Okay," Jules said. "I'll get to work on the food."

Margo knocked on Kat's door. "Kat? Are you up?"

The door opened and Kat stood there in her

robe, her hair damp around her shoulders. "Morning."

She looked better than Margo had anticipated. "Good morning. Would you like to join us for breakfast? We're making pancakes, eggs, and bacon."

Kat looked past Margo to where Cash was setting the table. "Is there coffee?"

"Yes."

"Great. Just let me get dressed and I'll be out. Do we have any fruit left? I could really go for some fruit."

"I'll see what's in the fridge," Margo promised. She left Kat to get herself together and went back to the kitchen. She found grapes in the fruit and vegetable drawer, so she took those out and washed some in a strainer, then put them in a bowl and added them to the table.

She went back to the kitchen. "What can I do, Jules?"

"Um…" Jules looked around. "Bacon?"

"All right."

While Jules made pancakes, Margo took care of the bacon. She started a second pan, adding some butter and a few spoonfuls of bacon grease, then got the eggs going, too.

Kat joined them in shorts and a tank top. She got

coffee for herself, then lifted the pot. "Anyone else want a refill? If I can empty the pot, I'll make another."

Cash, who was now sitting at the table, scrolling through his phone, raised his cup. "I'll have some, Kitty Kat."

With a smile, Kat went to fill his cup. Margo caught Jules's gaze and gave her a little grin to imply how nice the cousins were to each other.

Jules nodded and flipped a pancake. "Cash? Can you get the syrup out? And take this butter to the table."

He unfolded his lanky form from the chair. "On it."

Before long, they were sitting down to a lovely breakfast. As everyone filled their plates and tucked in, Kat sat up straighter, a curious look on her face.

She cleared her throat lightly. "First of all, I want you to know that I'm fine. Doesn't mean I'm not angry or upset, but I'm not going to let Ray's cheating ruin me. I am...rising above it. And him. Because he's not worth it."

"Good for you," Cash said. "He still deserves a punch to the throat."

"Cash," Jules said, shaking her head.

Margo cut a piece from the single small pancake she'd allowed herself. "He's not wrong."

Jules glared at her. "Mom, please."

Margo just shrugged. "Go on, Kat."

"Thanks, Grandma." She popped a grape into her mouth and ate it before continuing. "Secondly, Mom and I are going to work on a plan to stay here in Diamond Beach. Providing Mom actually gets to keep this house. If not, I'm not sure what we'll do, but we'll cross that bridge when we come to it. Anyway, I'm going out to talk to a few local charities to see if they might be interested in putting me to work."

"Wow," Jules said. "Good for you. And you guys are serious about staying? I know Danny wants your mom to open that bakery with him but...I guess I didn't really think she'd stay."

Margo put her fork down. "When did all this happen? What bakery?" She knew she'd been gone a lot lately, but how much had she missed? Quite a lot, she guessed.

Jules and Kat both explained in tandem.

Margo was amazed. "I knew she was going out with Danny this morning, but I thought she was going to breakfast."

Jules shook her head. "Nope. They're off to look at a possible location."

"Cool," Cash said. "Nobody bakes like Aunt Claire."

"It's happening pretty fast," Kat said. "But I think it's awesome. Why not go after what you want? That's what I plan on doing."

Margo agreed with her whole heart. She was suddenly very aware of how much she hadn't told her family. She'd mentioned Conrad, but only by his nickname, and she'd allowed them to believe Connie was a woman. That's what they'd assumed, and she hadn't corrected them.

She swallowed, nervous for reasons she couldn't quite name. "I, uh...I would love to stay here."

Jules blinked at her. "You would?"

Margo nodded. "I told Claire as much but at the time, she wasn't receptive. The thing is, I've made a friend and we've decided to try writing a book together."

"No kidding?" Kat said.

"No kidding," Margo answered.

Cash grinned. "Hey, that's epic. Like a cookbook?"

Margo snorted softly. "Not quite. A murder mystery."

His brows lifted. "You're going to kill someone off?"

Margo smiled, her nerves dissipating. "Several someones, if things go as planned."

"Go, Grandma." He nodded, giving his obvious approval.

"Is that friend the woman, Connie, that you mentioned?" Jules asked.

"Yes," Margo said. "But Connie's not a woman." She nonchalantly took a bite of bacon. "That's just a nickname. His name is Conrad and he's a former Marine."

Chapter Thirty-two

Trina stood with her grandmother in front of the big display of paint chips at the paint store, a bit overwhelmed by all the choices. There were *so* many shades of pink. And she loved almost all of them. No, that was a lie. They were all beautiful in their own special way. She just loved some a little more.

She sighed. "This is hard."

Her grandmother held onto Trina's arm. "That's why they offer the little samples. So you can pick a few you like and live with them. See which one you still like after a couple days go by."

"Oh. Right. Good idea." Trina picked the three that were speaking to her the loudest: Hot Lips, Crushed Berries, and Electric Blush. Then, just because it was also speaking to her, she snagged the sample of Rio Vibe, a hot pink that leaned slightly purple.

"Wonderful," her grandmother said. "Now, as soon as we find your mother, we can go to breakfast."

"She's getting the wallpaper sample books." Trina had done a lot of looking at salon interior design ideas online and she'd seen a few that had accent walls of incredibly bold, beautiful wallpaper. She figured she might as well see what was available.

This salon, thanks to her grandmother's generosity, was a once-in-a-lifetime chance to have her dreams realized. Within reason, of course. Trina had no intention of spending as much money as possible. That would just be dumb.

"Well, go find her," Mimi said. "My blood sugar's getting low."

Trina didn't think that was completely accurate. Her grandmother didn't actually have any blood sugar issues, despite her age. At least none that Trina had ever heard about and Roxie kept a pretty close eye on Willie. That was the nurse in her. But Trina wasn't about to make Mimi wait to eat. "She's coming now."

"Ma," Roxie said as she walked up to them with

wallpaper books in her arms. "Don't rush Trina. This is a big decision."

"No, it's okay," Trina said. "Is Ethan meeting us at the restaurant?"

Her mom shook her head. "No, he had another job he had to check on. But that's all right, because we need to have a little family talk."

Trina didn't know what that was about but she didn't like the sound of it. Family talks tended to be for the sharing of bad news.

For example, her mother had called a family talk to tell them that Trina's dad had passed away of a sudden heart attack.

She hoped whatever her mom was about to share, it wasn't that bad. She held up the paint samples. "Don't I have to pay for these?"

"No." Her mom smiled. "Those are complimentary. And I've already checked these books out so we can look at them at home. Let's go eat."

They went to the Hideaway Café, a little place just up the road that had only just opened a few months ago, according to Ethan, who'd told them about it. It was pirate-themed, which Trina thought was cute. She really liked the bright parrot-patterned wallpaper. How would that look in a salon?

Trina and her grandmother went to the bathroom while Roxie got a table.

They came back out and settled into the booth across from Roxie, then got coffee from Delta, the server who came to greet them and drop off menus.

Trina was pretty hungry and everything on the menu looked good, but she was more concerned about whatever her mom was going to tell them.

She set her menu down, unable to concentrate. "Are you going to tell us what's up?"

Her mom kept her eyes on the menu and shook her head. "Let's get our food ordered."

Thankfully, Delta came back pretty quickly.

Trina got a cheesesteak omelet with a side of tater tots. Her mom opted for the same omelet but with sliced tomatoes. Mimi ordered eggs benedict with grits, making sure to ask for hot sauce, too.

When the food arrived, Trina put her napkin on her lap, then braced herself for whatever her mother was going to say.

Roxie didn't disappoint. She sprinkled salt over her tomato slices. "We might have a problem."

Willie frowned as she shook the bottle of hot sauce into her grits. "Don't be coy. Say what you mean in plain words."

Roxie looked from Trina to her mother. "I think

Claire may have already heard from the lawyer. And I think she knows she's getting the house."

Trina's stomach dropped. Her appetite disappeared, too. She put her fork down. "What? How do you know that?"

Her mom leaned forward. "I talked to her at the shopping center but think about it. How is she going to be a partner in that bakery if she's not living here? Plus, she told me flat-out that she plans to stay in Diamond Beach. Well, where else is she going to stay if not in the beach house?"

Trina's grandmother put the bottle of hot sauce down. "You need to call that attorney right now."

"I already did when you two went to the bathroom. He wasn't in. I left a message telling him it was a dire emergency and that I needed him to call me back as soon as possible." Her mom made a face as she glanced at her phone. "You see how well that worked."

Trina shook her head. "I can't believe this. What are we going to do? That's our house, too. It's not fair."

Her grandmother, seated next to her, put her hand on Trina's arm. "Hush, now. Nothing's happened yet. Your mother is just guessing at what could have happened. We don't know any of that for sure until the lawyer confirms it, and if we can't get ahold of him, what makes you think Claire can?"

Willie glared at her daughter. "No more worst-case scenarios, you hear me?"

Roxie cut into her omelet. "Ma, she told me herself she plans on staying. How do you interpret that?"

Willie cut through one of her poached eggs, spilling sunny yolk onto the muffin beneath it. "I just don't think we should jump to any conclusions until we have actual facts."

Roxie sighed. "I'm not disagreeing with you, I just don't see what else she could mean. She clearly plans on staying in the house." She wiggled her finger at her mother and Trina. "If she thinks I'm giving it up without a fight, she's going to be surprised."

Her phone rang, making her jump. She exhaled and grabbed it. "Holy cow, it's the attorney."

"Well, answer it," Willie said.

Trina went still. She couldn't eat or think or do anything until she heard what the attorney had to say. She braced herself as her mother answered.

Roxie put the phone to her ear. "Hello? Yes, you've reached her." Silence for a few moments. "I see. Okay. I'll look for the email. Thank you."

She put the phone down, her face unreadable.

"Well?" Trina said. "What did he say?"

"Nothing. That was his assistant. But she said that Charles Kinnerman wants to have a video chat tomorrow morning to discuss the will. He's sending a link for us to click on that will connect us. A laptop would be best."

Trina shook her head. "Why couldn't he just tell us over the phone? Why do we have to wait?" She tried not to panic, but none of this sounded like good news to her.

"It's all right," Mimi said. "Listen, if your mother doesn't get the house, then I'll just buy us another one. You understand?"

Trina nodded and swallowed and forced a little smile, but it was hard at the moment. She felt guilty that her grandmother would spend so much on them. "Mimi, you're going to go through all that money awfully fast if you keep buying stuff for us."

But her grandmother just laughed. "Trina, my girl, if I buy a house for myself to live in, to be near my new business, how is that for you?" She gave Trina a big, exaggerated wink. "Sure, I'll let you live there. But come on, now. Just because I bought you a salon doesn't mean I'm buying you a house, too."

Trina chuckled. "I love you, Mimi."

"I love you, too." She patted Trina's hand. "And I don't want you to worry about anything, but especially not what your father might or might not have done, because there's nothing we can do to change it."

Across the table, Trina's mother shook her head. "That's not true. I can contest the will if it comes to that. Look, I may not have been married to Bryan as long as Claire, but that doesn't mean Trina and I should get nothing."

Trina recognized the fire in her mother's eyes. Roxie meant what she said. But she was also a little scared.

Trina understood. Because she was, too.

Chapter Thirty-three

*K*at hadn't brought much in the way of professional clothing, but she was hoping that the charities wouldn't be quite so formal as her regular place of employment, although she hadn't dressed up much for yesterday's meeting, because she hadn't brought work clothes with her.

Today, she wore her blue floral sundress with a white cardigan and white sandals. It was cute and with her new hair and a little more makeup than usual, she felt confident that she looked nice. And professional.

She took one last look in the mirror and knew something was missing. She just didn't know what.

She walked out into the living room. "Grandma? Are you still here?"

Her grandmother came out of her room. She was fastening an earring. "Right here. You look nice."

"Thanks, but I feel like the outfit needs something. It's kind of blah, right?"

Her grandmother assessed her, head to toe. "You could use a necklace and some earrings. A little white belt on that dress wouldn't hurt, either.

Kat pulled her hair back. "I'm wearing earrings and I don't have much in the way of necklaces. The belt, I don't know about."

"You need bigger earrings. With your hair down, those disappear."

"I have some larger hoops." Kat had always thought those were sort of...trampy. But maybe not. "I'll go put them on."

"And I have a necklace and a belt you can borrow. Meet you back here."

A couple of minutes later, her grandmother was handing her a thin white leather belt and a chain of open gold links. The necklace was bigger than anything Kat would normally wear, but the open links kept it from looking or feeling heavy. She put it and the belt on, then looked in the mirror in her grandmother's bathroom.

She nodded. The necklace added some sparkle

and the belt defined her waist, turning the casual sundress into something more polished. "Okay, you were right. Thank you."

"You're welcome. And good luck today."

"Thanks." Kat tucked her phone into her purse, grabbed her keys and headed out. She took the elevator down. Her phone rang as she was walking to her car. She checked the screen to see who it was.

Ray.

Of course he'd call. He probably thought he could explain his way back into her good graces. Or maybe he was calling to apologize. As if that was going to make a difference. She was about to ignore him and let the call go to voicemail, then changed her mind. Ray could be persistent. If she didn't answer, he'd just keep calling.

She tapped the button to accept the call. "We have nothing to talk about."

"Kat, please, don't hang up. I am so sorry."

"Sorry you got caught, you mean?"

"No, that's not what I—look, I'm sorry I did what I did. I really am. I was in a bad place and—"

"*You* were in a bad place? I'm sorry, did your father die suddenly and leave you to discover that he had another family you knew nothing about? No, wait, that was *me*." She was seething now, nearly enveloped with rage so pure it almost lifted her feet off the ground.

"Kat, I—"

"We are done, Ray. *Done*. You're a doctor, you should understand what that word means. Never contact me again."

"But I have—"

She hung up. As the anger drained out of her, she was left trembling and weak. She opened her car door and sat, leaving the door open and her feet on the ground. Something inside her was making her feel like she might cry again.

She refused to do that. She tipped her head back and blinked. She would not ruin her makeup. She would not ruin this day.

"You okay?"

She glanced over to see Danny Rojas walking toward her. She shook her head. "No, but I will be."

"Anything I can do to help?"

She smiled. He really was a nice man. "No. Just trouble with my ex. It'll all work itself out."

He nodded. "If he bothers you, and you want backup, you call me. I'm only next door."

Not once, in her entire life, had her father offered that kind of help. Kat wished she'd had a dad like that. "Thanks, but he's in Landry. I don't think he'll be showing up here."

"Glad to hear that. But the offer stands."

"Thanks." She hesitated for a second, then decided just to ask him what was on her mind. "Do you like my mom for her baking or do you like her for more than that?"

He chuckled softly. "I like your mom for both those reasons. But I enjoyed her company before I knew she could bake."

"Good answer," Kat said. "And thanks for being so kind to her. You've really lifted her spirits. My dad was..." She shook her head.

Danny sighed. "I know about your dad. I'm sorry for the way things turned out. That has to be hard on you, too."

"It has been, but you know, I've really started to like Trina. That's my half-sister."

"I know who you mean."

"Right." Kat shrugged. "I guess things work out sometimes in ways we can't imagine."

Danny glanced toward the house and smiled. "That's for sure."

Kat tucked her feet into the car. "Have a good day."

"You, too."

She made it to the end of the driveway before she realized she hadn't programed the GPS ap on her phone. She knew Diamond Beach well enough for only spending time here once a year, but she was going to need help finding specific addresses.

Her first stop was Helping Hands, a charity that helped families in need both locally and county-wide. She put the address in and drove, arriving twenty minutes later.

The office was located in an older outdoor shopping center that also had a nail place, a thrift shop, a Spanish-language church, and an insurance office. She parked and went in. There was no one at the desk, so she waited a moment, reading some of the notices on the bulletin board.

"Can I help you?"

She turned to find an older woman behind the desk now. "Hi, my name is Kat Thompson and I'm looking for a job."

The woman nodded. "Hi Kat, nice to meet you. I'm Joanna. I'm afraid we don't do job placement, but I can certainly direct you to an organization that does."

"Oh, no, I didn't mean—I meant I was wondering if Helping Hands was hiring. I want to do some kind of work that helps people. I hope that makes sense."

Joanna smiled. "It does. But we're almost entirely a volunteer organization, so any jobs we'd have available wouldn't be paid positions."

"I understand. I don't have a problem volunteering, but I need to be able to pay my bills, too."

"I hear you. Can I ask what sort of skill set you have?"

Kat went a little closer to the desk. "I'm currently employed as an actuary. Do you know what that is?"

"No, sorry."

Kat laughed. "It's okay. No one does. It means I work with a lot of numbers. Basically, I gather data that can be used to analyze risks and trends, and using that information, I help clients by making predictions for their future endeavors. It can be as simple as how much advertising a new product might need or as complicated as determining what state might be the best place to open another branch."

"I had no idea that was even a job."

Kat nodded. "It definitely is. The firm I work for employs quite a lot of us. But I really want to work in a field that means something, you know? Find a way to give back."

"I do know. I retired from working as a store manager and felt the same way. That's how I ended up here. I don't make much, but the real rewards are so much bigger."

"That's what I want. Real rewards."

Joanna glanced down at some papers on her desk. "Have you talked to anyone at Future Florida?"

Kat shook her head. She'd never even heard of them. "No, what kind of charity is it?"

"It's not really a charity, exactly. It's a foundation that gives grants to various Florida-based efforts. They donate to us every year. Not an insignificant amount, either. They do all sorts of things, from paying for a local firefighter's burn treatments to funding research into clean water initiatives for the state."

"I've never heard of them."

"I don't think a lot of people have. They tend to fly under the radar, but that seems to be the way they want it. From what I understand, the foundation was started by a group of retired friends who'd all done very well in their lives and wanted to give back to their home state. I've heard there's even an astronaut on the board."

"That is really cool. And what a great thing for them to do. Do you have an address for them? Or a phone number? I'd love to reach out to them."

"I can give you both," Joanna said. "Although I

don't know how much either one will help. They do have a local office, but they're a very private organization, and any requests for help are meticulously scrutinized. No idea if they're hiring, either. Still, it might be worth a shot."

"Thank you. It's a shot I'm going to take."

Joanna wrote down the information on a sticky note and handed it over. "I hope you find what you're looking for. And if you ever want to volunteer, please think of us."

Kat took the note and one of the charity's business cards. "I will. And thank you for your help."

She went back out to her car and looked up Future Florida on her phone. Nothing but great stories about good deeds. She was astonished by all the things they'd done. Funded a charter school. Restocked an entire library after a hurricane. Built a wheelchair-accessible house for a local police officer injured in the line of duty. Paid for surgeries, cancer treatments, the rehab of accident victims, hurricane relief.

She shook her head in amazement. This was the place she wanted to work. She looked up the address, finding the office in Diamond Beach that Joanna had mentioned.

Kat plugged it into her GPS, then said a little prayer.

Chapter Thirty-four

*J*ules changed into a tankini, then packed her beach bag with every possible thing she thought she might need, including two towels, her solar phone charger, her notebook and pen, several varieties of sunscreen, a bag of treats for Toby, extra poop bags, his collapsible water bowl, a foldable hat, a small package of wipes, and an extra pair of sunglasses.

With that done, she went out to the kitchen, Toby following her closely, and made sandwiches. Two turkey and cheese, two ham and cheese, and two roast beef and cheese. Toby got a scrap of roast beef. Okay, two scraps.

She bagged the sandwiches and put them in a rolling cooler from the laundry room along with some frozen ice packs. She then bagged the leftover grapes from breakfast and added them, three apples, six bottles of water, three cans of soda, a bag of potato chips, a bag of pretzels, a sandwich bag of baby carrots, a couple of apple cinnamon snack bars, and a small bar of dark chocolate, one of her weaknesses.

She ripped off a long sheet of paper towels, folded them, and added them to her beach bag, too. Cleanup at the beach was important.

Cash came down the circular steps and in through the sliding doors that opened into the dining room. He was in swim trunks, a tank top, and sunglasses. He had a towel thrown over his shoulder. "I'm ready."

"Great. Cooler's packed." She glanced toward Claire's room. "I thought your aunt would be out by now. Anyway, we need to grab the chairs and umbrella and whatever else you want from the storage closet downstairs."

"Is there still a skim board in there? Or a boogie board, maybe?"

"I'm sure there's something." She shrugged. "We'll have to look. You can take Toby?" She pointed. "His leash is right there on the counter."

Sitting nearby in case there would be more roast beef, Toby wagged his tail at the mention of his name.

"Mom." Cash shot her a look like she was being silly. "I'm not letting you carry that cooler. It's too heavy. I'll take that, you take Toby. Deal?"

She smiled. She'd been alone for so long she'd gotten used to doing everything herself. She imagined that was how Claire must have felt with Bryan always gone. "Thanks, honey. That would be great."

He grabbed the cooler by the carry handle, ignoring the fact that it had an extending handle and could be rolled, and went back toward the sliders.

Jules was about to go knock on Claire's bedroom door when it opened and she came out in a swimsuit and coverup, phone in her hand.

"Are you ready?" Jules asked.

"Almost." Claire was looking at her phone screen, but finally made eye contact. "I just got an email from the lawyer's office."

Jules went still. "And?"

Claire shook her head. "No news. Just a request that I join him for a video conference tomorrow for the reading of the will. I don't know why he can't just tell me what's in it now." She sighed. "Actually, I think I do know why. It's not good news. Otherwise, he'd have said something."

Jules thought her sister could be right, but she

didn't want that to be true. "Maybe it's just a formal-ity. Like he can't say anything until the will has been read. It could have been a stipulation of Bryan's will. You don't know."

Claire heaved out a breath, her eyes back on the screen. "Maybe. I do know that I want you to be with me when he reads it. Please."

"Of course I will."

"Thanks. With you and Kat and mom around me, I'll be all right, no matter the outcome." Her brow furrowed. "I hope. This is such a mess."

"You will be. I promise." Jules smiled. "You're still coming to the beach with us, right? You could use the distraction."

"Yeah," Cash said. "Come with us, Aunt Claire."

Claire nodded, giving her sister and nephew a quick, polite smile. "I am. Just need to throw a few more things in my beach bag. Two seconds."

She went back into her room.

Jules was worried about her sister. She hoped the beach did her some good. She looked at Cash, suddenly realizing what he was about to do. "You're not taking the cooler down the steps, are you?"

"I was going to."

Jules shook her head. "Elevator. Please." She was sure her son and his muscles were capable of handling the unwieldy thing, but she didn't want all of their food accidentally getting dumped out and ruined, either.

"Okay." He brought the cooler back and stood by the elevator.

"Go ahead and call it," she told him. "We'll be right there."

Claire came back out, now wearing her beach hat and sunglasses, with her beach bag in one hand. It looked as loaded as the one Jules was carrying.

Jules laughed. "I feel like we're taking too much stuff."

"Probably," Claire said. "You'd think we weren't going to be five minutes from the house."

"Mom, Aunt Claire, elevator," Cash called out.

Jules attached Toby's leash, and with her beach bag straps over her shoulder, headed to the elevator with her sister. The two of them, plus Toby, Cash, and all of their stuff, made a tight fit, but it was better than hauling everything down the steps.

Once the doors opened, they went to the storage closet and Jules used the key on a stretchy band around her wrist to open it. "I see the skim board. No boogie board, though. We need the umbrella and the anchor, and two chairs. Or three, if you plan on sitting at all, Cash."

"I don't need a chair." Cash snorted. "But we definitely need that." He pointed to the blue beach wagon with the big knobby tires that made pulling it over sand a breeze. It was folded and stored along one side of the space.

"That's what it's there for," Claire said. "Load it up."

Cash pulled it out, opened it up, and started adding things. He put the cooler in first, then two folding chairs alongside it, and managed to get the umbrella, anchor, and skim board in, too. "That's pretty full. Unless Toby wants to ride on top of the cooler."

Jules laughed. "His legs might be short, but when it comes to the beach, nothing stops him from getting there."

Toby barked as if in agreement.

Cash pulled the wagon while Jules and Claire followed behind. The beach wasn't crowded, which was just how Jules liked it. They found a spot quickly and got set up.

Cash screwed the umbrella anchor into the sand, then put the umbrella into it. "Is that good, Mom?"

"That's perfect. Thanks, honey." She pulled the chairs out and set one up on each side.

Claire spread her towel over one of them. "Thanks, Cash."

"You're welcome." He shucked his tank, kicked off his flipflops and grabbed the skim board.

"Cash." Jules pointed to her face. "Sunglasses. You'll lose them in the water."

"Nah, I have a cord on them."

"Okay." She still thought he'd lose them, but what did a mother know? She shook her head, amused, as she put her towel on her chair.

Claire sat and pulled her ereader out of her beach bag. "You can't tell them much. They have to learn it for themselves."

Jules knew that was true. She sat beside her sister. "Did you ever say anything to Kat about Ray? About him not being the right one for her?"

Claire snorted softly. "Once, not long after they started getting serious. I told her she was young and should date around. She didn't take it well."

"Do they ever?"

Claire shook her head, her brow furrowed. "I feel so bad for her."

"I do, too. And I'm furious at Ray. I swear, I feel like I could punch him."

Claire's mouth thinned down to a hard line. "Same. Although I might ask Danny to do it for me."

Jules snickered. "He probably would, too."

Claire smiled. "Yeah, he probably would." She sighed in a sort of happy, dreamy way. "Jules, what am I going to do? I like Danny a lot. No one's ever given me an opportunity like he has. I do not want to leave Diamond Beach and lose out on that. Or him. But if I don't get the house..."

"If you don't get the house, then we'll figure something else out."

Claire pushed her sunglasses to the top of her head and looked over. "Like what? I don't have any money."

"No, but I do." She thought about Jesse, and how enjoyable it was spending time with him. And then about how her creative mojo had returned. Maybe because of him. Or being here. Either way... "I don't want to leave, either."

Claire stared at her sister. "Are you saying you'd buy a place here?"

She nodded. "That's exactly what I'm saying. I'd sell my place in Landry, which is way too big for me anyway and something I've already thought about doing, and I'd find a house here that could accommodate all of us. You, me, Mom, and Kat, if she wants to be here. Cash, too. Why not?"

Claire's gaze seemed more liquid than it had a second ago. "You'd really do that?"

Jules smiled. "I would. I think part of the reason I haven't sold already is that even though the house is way too big for me, I was close to you guys. I'd much rather us be all together here."

Claire sniffed, but no tears fell. She seemed energized by Jules's words. "I'll sell the house in Landry and contribute whatever I can. I swear it. You're the best sister. I'm so grateful to have you in my life. I know I didn't show that early on, but I really do understand what a gift you are."

Jules felt a little misty herself now. "Thanks. I hope Kat and Trina can get to that point,, too."

Claire didn't look quite as enthusiastic about that.

Chapter Thirty-five

*W*illie opened up her purse and pulled out the cashier's check she'd gotten on the way over. She slid it over to the real estate attorney, Arnold Lipscomb, from where she sat at his conference room table.

"Thank you." In turned, he passed her the contract. "If you'll excuse me, I'll just go make a copy of the check for our records."

"Sure." She frowned at the papers in her hand. She wasn't good with contracts. She had no experience with them at all. Unless you considered the vows of marriage a contract, which she did. But even then her track record wasn't so great.

Ethan, who'd connected them with the real estate attorney, and Roxie were with her. Trina was at the house, calling salon supply companies, getting questions answered, ordering items, and organizing things.

Trina, Willie, and Roxie had only just finished lunch and were planning to enjoy a little pool time when Ethan had called to say the contracts had arrived at the attorney's office. They'd quickly changed out of their swimsuits and back into street clothes to drive over.

Willie had invited Ethan, asking him to make sure it all went the way it was supposed to. He'd been kind enough to agree.

Willie lifted her head to look at Ethan and Roxie. The legalese was making her eyes cross. "The attorney said everything looks good. I'm paying him, so I hope he's right, because I can't read any more of this. Not like I can understand much of it, anyway."

"Arnold is a good guy," Ethan said. "He's not about to do anything shady. He grew up in this town. I vouch for him."

Willie nodded. "And he must think a lot of you to fit us in so quickly."

Ethan smiled. "He's an old high school buddy. But the family you're buying the shopping center from wants it done asap, too."

Roxie laughed softly. "You have a lot of old high school buddies."

"I do," he admitted. "Is there something that's giving you pause, Willie?"

She shook her head. "Buying this place is just the biggest thing I've ever done. Biggest purchase for the biggest amount of money."

Ethan nodded. "I understand. If you've changed your mind, now is the time to back out. Once that's signed—"

"Not backing out," Willie said. She picked up the pen. "Just needed a second to let it sink in. I'm ready to sign."

Ethan stood. "I'll go get Arnold, then, to witness."

He returned with the attorney and a middle-aged woman a few minutes later.

Arnold sat beside Willie as she carefully signed her name on the line. Then his assistant, who was a notary, witnessed it and used her seal to make it official.

When that was done, Willie let out a sigh that took a few mental pounds with it.

Arnold smiled. "Congratulations on your new shopping center, Mrs. Pasternak."

"Thank you," Willie said. Then she looked at Ethan. "Now it's your turn."

Arnold pulled some paperwork out of a portfolio he'd brought in with him. "I've got that handled."

He put the contract in front of her. "This is a basic contract stating that you're hiring Ethan's company to do the remodel and repairs on the Beachview Shopping Center."

Willie didn't hesitate this time. She signed and pushed the contract toward Ethan. He signed, too, then passed it back to Arnold.

This time, he served as the witness, signing on a third line. He gave that to his assistant. "Barbara, would you get copies made of those?"

"Sure." She took the contract and left.

Arnold smiled at Willie. "Looks like you've hired yourself a contractor."

Willie took out a second check, this one in a much smaller amount, and pushed it across the table to Ethan. His first draw on the contract. Enough to get things moving. She glanced at her daughter. "Exciting, isn't it?"

"It is." Roxie grinned. "I almost can't believe it's official."

Arnold nodded. "It definitely is."

Ethan folded the check and put it in his pocket. "Work starts immediately."

Arnold's assistant came back with the copies of the contract, giving one to Willie and one to Ethan.

Willie folded her copy and stuffed it in her fanny

pack before standing up. "I guess we're all done here."

Arnold, Roxie, and Ethan all got to their feet as well. Arnold nodded. "We are. If you need me for anything, you just call me, Willie. But I'll have that lease agreement done for you in a few days, then you'll be ready to sign tenants up."

"Thank you. That's wonderful." She smiled. It was done. She owned the shopping center and Trina's dream was going to come true. Plus, her family would have the income from the property to live on. Even after she was gone, her girls would be taken care of.

Things were good. Better than they'd ever been. She owed Zippy a huge debt.

She walked out with Ethan and Roxie. They paused by Trina's car. Roxie was all smiles in Ethan's direction. "I'll see you soon, I guess."

Ethan nodded. "That's for sure. You'll be seeing a lot of me these next couple of months." He glanced at Willie. "I imagine you'll want me to get a For Lease sign up there pretty quick so you can get those other three units occupied."

"Yes," Willie said. Ethan had given them some paperwork from the previous owners that detailed what each unit had rented for along with what comparable units in other strip malls were going for. They'd done some quick math and come up with what to rent each unit for. "I'm going to talk to Miguel as soon as we get back and see if he and his son have made a decision about that end unit."

"I'll get started on the list of repairs that need doing," Ethan said. "Anything cosmetic and interior can wait for a bit, except for the salon, of course. I'll have a couple guys working in there by the day after tomorrow. But for the other three units, best to wait and see if you get any interest. Then the interiors can be tweaked to the new tenants' specifications."

"All right." Willie felt a good kind of nervous excitement. "That sounds reasonable. So long as we can get them cleaned up a bit. They look like they've been sitting. Which I know they have."

"Ma," Roxie said. "I can do some of that. They really just need to be swept out and fixtures wiped down, that sort of thing. Nothing I can't handle."

Willie considered that. "We can talk about it at home." Roxie got a funny look on her face, but Willie turned her attention to Ethan. "Thanks again for all your help."

He waved the contract in his hand. "Thanks for the work. You have my number. Text me with anything you need."

"We will," Willie assured him. She gestured at Roxie. "Let's go home."

Roxie didn't say anything, just unlocked the car and went around to the driver's side. When they were both in, she started the car and drove. A moment later, she spoke up. "Why don't you want my help, Ma?"

"Your help? You mean the cleaning?"

"Yes. What's wrong? You don't think I'll do a good job?"

Willie laughed. "You'd do a fantastic job! But I can afford to pay people to do that. I'd rather you stay home with me and help Trina with the salon stuff. I just didn't want to say in front of Ethan that I'd rather hire people. I don't know how much money he thinks I have, but that's my business."

Roxie glanced over, just for a second, before putting her eyes back on the road. "But being over there would mean I'd get to see Ethan more. And I could keep an eye on how things are going."

Willie nodded. "Sure, sure. I understand that. I just figured we might be busy house hunting."

Roxie sighed. "Thanks for reminding me."

"Sorry, sweetheart. But I don't want anything getting in the way of Trina's dream. If we need a new place to live, we're going to have to figure it out fast.

Otherwise, we might have to look for a place to rent temporarily. And that might not be easy. Diamond Beach is more a rent-by-the-week than the month kind of place. And with summer coming, most of the good places are already booked up."

Roxie let out a sad sigh. "This whole house situation gets worse every time I think about it."

Willie hadn't meant to upset her daughter. "It won't be that bad. Maybe...if Claire really does end up with the house, she'll let us stay until we can find a place. That's not so much to ask, is it?"

Roxie snorted. "I'd be surprised if she gave us enough time to pack."

"Oh, stop that. I know you don't like her, and she doesn't like you, but that's just ridiculous. She wouldn't do that. She's not a monster."

"Yeah?" Roxie shot Willie a look. "What makes you such an expert on Bryan's first wife?"

Willie sighed. Her daughter was clearly upset and not thinking straight. "I believe Margo raised her better than that. Look, obviously, it's an uncomfortable situation, but you're both adults and I have no doubt you'll deal with the outcome appropriately."

Roxie took a deep breath. "I hope so."

Willie did too. "That reminds me, I need to check

in with Margo. See if she's done anything about getting some grief counselling. Plus, we have that play at the seniors center the night after tomorrow, remember? *Arsenic and Old Lace*?"

"I remember, but after we find out what the will says, the play might be the last of our worries."

"It'll be all right," Willie said.

"I appreciate the thought, but we can't know, can we? Not for sure." Roxie stared at the road ahead. "Not until we hear for ourselves what Bryan left us."

Willie hadn't meant to get her daughter wound up, but clearly she had. "I need to call Miguel."

"Go ahead," Roxie said. "Maybe that'll be some good news."

Willie dialed his number by tapping on his name in her contacts. She'd programmed him in right away.

He answered on the second ring. "Hello, there."

She smiled. "Hi, Miguel. How are you?"

"I'm talking to you. I can only be good."

She laughed to herself. He was so sweet. "I was calling to see if you and your son had made any sort of decision about the end unit? For your bakery? I texted you both the rent amount earlier. Did you get it?" She hoped it wasn't too much. Ethan had said the amounts she wanted to charge were very competitive.

"Yes, we did and we were both pleased with what you sent. And we like that we can get in on the ground floor, so to speak. We want the unit. We'd like to start work on it right away, too."

Willie exhaled. "That's fantastic. I'll have a lease agreement ready in a few days."

"Wonderful," Miguel said. "Feel free to bring that agreement over in person."

Willie giggled. "I'll do that."

Chapter Thirty-six

Claire sat in her beach chair and read for a bit in the hopes of getting her mind off the reading of the will, but she ended up reading the same paragraph over and over. She finally turned her ereader off and pulled out her notebook and pen.

Even if she didn't know whether she'd be here to open the bakery with Danny, she couldn't give up on the idea of it. Not when it was such a once-in-a-lifetime opportunity. A bakery, where her recipes would be featured. And where she'd actually be a partner, not just an employee.

How incredible was that?

If she lost the opportunity because of Bryan, she would...do something. She didn't know what yet, but just thinking about it riled her up. She exhaled and tried to calm down. The last thing she needed was high blood pressure.

She opened her notebook and looked at the lists of possible treats she'd started to come up with.

For the popcorn crispy bars, the list was practically endless. The ideas kept coming. She loved the idea of seasonal flavors, too. For the fall and winter months, they could do a bar with dried bits of apple, a dash of cinnamon, and a caramel drizzle. Maybe another with dried cranberries, orange zest and white chocolate chips. She jotted down Harvest Bar next to that along with a question mark.

For Halloween, she was thinking about some kind of candy-loaded bar. Popcorn with M&M's, pieces of peanut butter cups, maybe even other candy bars chopped up. Then sprinkled with plenty of orange and black nonpareils.

The possibilities for Christmas were just as good. She couldn't stop thinking about a peppermint bark bar. Bits of crushed peppermint, dark chocolate chips and a drizzle of white chocolate with red and green sprinkles. How festive would that be?

She loved the idea of an eggnog bar, too, but that would take some experimenting. Was there an eggnog syrup she could mix with the marshmallow?

Or develop into a drizzle? With a touch of nutmeg, maybe? Definitely something to work on.

For summer, she thought they might go more heavily into the fruit bars. Strawberries were big in Florida, so a bar made with dried strawberries, which went very well with chocolate, could be big. The tropical bar that she'd come up with, obviously, but then another with banana chips and chocolate sounded good to her, too. She might even turn the lemon popcorn into its own bar.

Some of her other ideas included a cookies and cream bar, a trail mix bar, and the one she thought might become a store staple, the key lime bar.

The variations were really unlimited. She hadn't been so excited about anything in a long time. And that was just for the popcorn bars.

There were plenty of other treats to consider. Cookies were their own category. She wanted to do big cookies, at least five inches across, so they were really showstoppers. There were brownies to think about, and blondies, too, with all their possible varieties.

Cupcakes were an easy item, just like big cakes that could be sold whole or by the slice. She had a couple of outstanding cakes in her repertoire. A flourless chocolate, an apple spice, a great lemon sponge, and the triple chocolate that had always been Bryan's favorite.

She supposed the cakes could be made to order as well, but if they got into personalized cakes for birthdays and weddings and such, they'd have to hire a decorator. Claire's talents only went so far in that direction.

Pies she could do but was less enthused about. There were a lot of places to get key lime pie in the area and she wasn't sure if they should compete with that. It would require a refrigerated display unit. Hand pies, however, an individual pie that could be carried and eaten because its filling was all contained in the crust, that was something she didn't think anyone else was doing.

She made a note of that.

Unique things she liked a lot. The popcorn bars had that in spades. So would the hand pies. And the flavors and fillings could be seasonal, just like the bars. Whatever made sense for the time of year.

Muffins weren't exactly unique, but if they sold coffee, which she strongly felt was a necessity if they were going to have seating for people to eat there, then they should have grab-and-go breakfast items, like muffins and pastries. She didn't want to get into doughnuts, though. Diamond Beach already had

Sandy's Donuts, a much-beloved local establishment.

She didn't want to do bread, either. Bread was a lot of work and it meant someone had to be in the bakery very early to make the dough and get loaves in the oven. This was a tourist town where people came to indulge. Sweets were where their business was.

What else was sweet and delicious and popular with tourists?

A new thought popped into her head, and she gasped. "Ice cream." Should they serve ice cream? It did go great with pie and cake. But maybe she was overreaching. Diamond Beach had several ice cream shops. She wouldn't be thrilled if those places started serving cake.

Jules looked over. "Did you just say ice cream?"

Claire snickered. "Yes, but ignore that. Just thinking out loud."

"About ice cream?"

"About the bakery. I can't stop thinking about it."

"And you shouldn't," Jules said. "Because it's going to happen. And you're going to be part of it."

Claire stared at the notes she'd made. "I hope so. I haven't wanted anything in my entire life the way I want this." She looked back at her sister. "This is a

new start for me, you know? A chance to do something that can actually support me. I might even be
able to save for retirement."

"It's going to happen," Jules said again.

Claire wished she could believe that, but she just
wasn't sure. She went back to her list. What about
cheesecake? They were really their own thing,
requiring a different sort of bake than a pie or a cake.
Was there enough of a market for them? Maybe
small ones would be better. Individual-sized
cheesecakes.

She liked the idea of anything that could
encourage a person to buy more. She'd been a part
of so many bake sales in her life, in charge of a few,
too, that she felt like that was something she knew
well.

People might be intimidated by the idea of
buying an entire chocolate cake, but thought
nothing of getting an assortment of cupcakes,
brownies, and cookies to take home for everyone in
the house.

She made a note at the top of her page. Individual sizes. Then underlined it twice.

Her phone vibrated in the pocket of her beach
bag. She put her pen down and dug out the phone.

It was Danny. She smiled as she answered. "Hi, there."

"We got it."

She could hear the excitement in his voice, but she wasn't sure what he was talking about. "You got what?"

"The shop. The bakery. The storefront we looked at. We're signing the lease as soon as the paperwork is ready. We made the decision. The bakery is happening."

Claire felt a surge of excitement run through her. The bakery was real. "That's fantastic!" Then she remembered about the reading of the will and her mood sunk again. "Listen, Danny, about the bakery..."

She really didn't want to tell him she might not be able to be a part of it. She didn't want to ruin his mood or kill his joy.

"Yeah?"

She took a breath and made herself smile so that her anxiety wouldn't come through in her voice. "I think it's going to be great. I have a ton of ideas. And I can't wait to tell you all about them."

Chapter Thirty-seven

Margo was amazed to find that Conrad was a surprisingly capable typist. Better than she was. Then again, he did write two columns for the newspaper. She supposed all of that practice had helped hone his skills.

His typing talents were why he was seated in front of the computer and she was pacing the room he'd turned into an office. It was a very manly space. Lots of military memorabilia from his days as a Marine, along with some other framed mementos and items from his past. His desk was a big, dark wood thing, scarred from years of use. Across from it was a leather sofa with a single throw pillow bearing the Marine emblem. The room held the lingering scents of leather and Conrad's aftershave and the coffee they'd been drinking.

She liked the room. She felt the masculine aura

helped put her in the right mindset for the sort of book they were writing. A dark thriller. That's how she'd positioned it in her head. And a dark thriller, to her, had a masculine kind of energy.

No clue where all of that was coming from. She'd tried to explain it to Conrad, who'd done a lot of nodding. He'd called it her creative brain at work.

Whatever it was, it had helped her come up with some character names and a setting for the book, as well as a working title, which they'd decided would be *The Widow*, unless something better occurred to them.

She imagined it would. They were in the very earliest stages of creation, and nothing was set in stone.

Conrad wasn't typing anything at the moment. Just staring at the screen in front of him, where the only words were Chapter One. "I think we need to keep the twin a secret. At least until the midpoint of the book. I'm not saying we don't mention her, I just don't think she should be on screen."

"I hate to disagree with you," Margo said. "But in this instance, I think you're wrong. I don't want it to feel like a cheap trick that we've just suddenly pulled an identical twin out of thin air. She should be on the page immediately. An active part of Rachel's life.

Even part of her grief recovery. And I think we need to write Jennifer's character in such a way that the reader falls in love with her and thinks Rachel is the killer. Not Jennifer."

Rachel and Jennifer were the names they'd decided for their twin characters. Rachel was a talented, slightly cold surgeon; Jennifer, a caring, deeply empathic psychiatrist. Both women were competitive, both beautiful, both troubled in their own ways.

Conrad's hands stayed off the keyboard. "They're already going to think Rachel's the killer because she's good with a scalpel. Anyone who doesn't think that's a big clue has never read a thriller before."

"I agree with you on that. A real stroke of genius giving her that kind of career path. But I don't want the reader to have an ounce of suspicion toward Jennifer." Margo wiggled her fingers. "The secret psychopath."

Conrad snorted. "She is a truly interesting killer."

Margo smiled. "Thank you."

He was still looking at her, his gaze curious and amused and admiring all at the same time. "You have a remarkable brain, I must say. Devious. In the most appealing way. I suppose I shouldn't find that sexy, but I do."

She laughed, not at him but at how he made her feel. Sexy was not a word that had been applied to her in more years than she could count. She stopped pacing to sit beside him again. He'd brought in a chair from the other room and given her the more comfortable desk chair, a big, padded leather thing with brass studs that fit the room's vibe. "You're going to make me blush."

"Am I?" He looked into her eyes, pinning her with his intense gaze. Then he leaned in and kissed her, pressing his mouth softly against hers with enough insistence to let her know he meant it. "How about now?"

She didn't answer for a few moments, letting the feeling of the kiss linger because it made her happy. Conrad made her happy. She smiled and touched his cheek, a blissful kind of calm flowing through her. "Thank you."

"For the kiss?" His eyes sparkled.

Her smile widened. "For pulling me out of myself. For convincing me to do this."

"You mean the book?"

She shook her head. "I mean all of it. I mean...us."

He leaned in and kissed her again. She kissed him back this time. It was amazing what that little point of contact could do. It erased her age, erased the hurts of the past, planted her firmly in the present, and made her realize that she had so much more life left to live.

She couldn't stop smiling. She broke the kiss and took a breath. "I know how the book opens."

Conrad sat up a little straighter, his hands poised over the keyboard. "I await your orders."

"Hang on a second, let's talk it through first."

He put his hands back in his lap. "All right. How do you see the opening scene?"

"Rachel kisses her husband goodbye as she heads off to the hospital. We see her in a typical day. Getting ready for surgery. Maybe even in the midst of surgery. Then a call from the police and her husband's been found dead."

Conrad nodded. "Where was he found? How? This is all Jennifer's doing, right?"

"Right." Margo got up again and returned to pacing. "But it's got to look like Rachel's done it. I think...poison. In his coffee maybe? Maybe in the sugar. And only he uses sugar, not Rachel. That would work, wouldn't it?"

"Yes, definitely. We just need to make sure we have the right kind of poison."

Margo stopped pacing. "No, wait. Not poison. Some kind of medicine that would induce a heart attack. Something both sisters would have access to."

He pulled up a browser window, a search engine ready to go. "We need to research this."

She sat beside him again. "Okay."

He typed in *legal drugs that cause heart attack* and hit Enter. Then he looked over at her. "This is fun, isn't it?"

She nodded. "It really is. Do you think..." She almost didn't want to say the words out loud in case she might jinx the project. "Do you think anything will come of it? Is there any kind of chance we'll actually get it written and published?"

"If that's what we want to do, we'll do it."

"I know you're a Marine, but you seem awfully sure."

"Because I have faith and I know what my own abilities are. And I believe you're just as strong-willed and determined as I am when you put your mind to something."

"But getting published, that's not something either of us can make happen."

"No, but we could self-publish it. There's a

writing group at the library and quite a few of those folks are self-published. Some make some money at it. Some don't. But we aren't really in this for the money, are we?"

She shook her head. "No, not really. But I wouldn't be opposed to money."

He laughed. "Neither would I." He lifted his hands to the keyboard and began to type.

Truthfully, she was doing this for the adventure of it. The new challenge that had already brought her back to life.

And, ultimately, for Conrad's company.

The kissing didn't hurt, either.

Chapter Thirty-eight

Kat had had a long day. A pretty unsuccessful one, too, sadly. She pulled down the drive toward Double Diamond and parked in her usual spot under the house. She sat there for a moment.

Roxie, Willie, and Trina were all at the pool. Trina and Willie were on lounge chairs, sunning themselves, and Roxie was in the pool, looking like she was doing some kind of water aerobics, bouncing up and down in a bikini that was small enough to raise Kat's brows.

Roxie didn't look half bad in it, though. Amazing for a woman her age.

Kat sighed and tipped her head back, the disappointment of her day returning. She'd been hoping for great things at Future Florida, but all she'd found was a receptionist at a desk. The woman had been kind enough and given her an email address to submit a resume to, but hadn't been able to offer any information on whether the foundation was hiring.

The rest of the charities Kat had visited were much like the first. Happy to have volunteers, but without any paying vacancies. Well, except for the last one. They'd been looking for a part-time fundraiser.

Not a terrible position, but not one Kat felt greatly qualified for. And it was only part-time. She hadn't asked the salary, but she already knew it wouldn't be enough for what she needed.

She wasn't even looking for that much, really. But it had to cover the basics. With enough left over that she could contribute to whatever living situation she and her mom were in. Health care would be nice, too.

She put her hands on the steering wheel and rested her head on them. "Maybe this was a bad idea."

Maybe she was expecting too much. Just because she wanted to change her life didn't mean it was actually going to be possible.

She hated thinking that way. It felt defeatist. But today just hadn't given her the kind of happy, possible, new path kind of vibe she'd been hoping for.

She sighed and got out of the car, grabbing her purse. At least she could get her resume sent off to the Future Florida email. She'd have to look at her resume first and make sure it was up to date, which it probably wasn't. She hadn't been anticipating searching for a new job.

She locked the car and started for the elevator.

Trina waved excitedly. "Kat! Kat, come over!"

Kat didn't want to, but she did anyway. "Hey."

"Why don't you throw a suit on and come join us?"

"Um, maybe. I have a little work to do first, though." Kat hesitated, then decided there was no reason not to share. "I was out job hunting today."

"Yeah?" Trina lifted up slightly, her grin big. "That's awesome." Then her smile faded. "You're definitely staying here, then. Right?"

Kat shrugged one shoulder. "That's the plan. I mean, I really don't want to go home after..."

But she hadn't told Trina about Ray. Kat sighed. "Listen, let me go do what I need to do and then I'll come back down and we can chat, okay?"

Trina nodded. "That would be great." She patted the empty lounge chair beside her. "You can sit right here."

Kat nodded. "Be back shortly." She really didn't know how long it would take her to get her resume up to date, but she wasn't going to rush through it, either.

She went upstairs and straight to her bedroom. She tossed her purse on the bed, then opened up her laptop and sat. She went into her documents and clicked on her resume. Just as she'd thought, it wasn't up to date.

With a sigh, she started typing. Mostly adding things, like her current employment, and a few extracurricular things she'd done, such as a cancer walk to raise money for breast cancer.

That had been Ray's doing, because his office had been sponsoring the walk. All of his nurses had done it, too.

Which was how Kat had met Heidi.

Pretty, bubbly, curvaceous, available Heidi.

Kat stared at the laptop screen without really seeing it. Her mood dropped further. She'd already had a less than optimal job search. She didn't need to wallow in what Ray had done to her, too.

What could she do to boost her mood? Hanging out by the pool with Trina wasn't a bad idea. But then she thought of another.

She grabbed her phone and texted Alex. *Hey.*

Would you like to go out for pizza or something tonight?
Would love to hang out.

Maybe that was too needy. But she wanted to see him. She needed the reminder that someone found her attractive and appealing.

Thankfully, it didn't take him long to respond. *I'd love to. I'm on shift tonight, but if you don't mind hanging at the firehouse, that would be great.*

She smiled. *I'd love to see where you work. What time?*

Six?

See you then. She added a smiley face for extra emphasis. Seeing the firehouse would really be cool. She imagined she'd be meeting some of the guys he worked with, too. Was that like meeting his family?

She might have to ask Trina to help her pick out a good outfit. Cute but not too over the top. She wanted his work buddies to like her. She went back to her resume, read it though one more time, then attached it to an email with a quick note and hit Send.

At least that was done. She changed into a floral-print bikini, threw on a pair of shorts and a tank top, grabbed a towel and a hat and went downstairs.

Trina was in the same spot but Willie had joined Roxie in the pool. They were floating on noodles and talking. Trina had a trashy gossip magazine in her hands, but she closed it as Kat walked over.

Kat spread her towel over the lounge chair. "Hey."

"Hey," Trina said. "Did you get all of your work done?"

Kat nodded. "I did. And I made a date with Alex for tonight. I'm going to the firehouse to hang out with him there, since he's on shift. Maybe you could help me pick out an outfit?"

"You bet." Trina bit her lip. "I wonder if I should text Miles and see about doing the same. Would you care? I'd love to see him but I don't want to get in your way."

Kat shook her head. "You wouldn't be in my way. I mean, the firehouse is a big place, right? It's not like we have to hang out together just because we're both there." She really wanted to talk to Alex alone. To tell him about Ray, for one thing, but also about her decision to look for work in Diamond Beach, because she planned on staying here.

"Right." Trina got her phone out and sent a text, presumably to Miles. Then she put her phone next to her on the lounge chair. "You must be super curious about tomorrow, huh?"

Kat frowned. "What about tomorrow?"

"The reading of the will. Didn't your mom tell you?"

"No. I haven't seen her since I left this morning. I haven't seen any of my family. Hang on." She'd just been in her inbox, but there hadn't been any messages from her mom. No texts or missed calls, either.

She looked up again. "No one said anything to me. Shouldn't we be driving back to wherever the attorney is?"

Trina shook her head. "No, it's a video chat thing. My mom got sent a link, so I'm sure your mom did, too."

"I should text her. Just a sec." Kat typed quickly. *Just heard there's a will reading via video chat tomorrow?*

She put her phone next to her like Trina had. She stared at Willie and Roxie in the pool as she spoke to Trina. "What do you think is going to happen?"

Trina shrugged. "I don't have any idea." She glanced at Kat, a look of concern on her face. "If your mom gets the house, do you think she'll kick us out?"

"What?" Kat would have laughed if Trina hadn't seemed so worried. "No. What would make you think that?" Although at some point, she figured her mom would want them gone. Probably.

"Well, she and my mom aren't exactly the best of friends."

"Would your mom kick us out if she got the house?"

Trina shook her head. "No way. My mom's not like that. She might not like your mom, but she's not spiteful."

Kat would have thought otherwise, but she didn't know Roxie. And she'd begun to have trust in Trina. "Listen, whatever happens tomorrow, let's you and I do our best to keep the peace between our families. What do you say?"

Trina nodded, a small smile returning. "I say that's a great idea." Her phone chimed. She picked it up and looked at the screen. "Miles said he'd love to hang out but I'd have to come to the firehouse."

"Cool. We can drive together," Kat said. "If you want."

"I'd love that. Listen, if you're looking for a job, I might know of something. Won't be for a little bit, though."

"Yeah?" Kat adjusted the back of her lounge chair so it reclined a little more. "What is it?"

Trina hesitated a moment. "You could always

come work for me. As a receptionist. Or something. At my new salon."

"You got a job?"

"You could say that." Trina grinned. "And I'd be happy to give you one, too."

"Give me one?" Kat was confused.

"Why not? If I own the place, I can hire whoever I want. Being the receptionist isn't too hard. You could pick it up like that." Trina snapped her fingers.

"Wait. You *own* a salon?"

Trina glanced toward the pool. "I do now, thanks to Mimi. She bought a whole shopping center and one of the units is going to be my salon. And one of the units is going to be the new bakery where your mom and Danny Rojas are going into business together."

Kat just stared at Trina. Apparently, she'd missed quite a lot while out job hunting.

Chapter Thirty-nine

*C*ash's appetite continued to impress Jules. He sat on a towel in front of her and Claire, eating. He'd already had two sandwiches, an apple, a trail bar, half a bag of chips, and was starting on a bunch of grapes. She took another bite of her apple as she watched him glance toward the cooler like he was thinking about seeing what was left.

"Where do you put it all?" Claire asked him.

Jules swallowed. "I was just thinking the same thing."

He finished whatever he was chewing. "Aunt Claire, I need to keep up my strength."

She just shook her head, smiling.

He gestured at her with a grape. "It's too bad there weren't any of your kitchen-sink brownies in there."

Claire laughed. "I haven't made those in years. In

fact, the last time I made them might have been for your graduation party."

He popped the grape into his mouth. "I love those things."

Jules took another bite of her apple. "I've made you brownies."

"Yeah, and they're good and everything, but they're not like Aunt Claire's." Cash shrugged. "Sorry, Mom."

Claire got out her pen and notebook. "I should put them on the list for the bakery."

Jules was blissfully happy. She had her dog, her sister, and her son with her for a beautiful day at the beach. The water and sky were pristine blue, the breeze was just right, even the waves looked postcard perfect. What more could she ask for?

"Jules?"

Toby jumped up, his little tail wagging, and stared past Jules.

She looked over and saw Jesse walking toward them, Shiloh at his side. Jules waved. "Hi."

"Hey, I thought that was you. Just not used to seeing you with an entourage."

"This is my sister, Claire, and my son, Cash." She looked at them as she gestured to Jesse. "This is

Jesse. He owns the Dolphin Club. And that's his dog, Shiloh."

Cash reached out and gave Shiloh a scratch on the head. "Pretty dog."

"Thanks," Jesse said. "I think she's got a little crush on Toby."

Cash laughed. "Nicely done, Tobes."

Jesse smiled. "Nice to meet you both." He pushed his sunglasses up onto his head as he ducked under the umbrella. "I didn't know your son was here with you."

"He just arrived." She tipped her head toward the sand. "Come join us. If you have a minute."

"Actually, I don't. I was just taking Shiloh out for a quick walk before I left for the club. Sorry. I'd much rather hang out with you guys." He glanced at Toby. "You could walk back with us. It's just a little ways up the beach."

Jules got up and grabbed Toby's leash, which was tied around her chair leg to keep him from wandering off. "Sure." She glanced at Claire and Cash. "I'll be back."

Claire, who was all smiles, nodded. "Have fun."

"Yeah," Cash said. "I'm headed back into the water anyway." He got up and grabbed the skim board. "Nice to meet you, Jesse."

"You, too, Cash." He smiled at Claire. "And you."

Claire just grinned back at him. "It was *very* nice meeting you. Maybe we'll get to see more of you?"

Jesse laughed softly and looked at Jules. "Maybe."

She shot Claire a look. "Don't you need to work on your list for the bakery?"

"Mm-hmm," Claire said, returning Jules's look with one of her own.

Jules ducked out from under the umbrella, bringing Toby with her. "Come on."

She and Jesse headed toward the water to where the sand was hardpacked enough to make walking easier.

"I didn't expect to see you today. Nice surprise," he said.

She nodded, smiling a little. It was a very nice surprise. "How are you?"

"Good," he said. "How's the songwriting coming?"

"Also good. Been working on the music now but taking a bit of a day off since my son got here. I'll be back at it soon, though."

"Is he your oldest or youngest?"

"Youngest. My baby." She sighed. "He's struggling a little with what to do with his life."

323 Shifting Sands At The Beach House

"Not a musician like his mom and dad?"

She nodded. "He is and that's the problem. We left big shoes to fill, and I don't think his heart's in it. In fact, I know it's not. He just wanted to do what he thought would make us proud. Especially his dad."

"What's he want to do instead?"

She shook her head. "I don't know. I don't think he knows, either. I've tried to ask him a couple of times since he got here, but he shuts down. Doesn't want to talk about it. He will when he's ready, I know, but I wish he'd talk to me. I'd love to help him figure it out."

"How old is he?"

"Twenty-six."

"That can be a hard age. Especially if you're still not sure what you want to do with your life or where it's going."

She nodded, her heart aching for her son. Today was fun. But she really needed him to open up to her.

Jesse nudged her slightly with his elbow. "He'll be okay. I know you're worried about him. But he's got a fantastic mother."

She smiled. "Thanks. Hard not to worry about them, no matter how old they are."

"I know. Savannah's nineteen and I think I worry

more about her now than I did when she was six. Of course, at six, she knew everything. She's only just coming to realize that's not true, and that old dad isn't as dumb as she thought I was."

Jules laughed. "I'm sure she adores you and thinks you speak nothing but words of wisdom."

"I try." He slowed down to let Shiloh sniff some seaweed. "I'd ask you out again, but I imagine you want to spend as much time with Cash as you can. But I would love to see you again."

"I'd like to see you, too." Toby used their reduced pace as a chance to sniff Shiloh, who was quickly becoming one of his favorite dogs. "Maybe I could bring Cash over to the club later. At least say hi."

"I'd like that. We could have dinner, if you want. My treat."

Jules grinned. "Do you know how much a twenty-six-year-old man can eat? I appreciate that, but I'll feed him tonight. His grandmother would probably like to see him."

"Well, come by for dessert then. And he can eat all he wants. It's worth it if I get to see you."

"Okay, but consider yourself warned."

"So noted." He snuck a quick kiss. "I've missed you."

She realized she'd missed him, too. She nodded. "Me, too."

He pointed inland. "I'm right here, so I'll say goodbye. Until tonight."

"Until tonight."

"Come on, Shiloh." He got her moving and took a few steps backwards, smiling at Jules. "See you later."

She waved as Toby tried to chase a seagull. "Later."

She waited until he turned around before walking back. She liked Jesse a lot. She'd yet to tell him she was thinking about staying in Diamond Beach, though. Would it change his attitude toward her personally? She didn't want to think it would.

But she also knew that he might just be thinking of this as a minor flirtation with someone whose music he really enjoyed. She didn't often think of herself as a star, but she knew he loved her music. That he was a fan.

He wasn't hoping to make her a notch on his bedpost, was he? She hadn't gotten that vibe off of him, but her history with men had conditioned her to be suspicious.

Telling him she was staying in Diamond Beach

would either make him happy. Or make him disappear.

She had to wonder which result she'd get. She kicked up a little sand as she went back to their spot on the beach. Maybe she'd bring it up tonight and see how he reacted.

Cash would be there with her, and she hadn't said anything to him about staying in Diamond Beach, either. She didn't think he'd care. He'd probably love it. He'd always wanted to be closer to the water when he was a kid.

Claire looked up as Jules approached. "That was quick."

"He has to go to the club." Jules sat down and tied Toby's leash to the chair leg again. "But I'm going to see if Cash wants to go over later for dessert. After family dinner."

"That would be fun." Claire pursed her lips. "Jesse is very attractive. And young."

"He's not that much younger than me." Jules had pretty much expected those sorts of comments. She just smiled at her sister, then leaned back and adjusted her hat. "But he is also a really good kisser."

Chapter Forty

*R*oxie walked up the pool steps and grabbed her towel off the chair where she'd left it. Trina and Kat had been in a pretty deep discussion for a while now and she was dying to know what they were talking about. Whatever it was, it had to be riveting. Trina hadn't looked at her magazine since Kat had shown up.

Willie was still floating.

Roxie wrapped the towel around herself, sauntered over, and took her seat next to Trina, giving Kat a quick smile. "Hello, there."

"Hi," Kat said. "Trina was just telling me about the will reading tomorrow morning. I hadn't heard yet. I was out all day."

Roxie nodded. Curious that Claire hadn't shared that information with her daughter. "Should be interesting."

"No doubt," Kat said.

Roxie sat back. "I wondered what you girls were talking about."

Trina smiled. "I was telling her about the new salon, too."

Roxie just nodded. She would have assumed Kat had known about that, too, since Claire had been to the shopping center with Danny to look at the bakery location. But then again, maybe Claire wasn't ready to commit to that with Danny.

Or Claire might not want her daughter to know how serious things were between her and the next-door neighbor.

Weird, but not Roxie's business. She exhaled a short breath. Wasn't much chance of keeping a thing like that secret for long. Not when they were all sharing a house and Danny's new landlord was living on the first floor.

"Ma," Trina said. "Kat and I are going over to the firehouse for dinner. Miles and Alex invited us."

"That's nice. Kind of an exciting place to spend an evening."

Trina grinned. "I'm going to see if I can go down the pole. If they have one."

Kat laughed. "Oh, I bet the guys would love that."

Willie got out of the pool and came over to dry

off before laying down next to Roxie. "You girls should get in that water. It's gorgeous."

Kat got up. "Maybe we should. Come on, Trina. Let's go for a dip."

"All right." Trina put her magazine on the ground.

The girls went into the pool, leaving Willie and Roxie alone. Roxie leaned over toward her mother. "Kat only just found out about the will reading from Trina. Why would her mother not tell her?"

Willie frowned. "Beats me. Kind of strange, though, right?"

"It is." Roxie nodded. "I think Claire knows something. I just don't know what it might be."

"Maybe," Willie said. "Then again, she might just not have gotten around to telling Kat."

"Maybe." Roxie adjusted her sunglasses. "Trina and Kat are going to the firehouse to have dinner with the two guys they went out with the other night."

"Oh?" Willie grinned. "I might call Miguel up. See what he's doing. Maybe he'd like to come over and watch a movie with me."

"If you do that, I'm calling Ethan." Roxie settled back against the lounge chair.

"You just saw him today. Don't you think you're pursuing him a little hard?"

"Am I?" Roxie frowned. Her mother was probably right. "I guess I should wait for him to contact me. I just...like him."

"I know. And I understand. But he's our best chance of getting that place up and running for Trina right now. We need him and his talents. I don't want anything to drive him off. Not saying that's what you'd do, but just take it slowly with him. Make him want to make you happy."

Roxie just nodded. She couldn't argue with her mother. The woman had a way with men that was undeniable. And Willie was right about them needing Ethan. They all had to make getting the salon open their focus.

She glanced down at her phone, which wasn't easy to see in the sun. She cupped her hand around it to give it some shade. No new messages, missed calls, nothing. She put it back down and closed her eyes.

When she'd told Ethan goodbye today, he'd said he'd talk to her soon. What did that mean? She thought it had meant later today, but she could have misinterpreted his words. Maybe he'd meant in a day or two.

He did have a new project on his plate now. The shopping center needed a lot done. The salon, especially. And now that Danny and his father were taking the end unit, it was on the list as well.

Her mother was right. She needed to let him respond next. She was so out of the loop on dating and relationships, she didn't know what she was doing.

That's just how she was sometimes. When she liked something, she pursued it wholeheartedly. That's how she'd ended up with Bryan. She'd liked him right from the beginning. And she'd let him know.

If only she'd known he was already married. Of course, she wouldn't have Trina then, and Trina had made her life worthwhile. There were times when Trina had *been* her life.

When Bryan had been away so often and it had just been her and Trina, sometimes her mom, too, if she was in between marriages, those days had been magical. They'd become such a tight unit. The girls against the world.

Trina had adored her father, there was no doubt about that. But she'd definitely come to understand that her mother was the foundation of her life.

Roxie didn't regret that. Especially now that

Bryan was gone. Especially with the way he'd left them with so many questions and the weight of his betrayal to deal with.

All of that was why she didn't feel bad about Ethan.

Why shouldn't she spend time with a nice guy? It wasn't like she was trying to find another husband. She just wanted to be with someone who was a hundred percent there for her in the moment.

Bryan hadn't been great at that. It wasn't unusual for him to be distracted by something on his phone or, in the earlier days, by a message on his pager. She'd always thought it was work. She knew better now.

She sighed softly. She'd let Ethan be. Let him reach out to her when he was ready. There was no reason to rush things. They'd be seeing a lot of each other over the next few months. If something was going to happen between them, it would work itself out.

And if not? He was still a nice man and an enjoyable dinner companion. She wasn't going to have as much free time anyway when the salon opened. She'd be helping Trina in any way she could.

She might not even have time for a man in her

life. Or she might just be too tired at the end of the day.

Her phone vibrated. She glanced at it, shielding it from the sun again. She almost laughed at herself.

Steaks at my place tonight? If you're not too busy?

Still smiling, she texted Ethan back. *I'm not busy at all.*

Chapter Forty-one

Claire helped pack everything up, and Cash loaded it all into the wagon. She'd been under the umbrella most of the day, so she didn't think she'd gotten too much sun. "Today was just what I needed. I can't believe we spent all day out here, but it was so nice. Thanks for inviting me."

"Of course," Jules said as she wrangled Toby. "It was a great day."

Cash nodded. "I wish I could do this every day."

"You could if you were a lifeguard," Claire said.

"Yeah." He glanced down the beach toward one of the lifeguard stands. "You think they get bored?"

"Maybe," Jules said. "But staying on alert is sort of part of the job."

"True." He looked a second more, then grabbed hold of the wagon's handle. "Ready?"

Claire and Jules nodded at the same time.

As they approached the house, Claire saw Kat and Trina by the pool. Kat saw her at the same time and waved. "Hey, Mom. I didn't realize you were at the beach."

"All day," Claire said. "How was the job hunt?"

"Eh," Kat said. "It was all right." She put her hand on Trina's arm. "Trina, that's your cousin, Cash."

Trina jumped up and stuck her hand out. "It's so nice to meet you."

Cash shook her hand when he reached her. "Yeah, you, too."

As they chatted, Claire went over to Kat and sat on the chaise Trina had just vacated. "Listen, I got some news from the lawyer today."

"About the reading of the will tomorrow morning?"

Claire blinked. "Yes. How did you know?"

"Trina told me. Why didn't you tell me when you found out?"

"I didn't want you to worry about it while you were looking for a job. I figured you had enough going on."

"Oh." Kat shrugged. "You still could have told me. Knowing about the reading of the will wouldn't have upset me."

"No? Well, I'm sorry then. I thought it might." Claire exhaled. "It upset me."

"Why?"

"Because if it was good news, he would have just told me. Not sent an email with a link for a video conference."

Kat seemed to think about that. "It might not be bad news. Maybe it was just how Dad wanted it?"

"Maybe."

"You also didn't tell me about the whole bakery thing with Danny Rojas."

Claire smiled. "It was too much to tell you in a text and besides, I wanted to do it in person. I am *really* excited about it. It all happened so fast, but it will mean having a job I love and a chance at rebuilding my life in a way I never expected."

Kat made a funny little face, her mouth pursing. "Not to mention you'll be around Danny a lot."

Claire laughed. "That is definitely a bonus."

"Well, I said I would support you in whatever you wanted to do, whatever made you happy, and this certainly seems to be doing that."

"It is," Claire said. She inhaled, her whole body filled with sunshine in a way that had nothing to do with the day she'd just spent at the beach and everything to do with Danny. "He does, too."

"Good for you," Kat said. "Speaking of things that make us happy, I'm going over to the firehouse for dinner tonight with Alex."

"You are? What time are you leaving?"

"Probably around quarter to six."

Claire looked at the time on her phone as she got to her feet. "That gives me almost two hours. I can swing that." She looked at Kat again. "I want to make you something to take. Something to share with all the firemen. Would that be all right?"

"I don't see why not. You want help?"

Claire shook her head. "Nope. I got this. My only stipulation is that I want feedback."

Kat laughed. "I'm sure they can do that."

"Great. See you inside." Claire rejoined Jules, Toby, and Cash at the elevator. They'd already returned the beach things to the storage closet and were holding the doors for her.

"Thanks for waiting." She got on and mentally ran through the ingredients she had on hand. She'd need to dig around in the pantry to see what else was in there. She still had plenty of popcorn, that was for sure.

"You look lost in thought," Jules said as the doors closed.

"Cash's comment about those brownies I used to make got me thinking. A new recipe I want to try."

Cash grinned. "Do I get to sample it?"

Claire nodded. "I'll make sure you get some."

"Then I already think it's delicious."

Claire and Jules both laughed, but Claire had a question for him. "What did you think of your new cousin?"

"She seems super nice," Cash said. "She offered to give me a haircut. If I wanted one."

"You could use one," Jules said.

"Take her up on it," Claire added. "She's really good with hair."

The doors opened and they got off, except for Cash, who was going up to the third floor. "Text me when you need me to taste test, Aunt Claire."

"I will," she promised.

"What are you going to make?" Jules asked.

"I'm not sure yet. I need to see what ingredients I have left."

"I'm off to shower. I can manage dinner for us tonight, if you want."

"That would be great. Kat is going to the firehouse to eat with Alex, so it'll just be the three of us. And Mom, if she ever gets home."

Jules nodded. "I'll text her and find out."

Claire opened the pantry doors. "Okay, what's here?" Her mind was already busy with the idea she'd had. Kitchen-sink popcorn crispy bars. Would it work the way it did with brownies? Or was she getting too ambitious?

She'd soon know. She gathered the main ingredients of marshmallows and popcorn, then got out salt, butter, and two disposable aluminum pans. She'd make two batches, both the same, then cut them up into squares so she could save some for Cash and send the rest to the firehouse.

She might take a few over to Danny, too, depending on how they came out.

She put the butter and marshmallows on to melt, then went back to the pantry. Her kitchen-sink brownies included M&M's, potato chips, pretzels, all of which she had, plus chopped up Oreos. Which she didn't.

Frowning, she tried to think of what else she could use, but there really wasn't a substitute for Oreos. She'd been planning on trying a cookies and cream bar, anyway. Might as well get the supplies to do it.

She turned off the stove and put a lid on the pan. The butter and marshmallows would be fine until she got back from the store.

Chapter Forty-two

Margo couldn't believe they'd actually written two chapters. It felt...monumental. She was amazed at what she and Conrad had accomplished. She glanced over at him. He was behind the wheel of his Ford pickup truck, driving her home.

"We got a lot done today," she said.

He nodded, looking proud. "We sure did."

"More than I thought we'd do." She smiled. "We work very well together."

He gave her a quick look. "Very well." He put his eyes back on the road. "Are we writing again tomorrow?"

She wanted nothing more. "Yes. If you're available?"

He laughed. "For you? I am always available."

"Don't you have to write your columns?"

"I'm weeks ahead on those. I write them as they come to me, which sometimes means I have four or five ready to go at a time. No worries there."

"All right, good." She liked how organized and on top of things Conrad was. Those were qualities she found admirable. And also not surprising for a man who'd been a Marine. He was definitely squared away, a phrase he'd taught her earlier today. "We still need to work on our detective."

Conrad nodded. "I'm doubling up on my vote for him being a Marine."

She held her laugh. "I'm fine with that. But he's got to be a cop first."

"Maybe. Depends on the situation."

She just smiled. "I really like working on this book with you. I had no idea we'd get so much done today."

"I don't think that will continue. Not trying to be a downer, just being realistic. We're sort of in the honeymoon stage now. Everything is new and easy but the farther along we get, the harder it'll become. The plot will complicate, too. We'll figure it out, though. Two brains are better than one." He snorted. "Especially when one of them is yours."

"Now you're just flattering me. There's no need. I already like you."

"I'm not flattering you—well, maybe I am. But it's true. Your mind works in interesting ways." He pulled into the driveway of the Double Diamond and parked just before he would have pulled under the house.

She unlatched her seatbelt but didn't open the door. Instead, she turned toward him. "Would you like to come in for a moment? Meet my family?"

His brows rose slightly. "You sure about that? They might think that means something."

They would. Without a doubt. But she didn't care. "Conrad, we're co-writing a book. That's not a small project. We're going to be spending a lot of time together. I'd like them to meet you. And you them."

"I'd be happy to." He turned off the engine. "Are they going to be mad at me for how much of your day I've taken up?"

She shook her head. "I do what I want with my time. Tomorrow, I hope to have breakfast with my grandson again, but then I'm sure he'll be off doing his own thing. Just as the rest of them will be. Just as I will be."

"All right."

They got out and went to the elevator. Margo was a little nervous, but she supposed that was normal.

She was about to introduce a man she cared about to her family. That had never actually happened before. It was uncharted territory.

She had no idea what to expect.

The doors opened, they rode up to the second floor and got out. Claire was at the kitchen island, cutting some kind of treat into squares. "Claire? This is my friend, Conrad. Conrad, my daughter, Claire."

"Pleasure to meet you," Conrad said.

Claire straightened, the long knife still in her hand. She stared for a moment, then nodded. "Hi, Conrad. Nice to meet you, too."

He put his hands in his pockets and kept his eyes on the knife. "Whatever you're making looks good."

"They're popcorn crispy bars," Claire replied. "These are the kitchen-sink variety. They're still a little warm, but you can try one if you like."

He took a few steps close. "I might spoil my dinner, but I've never heard of popcorn crispy bars. I just might have to. Just a small one, though."

"If you like Rice Krispie Treats, you'll probably like these." She cut one of the squares in half, then put both halves on a small paper plate and slid it toward him. "These are going to be featured at the new bakery I'm helping to open. It's a Mrs. Butter's Bakery."

Conrad squinted at Claire. "As in Mrs. Butter's Popcorn?"

"The very same."

He picked up the bar and took a bite. After a few chews, he nodded. "I've never had anything like this. It's good. Really good. The salt and the sweet combined with the chewiness and the crunch...it's everything you could want." He pushed the plate with the other half of the bar toward Margo. "Try that."

Margo wasn't a fan of most sweets or too much sugar. Or carbs. But this wasn't just any sweet. She picked up the bar. It was sticky. "Are those...pieces of potato chips?"

"Yes," Claire said. "That's why they're called kitchen-sink bars. They have a little of everything."

Margo took a small bite. The bar was very sweet —to her, anyway—but the salt helped balance it out. "I can definitely see the appeal."

Claire laughed and looked at Conrad. "High praise from my mother."

Jules came out from the bedroom. "I thought I heard Mom." She smiled at Conrad. "Hello."

"Hi. I'm Conrad. A friend of your mother's from book club."

Jules made a face. "Book club?" She looked at Margo. "Since when do you go to book club?"

"I just started," Margo answered. "It's at the library. Anyway, Conrad and I have decided to write a book together. We started it today."

"Get out," Jules said. "That's pretty cool. What's it about?"

Claire chimed in before Margo could say anything. "Probably murder."

Conrad laughed. "Affirmative."

Footsteps on the outside stairs were followed by Cash coming in through the sliders. "I'm here to taste test."

"Conrad," Margo said. "This is my grandson, Cash."

Cash came over, hand extended. "Hey, there. Are you my grandma's new boyfriend?"

Margo stopped breathing for a moment while on either side of her, Claire and Jules seemed to be having some kind of fit. Margo cleared her throat and was about to say that Conrad was just a friend when Conrad answered him.

"Yes, I am." He shook Cash's hand. "That all right with you, young man?"

"Sure it's all right." Cash smiled and held on to

Conrad's hand. "So long as you don't make her cry. Then we'll have trouble."

Conrad laughed and looked at Margo. "I like this one a lot. Good lad. You've got to protect the women in your life."

"What's all the noise out here?" Kat came out from her bedroom, looking dressed to go somewhere, makeup done, hair smooth and silky, wearing tight jeans, sneakers, and a gray Diamond Beach Fire Department T-shirt tied at the waist so that it hugged her body. "Hi, Grandma."

"Hello, Kat. I've brought Conrad up to meet everyone." Margo hadn't actually thought everyone would be home. "Conrad, this is my granddaughter, Kat."

"Hello, there. Good to meet you."

Kat grinned, hands on her hips. "You, too. So you're the man my grandmother has been spending so much time with lately?"

Conrad nodded. "Guilty. I hope I haven't taken her away from you too much."

Kat's smile remained as she shook her head. "I'm happy to see her happy. Are you staying for dinner? If so, I wish I was going to be here, but I'm headed out."

Conrad shook his head. "No, I should get home myself."

"Stay," Jules said. "We're not having anything fancy. Pasta with meat sauce and salad."

He glanced at Margo.

She hadn't expected her family to welcome him so warmly. But she was glad about it. She nodded. "Stay. If you want."

"All right." He smiled. "I will."

Chapter Forty-three

Kat held the dish of popcorn bars in front of her as she and Trina walked into the firehouse. They didn't go much farther than a few steps inside one of the big open bays. The brilliant red firetrucks and white ambulances were all lined up, paint shiny, chrome gleaming, looking very much like they were ready to leap into action. Which she supposed they were.

Trina leaned in closer. "Where do you think everybody is?"

"Not out here," Kat answered.

Then they heard voices. Laughter and cheering. They both looked at each other. Kat snorted. "I think we found them."

They followed the sounds back through the garage bays, through a door, and into a big lounge area with leather couches, chairs, a long dining table, and a massive, big-screen TV. There was a baseball game on, and the seats were filled with firemen. And, apparently, paramedics, since Kat spotted Miles.

She and Trina stood at the door. Kat was a little intimidated to be facing that many firemen at once.

Then Alex saw her and stood up. "Hey, Kat, you're here. Hi, Trina."

Miles looked over and immediately got to his feet, smiling. "Hey, Trina."

The two guys came over. A few of the other firemen smiled in their direction but no one said anything.

Kat held the pan out to Alex. "My mom made these. To share with everyone. They're a new recipe, so she'd like to know what everybody thinks about them. Even if they don't like them."

He took the pan. He looked so good in uniform. "Judging from the looks of them, there will be no bad comments." He leaned over the dish and kissed her, short and sweet. "I'm glad you came."

"I'm glad you invited me."

He nodded at her attire. "Good choice of shirt."

She smiled. "Thanks." She'd gotten it for signing up for the sandcastle-building contest, the whole reason behind how they'd met. It had seemed appropriate.

Miles and Trina had already headed back into the room.

Alex hooked his thumb over his shoulder. "We're about to eat. Larry made red beans and rice with smoked sausage, and we're having that with salad and there's garlic bread, too."

"Who's Larry?"

"Firehouse cook. He's a fireman, too, but his main duty is he keeps us fed." Alex lifted the pan of popcorn bars. "He'll really like these. He always enjoys when people bring us stuff. Says it shows that we're appreciated."

"Good." She had no idea they'd be eating with the entire crew. Her nerves kicked in. "Are you sure no one will mind that Trina and I are joining you?"

Alex laughed. "No, I promise. It's nice to have guests. Doesn't happen often. Of course, if we get a call in the middle of dinner, you'll basically be on your own, but let's hope that doesn't happen."

"Right."

"Come on. I'll introduce you to Larry."

She walked with Alex down a small hall and into a big kitchen that was equipped with more industrial appliances than residential. A large man who looked like he could have been a retired pro-wrestler stood at the stove, stirring something in an enormous pot.

"Larry," Alex called out. "We have dessert. And a visitor. My friend, Kat."

Larry turned. "All right." He grinned at Kat. "Nice to meet you. Did you make those for us?"

"No, my mom did. She's a big baker."

"Sounds like my kind of woman," Larry said. "Are those Rice Krispie Treats?"

Kat shook her head. "No, popcorn crispy bars. Sort of similar, but popcorn instead of rice cereal. I'm supposed to tell you they're a prototype for what will be served at the new Mrs. Butter's Bakery when it opens. They're made with Mrs. Butter's popcorn."

Larry put down the big spoon in his hand. "No way. I love that stuff. I've never had a bar made with popcorn before. I love the idea, though. Makes so much sense."

Kat felt some relief. She was afraid the firemen might think they were silly or weird or something.

Larry gestured at Alex. "I'm about to ring the bell. Better tell those boys to get in their seats and say grace."

"You got it," Alex said. He looked at Kat. "The

chaplain says grace. And we already added two chairs for you and Trina."

Kat grinned. Her nerves were just about gone. "Nice."

"Ready to meet the crew? Don't worry if you don't remember names." He tapped the silver name tag on his chest. "We're good with last names, too."

"I'll do my best."

They went back out to the big lounge, and he waved his hands to get their attention. Someone turned down the volume before he spoke. "Larry's about to ring the bell. He said to sit down and say grace. But first, everyone meet Kat."

What looked like a dozen guys waved back and all said hello at the same time.

Kat waved and smiled.

Then Alex pointed to Miles. "Your turn."

Miles cleared his throat. "This is Trina."

Everyone said hello to her, too. Then the chaplain stood up and said a quick prayer over the food. After that, they all moved to the table.

After being introduced to the fire chief, a man named Ed Walters, Trina sat next to Miles and Kat beside Alex. Each place had a large plastic tumbler of ice water, unless someone had gotten themselves something different to drink.

She sat quietly, putting her napkin on her lap, and just observed. It was obvious this crew weren't just co-workers. They joked and carried on like family.

Very different from her job.

Larry and two other firemen brought big serving platters filled with food to the table, then they took their seats as well. The food looked all right and smelled great, but rice and beans, even with the sausage, wasn't something Kat was used to eating as a meal.

Kat leaned toward Alex. "I don't think I've ever had red beans and rice before."

"RB and R," Alex said, smiling. "We love it. It's really good. We have it a couple times a month. Larry's from Louisiana. He's a great cook and his traditional dishes are the best. His gumbo is unbelievable."

"I'm really curious to try it now." She helped herself to a scoop of the beans and rice as Alex held the platter for her, then took a small piece of sausage, a piece of garlic bread, and a large serving of salad. She drizzled that with ranch dressing from a bottle already on the table, then glanced around at everyone else.

The conversation had died down a bit as the men

focused on the food. She took a bite and instantly understood why.

The red beans and rice, along with whatever seasonings had been used, were delicious. There was a smoky flavor to them, which she realized came from the sausage after she tasted it, too. She nodded at Alex. "Okay, I get it now. This is amazing."

"Right?" He grinned. "Told ya."

Miles and Trina were on the other side of the table. Trina caught Kat's eye. "This is really good."

Kat nodded. "It is."

The chief nodded. "Fantastic meal, Larry. As always."

Everyone agreed with the chief, adding their compliments. Talk of the baseball game started up, along with a few questions for Kat and Trina about where they were from and how they were enjoying Diamond Beach.

Both Kat and Trina answered with the information that they were about to make Diamond Beach their permanent home. Alex and Miles seemed happy to hear that.

Larry gestured at the two of them with a piece of garlic bread. "Are you two related?"

Trina nodded. "We're half-sisters. Different moms."

Kat smiled at Trina. "Although the half seems to matter less and less."

As the meal came to an end, Larry got up and went back to the kitchen. A few other firemen helped clear plates and take the big platters in.

Larry returned with the pan of popcorn crispy bars. "From the mother of one of our guests tonight, Kat."

The men applauded, making Kat laugh. "You haven't tasted them yet. But when you do, my mom wants feedback."

Larry put the pan down in the middle of the table. "Apparently, these will be one of the items on sale at the new Mrs. Butter's Bakery that's opening soon." He sat down and took a bar, along with everyone else at the table.

He took a bite and nodded, making a sound of pleasure as he chewed. "I've never been so happy to be a guinea pig."

"Agreed," said another man. "I could definitely eat more of these."

Even the chief nodded. "Tell your mother she's got a hit on her hands."

"I will." Kat smiled. Especially when a few of the guys went in for seconds.

The whole table seemed to be enjoying them,

and as the meal ended, Kat sent her mom a quick text. *Bars were a big hit. Not a single one left.*

Then she tucked her phone away and turned to ask Alex if she could help clean up. She figured it would be a lot of work, but she didn't mind. The men had been kind and welcoming and she wanted to pitch in.

But as she opened her mouth, an alarm went off and a light in the room began flashing. The chief came back into the room. "Missing child on the beach. All units. Priority One."

"Sorry," Alex said. "Gotta go. Text you later."

And just like that, he and Miles and every other paramedic and fireman in the building rushed out of the room, leaving Kat and Trina alone.

Together, they walked to the door and watched the men suit up and climb aboard the trucks, then the trucks sped out of the bays, lights on, sirens blaring.

In moments, Kat and Trina were the only ones there.

Kat took a breath. "Well, Alex said that might happen."

Trina nodded. "Miles did, too."

Kat looked at her. "I bet they didn't have time to finish the cleanup after dinner."

"Probably not," Trina said. "You think we should take care of that for them?"

Kat smiled. She'd been waiting to do something really useful. Now she was getting the chance. "Yeah, I do."

Chapter Forty-four

Jules hadn't had to do much convincing to get Cash to go to the Dolphin Club with her, not after she'd told him about performing there at the last minute. The promise of free dessert had probably helped, though.

He'd already had two of Claire's kitchen-sink popcorn bars and declared them as good as the brownie version, much to Claire's delight.

As they went into the club, they were stopped for ID and to pay cover. The man checking the IDs shook his head at her money. "Julia Bloom? You're comped. You're on our VIP list." The man smiled. "I like your music, too."

Cash grinned. "VIP? Way to go, Mom."

She laughed. "Don't act that surprised." She nodded at the bouncer. "Thank you."

"Jesse's in his office," the bouncer said. "He said to let him know when you arrived."

"We'll head there now." She linked her arm through her son's. "Come on, it's this way."

He was all eyes as they walked through. "This place is pretty cool. I wasn't expecting this. I thought it would be more...I don't know."

"Stuffy? Outdated?"

"Yeah, something like that. Jesse knows what he's doing. It's really got a cool, tropical thing happening."

She thought so, too. At his office door, she didn't have to knock.

He opened it as they arrived and smiled. "Hey, there. I'm glad you guys came." He pointed at Cash. "Dessert?"

"I never say no to dessert," Cash said as he followed Jules into Jesse's spacious office. "What have you got?"

"Key lime pie, naturally. Plus, a killer chocolate cake, an apple dumpling with ice cream, and a sandbar sundae. The sandbar sundae is the only thing we really make in-house, but they're all good."

"What's a sandbar sundae?" Cash asked.

"Basically a s'mores sundae. Vanilla ice cream with hot fudge sauce, marshmallow cream and a liberal dose of graham cracker pieces, plus whipped cream and a cherry."

"Wow. That actually sounds pretty good." Cash nodded. "I'll have that."

"Good man." Jesse looked at Jules. "How about you?"

She shook her head. "I'm good."

"We have a sugar-free cheesecake," Jesse said. "I'll share a piece with you."

"Yeah?" Jules nodded. "Okay. But I might not have more than a few bites."

"No problem." Jesse picked up the phone and dialed one number, then ordered the food. When that was done, he returned to his desk chair.

Jules and Cash sat on the couch across from his desk.

Jesse smiled and made eye contact with Cash. "Will you be here this weekend? The Killerbees are playing."

"Seriously?" Cash seemed impressed.

Jules had never heard of the group.

Jesse nodded. "I can get you backstage if you want."

"That would be amazing. I'd love to see them. I mean, they're next-level cool." Cash's brows pulled together, and he looked at Jules. "Did you set this up? Some kind of thing to make me want to stay with music?"

She held her hands up and shook her head. "I don't even know who the Killerbees are. This was all Jesse."

Cash returned his attention to Jesse. "Thanks, man."

"You got it. I'll give you a tour of the club later, too, if you want."

"Sure," Cash said. "I worked at a place like this in L.A. for a while. Not exactly like this. It was smaller and more focused on open mic nights. You ever do anything like that?"

Jesse shook his head. "No, but I've thought about it. Maybe I could pick your brain about that. If you wouldn't mind."

"Nah, happy to share," Cash said. "It was always entertaining, good or bad. And it brought a lot of producers into the joint. Which in turn brought better acts in. Kind of win-win, you know?"

"Sounds like it," Jesse said. "How did the club get it started?"

Jules just smiled. This was the most Cash had talked about music or the music industry since he'd arrived. Somehow, Jesse had got him to open up. She decided to give them some space. She stood up. "Just going to run to the ladies. Be right back."

She excused herself and went down the hall to the bathrooms. When she got back, Jesse and Cash were still talking music, although Cash was doing so in between bites of the biggest sundae she'd ever seen.

She laughed. "Is that a fishbowl or a sundae?"

Jesse grinned. "I forgot it was meant for two. I don't think that's going to be a problem for Cash, though."

Cash shook his head. "This thing is epic."

Jesse handed Jules a plate of cheesecake, a much more realistic serving size, decorated with a fat dollop of whipped cream and a fan-sliced strawberry along with a nice serving of blueberries, blackberries, and raspberries. "For you. Eat what you want. I have to run up to the front and I'll be right back."

"Okay." As he left, she eyed Cash's sundae. "I might need to get a taste of that."

He handed her a clean spoon off the saucer and sat back. "Help yourself."

She took a bite, the cold creaminess and warmth of the hot fudge mixing perfectly on her tongue. She swallowed. "That is...what did you say? Epic?"

He laughed and nodded.

She licked the spoon. "Jesse's a good guy."

"Yeah, he is. He's super chill. I like him a lot. If there were more people like him in the industry, I might have stuck it out longer." Cash sighed. "But there aren't."

"Whatever you want to do, I'll support you. I mean that. Anything. I don't care if you want to be a professional dog walker."

He snorted softly. "That doesn't sound too bad." He sighed again. "The thing is, I don't know what I want to do, Mom. I just feel...lost."

"That's okay, too. You don't need to know right this instant. Maybe you need a couple of weeks to just do nothing and see what sounds interesting."

He shook his head. "I can't just do nothing."

"Then get a job that doesn't matter but puts some money in your pocket."

"You mean in L.A.?"

"I guess I was thinking here. But if you want to go back to L.A.—"

"I don't." He looked at her. "I'd rather stay here. But I know you're working on stuff for the new album and I don't want to be in the way of that, either."

She smiled at him. "Honey, you're my son. You could never be in my way."

"Yeah," he said. "I could be. We both know that. But if I got a job, that would help, wouldn't it? I'd be out of your hair some."

"You're not in my hair now."

"You know what I mean."

"I do." He was such a good kid. She wished she could snap her fingers and fix everything for him.

Jesse came back in. "Is there any cheesecake left?"

She nodded. "Plenty. I was preoccupied with the sundae."

"Hey, um, Jesse?" Cash said.

Jesse sat in his desk chair. "Yeah?"

"Would you want some help with that open mic night thing? I was thinking maybe I could help you run it or something."

Jules held her breath. Was Cash really asking Jesse for a job?

Jesse grinned. "I had the same thought as I was walking back." He stuck his hand out. "Consider yourself hired."

Chapter Forty-five

Willie sat snuggled up against Miguel on the couch in the living room of the Double Diamond's first floor. She'd never been so happy on this couch as she was in that moment. "This is nice."

Miguel nodded and patted her hand. "Like a dream come true."

She laughed. "You say a lot of sweet things."

"All true," he said with a wink. "Which is the only reason I say them."

They were watching an old movie, *It Happened One Night*. Willie sighed contentedly. "I always did have a thing for Clark Gable." She cut her eyes at Miguel. "You look a little like him."

Miguel frowned. "Are you saying I have big ears?"

She laughed. "No, I'm saying you have that same

kind of charm and masculinity." He really did. She was completely smitten.

He grinned. "Now who is saying sweet things?" He put his arm around her, and she leaned in.

He was warm and the spice of his aftershave tickled her nose. She could feel herself falling for him in a way that she hadn't exactly wanted to. She wasn't fighting it. The heart wanted what the heart wanted. But there was no way she was getting married again.

She had too much going on with the shopping center and the salon. She needed to focus on her family. For all she knew, Roxie might be about to find out she had no claim to the beach house tomorrow morning, then they'd be scrambling for a place to live.

No, Miguel was a lovely distraction. A great companion. A marvelous kisser. He had a fantastic sense of humor, a terrific way of sharing his culture with her, and the man could dance. But he wasn't about to become her fifth husband.

She had no doubt he wasn't even contemplating that. It was pretty clear to her that he wanted the same thing she did. Someone nice to fight off the loneliness of old age with.

In that regard, they were perfectly matched.

Loneliness was one of the three great downfalls of getting old. The other two were becoming invisible and being forgotten. She hoped Zippy hadn't felt any of those things in his final days.

She was blessed to have her daughter and granddaughter around her, just as Miguel was blessed to have his son and grandchildren. But so many of her peers weren't as fortunate. If she thought about it too much, it made her heart hurt.

"What's wrong?" Miguel asked. "There are tears in your eyes."

Were there? She wiped at her face but found no wetness. She shook her head. "I was thinking about how fortunate we are to have family around us. Not everyone does, you know."

He nodded solemnly. "I know. I see the old men sitting on the park benches sometimes and I think but for the love of God and family, that could be me."

"Makes me sad."

"Me, too." He tightened his arm around her, pulling her in closer and kissing the top of her head. "But that won't happen to us."

"I hope not. I don't mean to say that I think it will, but life isn't always predictable."

"No, it isn't." He pointed at her drink. "You want another gin and tonic?"

"This one was enough."

"I don't know how you drink that. Tastes like floor cleaner to me."

She snorted. "Have you had a lot of floor cleaner?"

"No, but I bet that could strip the varnish off a dresser."

"I know, rum is the only thing really worth drinking, right?"

He smiled. "That's more like it."

She didn't mind rum, but it was a heavier drink to her. Or at least the drinks it went into were. And she didn't want a rum and Coke. The caffeine would only keep her up. She had enough trouble sleeping some nights as it was.

She picked up her glass and swirled the lime and the half-melted remains of the ice around. "Maybe I should quit drinking altogether. Probably not good for me."

He shrugged. "I don't think a little can hurt you."

"No, but I should take better care of myself."

"I wouldn't mind taking care of you." He leaned forward, twisting slightly to see her better.

She looked at him. "You do just fine when we're

together." He did, too. He was always looking after her, making sure she had whatever she needed, checking that she wasn't too hot or too cold. He was very nurturing that way.

"But who looks after you when I'm not around?"

"My daughter and my granddaughter. I promise, they do a marvelous job."

"Good." He sat back. "You know I'm just a phone call away if you ever need me, though."

"I know." She also knew that might change tomorrow. She hoped it didn't. She liked very much being right next door to him.

But she supposed Claire felt that way about Danny, too. Would Claire's relationship with him make her more sympathetic to Roxie if Claire inherited the whole house? Willie hoped so. Although she prayed that they wouldn't be displaced.

She didn't want to mention it to Miguel, but then again, what was she going to tell him if he found them suddenly packing all of their things into the car?

Maybe she *should* tell him. But in a gentle way. If that was possible. She didn't really want it to come as a big shock. Or for him to find out from another source. People in their age bracket didn't always do well with surprises.

She picked up the remote and paused the movie. "Listen, Miguel. There's something I need to tell you. It's probably not going to happen, but just in case, I want you to know ahead of time."

His brows furrowed in concern. "What is it? Is everything all right?"

"I don't really know just yet." She smiled to soften her words. "My late son-in-law's will is being read tomorrow morning. My daughter should know then whether or not she gets to keep this house. And if we can stay here."

Miguel blinked twice before speaking. "You mean you might be leaving?"

"Only this house. I'll buy another one. And get us a place to rent in the meantime, if need be. But we won't be next door anymore."

He frowned. "I do not like the sound of that."

"Neither do I. But I wanted you to know what was going on in case it happened. Better than you being unprepared for it."

He nodded. "I suppose. Yes. Thank you for telling me. I will be heartbroken if you have to leave."

She would, too, she realized. She tried to keep smiling. "I'm sure it won't happen. There's no way Bryan wouldn't have left her this place. That mermaid mural on the elevator floor? He did that for Roxie. Said she was as beautiful as any mermaid hoped to be. That has to mean something, right?"

"Right." Miguel didn't look convinced, though. With a little effort, he turned toward her. "There is something that might help. Something I could... offer you. Or rather, something we could do."

Willie was instantly intrigued. "What?"

Miguel took a breath, cleared his throat slightly, then clasped her hand in his. "You could marry me."

Chapter Forty-six

Trina finished wiping down the firehouse's big dining table and went back into the kitchen with a real sense of accomplishment. "All done out there."

"Great." Kat pressed the start button on the dishwasher and closed the door. "I hope we did everything right."

Trina had helped her sister handwash the big stuff first. "I'm sure we got close enough. And really, they'll be happy just that they don't have to do it themselves, don't you think? They won't care if something isn't exactly right."

Kat nodded. "Good point." She smiled. "It was a lot of work, but I'm glad we did it. I feel like we really accomplished something good."

"Me, too." Trina put the cleaner and paper towels away, her thoughts returning to the alarm that had cleared out the firehouse. "I hope they find the missing kid."

"I can't imagine how frightened the parents must be." Kat leaned against the counter. "Do you think we should wait around? Or just go home?"

Trina pulled out her phone. "There's no text from Miles. He said he'd let me know if there were any updates. If he could. They must still be searching. I say we go home."

"Okay." Kat shrugged. "My phone hasn't buzzed, either, so I'm sure there's nothing from Alex. Kind of a bummer we didn't get to hang out longer, but it was fun meeting them all and having dinner with everyone."

"It was," Trina said. "They were all really nice. And they really liked your mom's popcorn bars."

"They did." Kat smiled. "She'll be glad about that."

Kat drove them back. On the ride home, they chatted about the different firefighters and about the food and whether they'd get to visit the firehouse again.

Trina hoped they did. "I told Miles about the salon. He was genuinely happy for me. I like him so much. He's so smart. And a great listener. And he seems to really like me. I don't know why I've never been able to find a guy like him before."

"Maybe it wasn't the right time in your life," Kat said. "Or maybe the guys here aren't as small-minded and set in their ways as the guys at home. I don't know what it's like where you live, but in Landry, everybody knows practically everybody. Which means everyone knows your history."

Trina nodded. "Port St. Rosa is like that, too. It's such a small town. Most of the datable guys my age I went to high school with and that's enough reason not to want to go out with them." And for them not to want to go out with her. Trina hadn't had a lot of friends in high school. A few. But they'd been kind of outcasts at the same time.

Kat laughed. "I can understand that." She turned onto their street. "Don't you think that a guy like Miles is just more open-minded than most? He's a paramedic. He's seen what people are capable of doing to one another. Bad stuff. I think someone like you, someone who's happy all the time and sees the bright side to everything is probably like a gift to him."

Warmth swept through Trina. "You think I'm a gift?"

"To someone like Miles? Heck, yes. Can you

imagine the awful things he's seen? Why wouldn't he want a ray of sunshine in his life?" Kat shook her head. "All those guys who thought you were too much were idiots."

Trina grinned. "That's such a nice thing to say."

"Well," Kat sighed. "I have to confess that I thought you were too much when I first met you. But now that I know you? You're just being you. And I was a lot more cynical." Kat's face suddenly fell. "I've had my eyes opened, though."

Trina didn't know what that meant.

Kat pulled down the driveway and parked under the house.

"By what?" Trina asked when Kat didn't say anything more.

Kat turned off the engine, then looked at her sister. "I meant to tell you earlier by the pool but we got sidetracked. I found out Ray was cheating on me. I caught him at my house in my bed with one of his nurses." She told Trina the whole story, including how Ray had called to apologize. "I didn't want to say anything earlier tonight because it's a heavy conversation and I didn't want to get into it right before going into the firehouse."

Trina nodded, her heart broken for her sister. "I completely understand not wanting to talk about it.

What a jerk. I am so sorry you had to go through that. He did not deserve you. And you definitely deserve better. Did you tell Alex?"

Kat shook her head. "I was going to, but I didn't get the chance."

Trina gave Kat's arm a little squeeze. "At least Ray got to see your new hair and how good you looked. Serves him right to realize what he lost."

Kat snorted. "Like I said, you always find the bright side."

Trina laughed. "That is sort of my gift, huh?"

Kat nodded but made no move to get out of the car, so Trina stayed put, too. For a moment, they sat in silence, then Kat said, "Do you think we're going to be okay tomorrow?"

"I...I don't know. I hope so. Our moms might not be, depending on how things go."

Kat leaned back in her seat and exhaled toward the windshield. "I know. That's what's worrying me." She looked over at Trina. "But we're good, right?"

"We're good, no matter what. We made our pact and we're going to stick to it." Trina was so glad she and Kat had discussed what to do, no matter the outcome of the will reading. It gave her peace she might not have had otherwise.

"I wish our moms could find a way to be friends," Kat said. "I think they'd be good for each other."

"My mom doesn't have a lot of female friends. When I was growing up, most of the other moms thought my mom was a bad influence." Trina frowned. "People do an awful lot of judging."

"They sure do." Kat opened her door. "I guess we should go in."

They got out and walked to the elevator together, got in, and each pressed the button for their floor.

When the doors opened on the first floor, Trina paused, halfway out. "See you tomorrow?"

Kat nodded. "Yes. 'Night."

"'Night." Trina walked toward the living room to see who was home. Her grandmother was watching a movie but there was no sign of her mom. Of course, her car was gone, so obviously her mom was still out. "Hey, Mimi."

"There's my girl. Come on in and sit a spell."

Trina smiled and went to the kitchen for a drink. "You want anything while I'm up?"

"No, I'm fine. How was your dinner? I didn't think you'd be home this early."

"The firehouse got a call, so they all left right after dinner. Missing child on the beach."

Mimi shook her head. "Terrible thing. Have they found the little one?"

"Don't know yet. I hope so. I hope the kid was okay, too." Trina took a seat on the couch. "Did Miguel come over?"

Her grandmother nodded. "He did. But we were both getting a bit sleepy, so he just left." She stared at Trina, eyes slightly narrowed. "Are you worried about tomorrow?"

"The reading of the will? Not really worried. I can't do anything about what's going to happen, so what's the point of getting worked up about it?"

"That's exactly right. Good for you."

"Besides, I have a plan." Well, she and Kat had a plan.

"I might have one myself," her grandmother said.

"Yeah?" Trina scooted closer. "You mean something besides buying a new house?"

Her grandmother nodded, a curious look in her eyes. "Miguel asked me to marry him."

Chapter Forty-seven

*R*oxie sat next to Ethan on his back deck. He didn't live directly on the water, but just across from it, meaning the Gulf was still visible from his deck. His house was up on stilts, too, giving him an excellent view.

Wasn't a big house, three bedrooms, two bathrooms, but it was one of the nicest places she'd ever seen. Not hard to tell that he was in the building business. Everything was high-quality and beautifully done, with the kind of small details that made big differences.

The deck was just as lovely. A good portion of it was screened, the rest left open. That was where he'd grilled the steaks.

Now they were on the couch in the screened area. He had a few candles flickering in glass jars.

Just enough to cast a romantic glow over everything. Farther out, the moon sparkled on the water.

The evening felt about as close to perfect as an evening could be.

She glanced over at him. "I know I said it already, but those steaks were really good."

He smiled. "The company's better."

She laughed softly. She could get used to this kind of attention. "The company is excellent."

He cleared his throat quietly. "You know...I never thought I'd end up meeting someone that morning I ran into you and your mom at the shopping center. Wasn't even on my mind."

"Mine either," Roxie said.

"I've kind of been avoiding a relationship. Divorce'll do that to you."

She nodded. Even though she had no experience with it herself, she could imagine. "I'm sure." She went still. "Wait. Are you telling me you don't want to see me anymore?"

He laughed. "No. I'm trying to tell you the opposite. And clearly failing. I like you a lot, Roxie. You're fun, but you're also sweet and kind and, honestly, the sexiest woman I think I've ever met in person. You're just the total package."

She grinned. She felt like she might have

blushed a little, too, but in the dim lighting, she was sure he couldn't tell.

He continued. "I just never thought I'd meet someone who interested me again the way you do. Especially not someone who was a widow. But you're not like any widow I could have imagined. I hope this isn't happening too fast, but I don't want to see anyone but you."

Before she could speak, he added to that. "And I know things could get sticky with the shopping center if you and I don't work out, but I'm hoping we work out just fine. And if we don't, then I'd hope we can be adult enough to still be civil to one another."

She nodded. "I'd hope that, too. I like you very much, Ethan. You're a kind man who's gentle and down to earth and you tell great stories. Not to mention, you seem capable of fixing or building just about anything. I don't want to see anyone else but you, either."

She turned toward him slightly. "But I do want to take things slow. I need to. I still wake up in the morning expecting to find Bryan beside me."

He nodded in understanding. "I can't imagine how hard that is for you."

"Well, he made it a little easier by not being

faithful. But there are times when the grief comes out of nowhere and hits me."

"You should take all the time you need. I would never want to get in the way of your grief. If you ever think I'm doing that, you tell me."

She smiled. "You've been really good about it. I think you've been a great distraction, too. There's a lot of my life that I need to sort out." She hadn't said anything about the reading of the will tomorrow. She weighed whether to share that.

"Anything I can do to help?"

She shook her head. "Just be patient with me. I may really need it in the next few days. Things may get crazy."

"Something going on?"

She let out a little breath and looked away for a second before answering. "The reading of my husband's will is tomorrow morning by video chat. I might get the house, but then again, I might not."

He looked horrified. "If you don't get the house, where will you go?"

"My mom and I talked about it and she's already decided to buy a place here in Diamond Beach, but that will take a while. We may have to rent something. I don't really know. All depends on how fast Claire wants us gone."

"You really think Claire would do that? She seemed so nice when I met her."

"She is nice, I guess, but I'm the other woman. I can't imagine she'll let us stay. Not if we have no legal right to the place."

"The other woman?"

"I told you about Bryan and his other wife?"

"Yes, you did."

"Well, he married Claire first. So, in her mind, I'm sure I'm the other woman."

He let out a hard exhale. "That's such a crazy situation. I thought my life had some weird moments but yours takes the cake."

She stared out at the water. "You can say that again." Then she cut her eyes at him. "What weird moments has your life had?"

He made a face and joined her in gazing out at the waves. "I told you I was divorced, but I didn't tell you the details. In a nutshell, my wife left me for my oldest brother."

Roxie almost choked. "What?"

Ethan nodded. "It's not something I talk about a lot. Town talks about it enough. But yeah, she did."

Roxie blinked as she tried to gather her thoughts. "I take it you don't talk to either of them much anymore."

He shook his head. "No. Neither does the rest of the family, really. Kurt went his way, and I went mine. He left the business and everything. He kind of had to. Wasn't like it would have worked if he'd stayed."

"Are they still together?"

"Far as I know."

"That had to be really hard. How did you get through it?"

Ethan paused as if collecting his thoughts. "It helped that my family supported me. My sister, my younger brother and my parents all told Kurt he'd made a mistake. He wouldn't hear it, naturally. But they stuck with me through the divorce and that made a difference. Especially to the kids."

She reached over and took his hand. "What a crappy thing to go through."

"Yes, it was." He laced his fingers through hers.

"I'm not so sure my late husband being married to another woman is actually worse than that. I think we might be tied for terrible marriage experiences."

He smiled, which was so nice to see. "Maybe that's why we get on so well. We understand all about the dark underbelly of life. We've experienced it, and we're still standing. Kind of makes us survivors."

"I hadn't thought about it that way. I like that. I like the idea of being a survivor."

He brought her hand to his mouth and kissed her knuckles. After a moment of silence, he spoke. "You guys could come here, you know. If you needed a place to stay until you found something."

"Here?" If he'd pushed her off the couch, she would have been less shocked. "At your house?"

He nodded. "Sure. I have the two guest rooms. You'd have to share a bathroom, though. And one of the bedrooms. We could figure it out."

She smiled and shook her head. "You are so sweet to offer, but I wouldn't want to turn your life into that kind of circus. We'd be on top of each other constantly."

His mouth hitched up in a lopsided smile. "I can think of worse things."

She chuckled. "You know what I mean. I appreciate the offer so much. It's beyond kind. But you're already working on the shopping center for us. You don't want us in your house, too, trust me. We'll find a place. It won't be too hard."

"The offer stands. I don't want you going homeless. Or, worse, leaving."

She leaned over and took his face in her hands and kissed him the way she'd been wanting to since that first night out at dinner. She kissed him slowly, reminding herself what a good kiss felt like.

What a good man he was.

A second later, his arms were around her and he'd lifted her onto his lap, her legs across his.

She inhaled as she let go of him, but stayed there in his arms, her head resting against his. It was unbelievably comforting. She had missed this kind of closeness. With Bryan around so infrequently, it was something she'd been missing for a while.

Finally, she lifted her head. "I should go."

"It's not that late."

"I know. But tomorrow is a big day."

He nodded. "Yes, it is. I'll walk you down to your car."

They held hands down the steps. He opened her car door for her. "I'm just a phone call away if you need me. For anything."

"Thanks." She kissed him again. Even if things didn't go like she hoped tomorrow, she had her family and she had Ethan.

She'd be all right.

Chapter Forty-eight

Margo had gone to bed early to do some reading. She'd brought a few books with her, as she usually did, but she'd put the historical novel aside in favor of the thriller she'd tossed into her bag as an afterthought.

Wasn't that she didn't like thrillers—she loved them. But this was a new-to-her author, and she often felt a little reluctance to read a new author. They could be so hit-or-miss. She'd figured if the book wasn't any good, she'd add it to the shelves on the first floor for someone else to try.

Now she was eager to see how it compared to what she and Conrad were writing. It was all she could think about. The book. And him.

Of course, that wasn't entirely true. The reading of the will was on her mind, as was the very real possibility that she'd be making Diamond Beach her home.

If things went badly tomorrow, if Claire and Jules decided this wasn't the place for them after all, if Kat wanted to return home, Margo still wanted to stay.

Perhaps that made her a less-than-perfect mother, but shouldn't she have some say in her life? Her daughters were grown women. They didn't need her like they had when they were young. Even her grandchildren were grown. And they definitely didn't need her. Not in a daily sort of way.

She'd finally found some happiness with Conrad. And writing the book made her feel like she had a purpose once again. Something she hadn't felt since Lloyd had died.

Now that she'd let her defenses down and made herself vulnerable, she couldn't just give up. She would fight tooth and nail to hang onto this feeling.

To hang onto Conrad.

She'd be a fool not to. But besides that, losing him and the newly discovered joy she was experiencing would break her in a way that even losing her husbands hadn't.

Somehow, she understood that. It felt instinctual.

She had to hold onto this.

She sipped the tea sitting on her nightstand,

then opened the book. It was called *Girl Gone Missing.* The title alone made her roll her eyes. Everyone and their brother put girl in a title these days, like it conveyed an instant bestseller.

Overused, in her opinion. Grossly overused.

She read the opening line. *Amanda Smith ran for her life, unaware it was the last run she'd ever go on.*

Margo reread the line, then frowned and closed the book. Nope. This wasn't something she wanted to read.

Just then, she heard the refrigerator open. Someone had come home. Probably Claire back from sharing her latest creation with Danny.

Margo tossed the book onto the bed, got up, and pulled on her robe. She carried her teacup out with her. Not Claire. "Kat, is that you?"

Kat turned. "Yep. Did I wake you? I was trying to be quiet."

"I wasn't sleeping."

"Oh." Kat glanced at the TV. "I thought if you were up you'd be watching your shows."

Margo shook her head. "I was reading. You're home early."

"Firehouse got called out on a missing child." She shrugged. "Trina and I came home."

"I see. I hope they find the child."

"Me, too." Kat got a sparkling flavored water out of the fridge, then shut the door. "I guess Aunt Jules is still out?"

Margo nodded. "So is your mom."

"You want to watch something? I'm not ready for bed yet."

"Sure. Let me make a fresh cup of tea. We can watch anything you want. You pick."

"Okay."

By the time Margo had her tea made, Kat had found a show. Something called *Criminal Intent*. Instead of her usual spot on the chair by the window, Margo sat on the couch with her grand-daughter, putting her cup on the coffee table. "How are you doing with that awful business with Ray?"

"I'm all right." An unexpected smile curved Kat's mouth. "Having Alex around is helping. Not just because he's like a substitute or something, but because he's shown me that there is so much more to life than Ray."

Margo smiled. She'd been trying to tell her granddaughter that for years. "I'm glad to hear that. Glad you're doing well. I'm sorry today wasn't more fruitful for you. The job hunting, I mean."

"Yeah, me, too." Kat sipped her water. "Something will turn up eventually." She grinned at her grandmother. "So. Conrad."

Margo nodded. "Yes?"

"He seems super nice. Very handsome, which doesn't hurt. And fit."

"He was a Marine. Although they say once a Marine, always a Marine. Seems to be true. He takes very good care of himself." Something that pleased Margo endlessly.

"You two have really hit it off, huh?"

"We have." Margo paused. "He makes me happy." The lightness of her mood made her more prone to sharing than usual. "This afternoon, we got stuck a bit on a decision about the book. So we went for a walk. There's a park not too far from where Connie lives. It was really nice."

She got lost in the memory, in the way his hand had felt holding hers.

"You've missed that, haven't you?"

Margo looked over. "Missed...walks?"

"No. I mean having someone to do stuff like that with."

Margo nodded. "I have. That's very true. Life can be gallingly hard sometimes, Kat. I suppose that's something you already know, though, isn't it? What with your father's nonsense and now Ray." She sighed. "At least it doesn't have to stay that way. I'm glad you've found this new young man. Is he nice?"

"Grandma, he's so nice. He's a fireman, for one thing, which already makes him something special, but he's just such a happy, easygoing guy."

"Ray was happy and easygoing." And that hadn't turned out so well.

"I don't mean like that. Alex knows what he wants out of life. He has a plan. He's definitely not a pushover."

Margo nodded. "I'm glad to hear that. Why don't you invite him to dinner some night so I can meet him? I'm sure your mother would like to meet him, too. And Aunt Jules."

Kat pursed her lips. "Yeah, maybe. I'd like to go out with him at least one more time first. I don't want him to think I'm overeager. Or have you lot scare him away."

"We won't scare him away. Not if he's as great as you make him out to be. But I can respect your decision to wait a little. Nothing wrong with playing the long game. Not a bad idea at all."

Kat laughed. "You never cease to amaze me, Grandma."

They watched the show for the next few minutes and Margo was glad she had. There was a part that talked about the DNA of twins that she found riveting.

Kat's phone vibrated with some kind of notification. She read it and gasped.

Margo's heart sank. All she could think of was that the missing child had come to a bad end. "What is it?"

Kat looked at her grandmother, her mouth open. "I-I sent this company my resume earlier today. It's a big charitable foundation located here in Florida; they have an office here in Diamond Beach. They just emailed me back. They want me to come in for an interview." Kat looked at her screen again. "*Tomorrow.*"

"That's fantastic!" Margo was thrilled for her granddaughter. Not just because it was undoubtedly a tremendous opportunity. But because it would be one more thing keeping her family in Diamond Beach.

Chapter Forty-nine

"I should go home soon," Claire said. "It's after eleven." She was never up this late on purpose. She'd even seen Jules and Cash returning from the Dolphin Club from her spot in Danny's backyard.

But she made no move to get up. Instead, she watched as flames crackled in the firepit in front of her. It was mesmerizing. Beyond the grass-covered dunes, the waves crashed against the shore, the distant sound a pleasant white noise. She could have sat there for hours more.

"Stay a little while longer," Danny countered. "It's not like you have a long drive home."

She nodded at the fire. "True. But I'm afraid you're going to get tired of me talking about the bakery."

He laughed. "I promise that is not going to

happen. Not when you're so full of ideas. I love talking about it and making plans. Not to mention, you keep bringing me such delicious things to eat." He put his hand on his stomach. "I'm going to have to get an extra workout in tomorrow."

"I'm really glad you liked those kitchen-sink bars."

"They were great. But I'm kind of a sucker for anything that's salty and sweet." A funny grin crossed his face. "I guess that's why you intrigued me so much when we first met."

She rolled her lips in as she tried not to laugh. "I was pretty salty, huh? I'm sorry about that."

"You weren't in a good place." He winked at her. "You've warmed up considerably, though."

Of course she had. Looking at him made it impossible not to want to be friendly. She still wasn't in the best place, not knowing what was going to happen with the house tomorrow, but she was better than she'd been when she'd arrived. All thanks to him.

He lifted a finger. "There is one thing about those bars I didn't like."

"Oh?" She sat up a little straighter, paying attention to whatever he had to say. "Too many pretzels? I had a feeling that was—"

"No." He smiled. "The name. I don't love the whole kitchen-sink thing. Some people might think that sounds less than appetizing. Kitchen sinks aren't always the cleanest of things. Or maybe that's just me."

"No, I can see that." She thought a moment. "How about Cash Bars? My nephew, Cash, is the one who inspired me to make them. I used to make brownies like that for him."

"Cash Bars." Danny nodded. "Yeah, I like that. Especially because those bars are going to make us some cash."

She laughed. "He'll love having something named after him."

"How old is he? Does he need a job? We're going to have to find some good help when we open. I could bring a few people in from some of the other stores, but I'd only have to replace them there."

"He's twenty-five. No, he's twenty-six now. I'd say he might need a job, but then again, I don't know what his plans are. He might be going back to L.A. for all I know."

Danny nodded. "Well, if you have anyone you think might be a good fit for the bakery, get their information. We should definitely start thinking about the team that's going to work there." He glanced at her. "I want you to be happy with them. They have to be able to create these recipes to your specifications."

She smiled. She'd never had that kind of responsibility before in her life. "Once we get close to opening, shouldn't we just hold a couple days of open interviews? Let people come in and apply?"

"Absolutely, and we will. But it never hurts to have a few folks lined up. Especially if they're people we already know."

"Unfortunately, I don't know too many people in this town."

"Once the bakery opens, everyone will know you." He laughed. "They'll want to be your best friend."

"Sweets can have that effect on people."

He kicked his feet up onto the edge of the firepit. "I really like hiring retired folks. There are a lot of them in this area, they have fairly open schedules, and they seem to understand the meaning of good customer service better than the younger generation. I'm sure that's something I shouldn't say, but it's true."

"I like the idea of hiring older people. A lot."

"Good. I'm glad we're on the same page with that." He shifted a little, getting more comfortable.

"There's something else I hope we can be on the same page with."

"What's that?"

"It's important to my father and I that we have a selection of traditional Puerto Rican pastries. I realize this isn't your area of expertise, so we'll have to find someone who knows how to make them. We have the recipes from my mother and grandmother. They've been handed down over generations."

Claire nodded. "I love that idea. I'd love to learn to make them, too."

"You would?"

"Definitely. I love learning new things. And if I'm going to be in charge of things, I really need to know how to make them. Otherwise, how will I know if they're not right?"

He smiled. "Okay. That's great."

"Do you think I could get copies of those recipes? Maybe take a crack at them?"

"You really want to do that?"

"Yes!" She leaned closer. "Look, I don't think I'm going to nail them straight off the bat. They're family recipes. You're used to them tasting a certain way. But trying them out myself, working with those ingredients, it'll help me understand them. I can't really explain it but recipes, especially old family ones, are like a language all their own. Sometimes, they're a love letter. Sometimes, they're in code. And sometimes, you have to learn to read between the lines."

"My mother and grandmother would have loved you." He shook his head. "We actually think that some of the recipes are incomplete. Both of those women were rather proud of their skills in the kitchen. We think they left out things or maybe didn't put the right amounts of things so that no one could ever fully duplicate what they made."

Claire nodded. "That doesn't surprise me. Have you ever tried making any of the recipes?"

"I haven't but Ivelisse has and nothing's ever really turned out exactly right."

"I still want a crack at them. Will you let me?"

"Of course. I can't wait to see what you come up with. Do you want to take them with you tonight?"

"Okay. But when I actually get around to making them will depend on what happens tomorrow."

"The reading of the will."

"Yes." She went back to staring at the flames. "You know, everything Bryan did, all the lies and deception, made me mad. But this? This last bit of control that he's exerting over us? It's made me furious. If he's left us with nothing, I am going back to my maiden name. I might anyway."

"You should. He doesn't deserve to be remembered if that's how he's going to treat you." The fire reflected in Danny's eyes, matching the tone of his voice. "A man should take care of the women in his life. Not because they're weaker or incapable, but because they are worthy of his protection. A man who fails in that isn't a man at all."

She smiled at him. Then she got up, went over to his chair, and kissed him. "Come on," she said. "Let's go have a look at those recipes."

Chapter Fifty

*K*at woke before her alarm, which she'd only set to make sure she didn't oversleep. Today was a big day. Maybe the biggest of her life, depending on how her interview at Future Florida went.

And the reading of the will, of course.

But she was far more energized about the interview. It felt like it could be a defining moment for her. For her life.

She was slightly panicked about what to wear. She exhaled and grabbed her phone. There was plenty of time to find an outfit. The interview wasn't until one in the afternoon. She looked at her messages.

Alex had finally checked in around three a.m. Relief flooded her as she read what he'd sent.

Found the kid hiding in a lifeguard station. All is well.

Thank you for cleaning up the firehouse. The crew was amazed and now they think you and Trina are the best girls we've ever dated. He'd added a big smiling face.

Which you are, he continued. *Chief says you're welcome here anytime. Maybe you guys want to come back tonight? About to crash. Text me soon.*

Then he'd signed off with a heart. Just seeing that tiny red emoji made the breath catch in her throat.

She reread the messages, savoring each word. Alex made her happy. There was no other way to describe the feeling he gave her. Happiness.

She thought she'd been happy with Ray. Now that she understood the difference between settling and real happiness, she'd never be all right with anything less.

Ray really had done her a favor. A terrible, hurtful favor, but one she could appreciate all the same. He'd made it so easy for her to walk away from him, guilt free.

She sent Alex a text back. *I'm glad the cleaning up went over well. Even more glad you found the missing child. BIG interview today. I'll text more as soon as I can.* She added a smiley face and a heart of her own.

Then she went out to make coffee. As much as she wanted to go for a walk on the beach, she felt weirdly nervous about leaving the house this morning. Like she should stay here until the reading of the will was over and she knew how things were going to go.

Her mother was sitting at the dining table, a cup of coffee next to her, some sort of old book in front of her.

"Morning," Kat said softly, since it seemed like her grandmother and Jules were still asleep.

Her mom looked up. "Morning. How was your night?"

"Good. Not as good as yours, though, apparently." Kat smiled before getting a coffee mug down. "What time did you get in?"

Her mom's little half-smile conveyed at lot. "It was nearly midnight. Danny and I were deep in conversation about the bakery." She nodded at the notebook in front of her. "He gave me a collection of recipes from his mother and grandmother. All kinds of traditional Puerto Rican sweets, cookies, cakes, and pastries. Things he'd like to sell in the shop."

Kat filled her mug and added sweetener before getting out the creamer. "That sounds really cool. Are you going to try to make some of them?"

"That's my plan. Some of them don't seem all that different from other things I'm familiar with.

Like the pineapple rum cake or these *mantecaditos*, which I'm probably not saying right, but they're basically just a shortbread thumbprint cookie filled with guava jam. But then there are a few that call for puff pastry, which is something I've always bought frozen."

She shook her head. "We can't sell things made from someone else's frozen pastry. Not in a bakery where everything is supposed to be homemade."

Kat shrugged as she took a sip of her coffee. "So make the puff pastry."

Her mother snorted. "Puff pastry isn't easy. It's a lot of work to get right."

"Mom, you're a rockstar in the kitchen. You can do anything."

Her mom smiled. "I appreciate the vote of confidence. Are you going out for a walk this morning?"

"I don't know. Are you?"

Her mom nodded. "I think I'd better if I'm going to be making and tasting all of these new things. Come on, get dressed. I know we have a lot ahead of us today, but a walk will do us good."

"Okay." Kat lifted her mug. "But I'm finishing this coffee first."

Once that was done and they'd gotten properly

dressed, they were out the door. Kat felt better about going for the walk as soon as they'd started.

"Your bars were a big hit last night at the firehouse," Kat said. "Big. They loved them."

"I was glad to get your message about them, but it's nice to hear again." Her mom's grin went ear to ear. "No complaints at all? No comments about how there could have been more or less of some ingredient?"

Kat shook her head. "The only complaint was how fast they disappeared."

"That is really good to hear. Danny didn't love the kitchen-sink name so we're going to call them Cash Bars."

"Cool. Cash will love that."

Her mom nodded. "I thought so, too."

"I have some more news," Kat said. "I have an interview today. With a big foundation. I don't even know what they're hiring for, but it sounds like a great place."

"What's the name of it?"

"Future Florida," Kat said.

"I've heard of them."

Kat glanced at her mom. "You have?"

"Yes. You remember that boy in your sixth-grade class who had a brain tumor?"

"Sure. Jimmy Pepperidge, right?"

"Right. Future Florida contributed a hundred thousand dollars to his medical bills."

"Get out. That's amazing. I don't remember that at all."

"I don't think it was widely known, but I was on the fundraising committee the school put together. His parents told us about it. I don't know much else about the foundation, but it seems like an incredible organization."

They chatted the whole way through their two miles, but Kat noticed that her mother avoided the topic that could only be described as the elephant in the room. The will reading. Kat didn't push it. She wasn't exactly eager to talk about it, either.

Nothing they could do or say would change the outcome, so what was the point?

When they got back, they went their separate ways to shower, then met back in the kitchen to figure out breakfast. Kat had thrown on shorts and a T-shirt, her phone in her back pocket, still undecided about her interview outfit. Her mom was in white capris and a soft coral top. Maybe what she planned to wear for the video conference.

They examined what was in the fridge, and what needed to be used up. Eggs, sausage, home fries and toast was what they decided on for breakfast. By then, Jules and Kat's grandmother were up, too. Jules took Toby out.

Cash magically came downstairs a few minutes before everything was ready to be served.

As they were sitting down at the table, Kat's phone vibrated with a message. She checked the screen, expecting Alex, but saw it was from Trina.

I think we should all watch the will reading together. What do you think?

Kat thought a second before answering. *It's okay with me. We're eating breakfast. I can ask.*

Okay. I'll ask here, too.

Kat put her phone down. "Hey, Mom?"

Her mother passed her the plate of sausages. "Yes?"

"Why don't we ask Trina and her family up to join us for the video conference? It would be easier to all be in one room. And I can hook my laptop up to the big TV in the living room so we can watch it from there."

Her mother stared at her so long, Kat thought for sure it would be a hard no. "I guess that would be all right." She looked around the table. "What do you guys think?"

Aunt Jules shook her head. "It's not for us to decide. You and Kat do whatever you want."

Her grandmother helped herself to some scrambled eggs. "I agree with Jules."

Kat's mom took another moment. "I don't know."

Cash snagged two pieces of toast. "It would seem like a gesture of goodwill, don't you think?"

Kat nodded. "He's not wrong. We might be able to have a civil discussion afterwards, instead of us each sticking to our floors and wondering what the other is thinking."

Her mother pursed her lips, silent for a few long moments. "All right. Invite them up."

Chapter Fifty-one

*A*s Jules sat in one of the dining chairs that had been turned to face the big TV, she realized she really had no dog in this fight. Yes, it directly involved her sister and her niece, but no matter the outcome, she'd already decided she was moving to Diamond Beach.

Anyone who wanted to was welcome to join her.

On the couch, Trina sat between Claire and Roxie. Jules's mom was in her usual chair and Willie had taken the gliding rocker at the other end of the couch.

She and Cash were on dining chairs behind the couch. Toby was at her feet. Kat was sitting on the floor in front of the television, connecting her laptop screen. Casting was what Kat had called it. Whatever it was, Jules thought it was pretty cool.

"Ten minutes," Trina said, reminding everyone

how close they were to the video conference going live.

Both Claire and Roxie seemed nervous. Understandably.

Cash was on his phone. As best Jules could tell using her peripheral vision, he was texting with a friend. She would have loved to read the text, but she didn't want to get caught being that nosy.

It was his business, after all. But last night's trip to the Dolphin Club had gone so well that Jules was dying to know what was on Cash's mind. They'd stayed longer than she'd expected. Jesse had given them a tour of the club, which Cash had really seemed to enjoy. Then they'd gone back to Jesse's office where he and Cash had mapped out plans for the Dolphin Club's first-ever open mic night.

Jesse had roped Cash into working it with him that night, although roped wasn't accurate. Cash had literally offered to help. In fact, he'd seemed eager.

Being paid for his time probably didn't hurt, but either way, he'd been genuinely excited about it.

Cash picked his head up and leaned toward her. "You know, you should do something for open mic night."

She frowned. "Me?"

He nodded. "Yes. Can you imagine the social

media that would get? The Dolphin Club's first open mic night and Julia Bloom shows up? It would be epic."

She gave him a look. "Did Jesse put you up to this?"

"No." He snorted. "But you gotta admit, it's a killer idea. Will you do it? Come on, just one song."

"I don't know." It would be an interesting way to try out the new song she was working on. "I'll think about it, okay?"

He smiled. "Okay. I'm putting you down as a definite maybe."

Jules snorted as Kat came back and sat down on the couch between Claire and Trina. Her laptop screen was now up on the television. She went into her email and opened the one from the attorney that Claire had forward her. In that email was the link to join the video call.

Kat clicked on it and a new screen came up, letting them know the host would let them in shortly. She set her laptop on the coffee table, which had been pulled further away from the couch. "They should be able to see us, too, now. Well, most of us. When they log on."

"Technology," Willie said, shaking her head.

"It's really something," Margo added.

"As soon as the call starts, I can adjust the volume, if need be," Kat said. "Hard to tell what it's going to sound like until there are voices."

Roxie leaned forward to look at Claire. "Very nice of you to invite us up."

Claire's smile was tight, but it was still a smile. "It was Kat's idea."

"No," Kat said. "It was Trina's idea."

Trina shrugged. "We really kind of decided it together."

The screen changed again. Now they were looking at a man about Bryan's age sitting at a big oak desk, bookshelves on either side of him, the wall behind him filled with diplomas and plaques and framed citations. There were even pictures of him with a few former presidents and a couple of golfing photos.

On his desk was a sheaf of paperwork and a laptop off to one side. They must be watching him from a dedicated video conferencing camera. Figures a law firm would have that kind of equipment.

Jules rolled her eyes. "So *that's* Charles Kinnerman."

Charles looked up from the papers in front of him. He pushed his reading glasses to the top of his head.

"Mom," Cash hissed. "I'm pretty sure he can hear us."

Jules shut her mouth.

"We're here, Charles," Claire said. "All of us."

At the sound of her voice, Charles looked over at his laptop. "Ah, yes, there you are. You really are all there." He smiled as if he found that amusing. "I guess you're getting on all right then?"

No one answered until Kat spoke up. "We're fine, Mr. Kinnerman. Just really curious as to what the will says."

Claire and Roxie both nodded. Willie crossed her arms. Margo frowned at the screen.

"Yes, I suppose you are. Let me get things moving then. As the executor of the will, I'm pleased to see you both, Claire and Roxanne. I am also pleased to tell you that the life insurance payments will be coming to each of you very soon."

Claire exhaled, visibly relieved.

Roxie just smiled and glanced at her mother.

Claire spoke up. "What about this house? We'd really like to know."

He nodded. "Of course. All of that will be answered shortly."

He took a sip of water from a glass that wasn't on

camera, put his glasses back on, then began. "I, Bryan Michael Thompson, do hereby nominate and appoint my dear friend, Charles Kinnerman, to act as the Executor of this, my Last Will and Testament. In the event that Charles Kinnerman shall predecease me or chooses not to act for any reason, I nominate and appoint his associate, Edward Richards, to act in his place."

"So much legalese," Margo muttered.

He went on. "I give and bequeath to Claire Thompson, should she survive me, all of my personal effects and clothing that remain in the Landry, Florida house, as well as that house and the property therein."

Claire frowned. "His personal effects and clothing?"

Charles just kept reading. "I give and bequeath to Roxanne Thompson, should she survive me, all of my personal effects and clothing that remain in the Port St. Rosa, Florida house and the property therein."

Roxie crossed her arms and leaned back. "Seriously?"

"As for the Double Diamond, the beach house located at 89 Gullwing Drive, Diamond Beach, Florida, I do hereby give and bequeath equal shares of that property and all its interior and exterior furnishings, artwork, and material goods, to my daughters, Katrina Margo Thompson and Katrina Wilhelmina Thompson."

Everyone went silent.

Charles continued on. "Finally, if any beneficiary under this will shall choose to contest this will or any of its provisions, any share in my estate given to the contesting beneficiary under this will is revoked and shall be disposed of as if that contesting beneficiary had not survived me."

"Hold up," Trina said. "What does that mean?"

Charles finally looked straight into the camera. "It means that if any of you decides to contest the will, anything you received from it will be taken back." He set the paperwork down. "Any questions?"

"Kat and Trina get the house?" Claire asked.

Charles nodded. "That's correct. Equal shares of it and all the material goods that go along with it. Any other questions?"

No one said anything.

He pushed his glasses onto his head again. "I'll be sending copies of the will along with some additional paperwork to both Katrinas this week. If you think of anything else, just give me a call. You have my number. Have a good day."

The screen in front of them went dark.

No one moved for a solid minute. Then Trina shrugged and looked at her mom. "I guess nobody's going anywhere."

Jules smiled. She guessed they weren't.

Claire's Popcorn Crispy Bars

Ingredients

Cooking Spray
4 tablespoons (1/2 stick) salted butter
1 (10-ounce) bag miniature marshmallows
4 cups of cooked kettle corn
Optional add ins and extras – candy pieces, melted chocolate for drizzling, etc

Instructions:

Grease both a spatula and a 13x9-inch pan with cooking spray so they're ready to go.

In a large pot, melt the butter and marshmallows on medium heat, stirring throughout.
Once butter and marshmallows are smoothly

combined, add popcorn and mix until well-coated. (Add any candy pieces now.) Use the greased spatula to spread the mix into pan. Let the bars cool completely in pan either on the counter or in the fridge if you're impatient.

Drizzle with melted chocolate if doing so, then cut into bars and enjoy!

Want to know when Maggie's next book comes out? Then don't forget to sign up for her newsletter at her website!

Also, if you enjoyed the book, please recommend it to a friend. Even better yet, leave a review and let others know.

About Maggie:

Maggie Miller thinks time off is time best spent at the beach, probably because the beach is her happy place. The sound of the waves is her favorite background music, and the sand between her toes is the best massage she can think of.

When she's not at the beach, she's writing or reading or cooking for her family. All of that stuff called life. She hopes her readers enjoy her books and welcomes them to drop her a line and let her know what they think!

Maggie Online:

www.maggiemillerauthor.com
www.facebook.com/MaggieMillerAuthor

Made in the USA
Coppell, TX
31 July 2023

19796104R00234